Naked Truth of Love

Donna Christopher

Naked Truth of Love

When the naked truth of love exists and your past comes back to haunt you, how far is one willing to go to protect their love or surrender in defeat?

Donna Christopher

Naked Truth of Love

Chosen Destiny Books Publishing

Copyright © 2017 by Donna Christopher

Dedications

I dedicate this book to my husband. Thank you for your patience, your love, your support, your understanding and for believing in my gift. You are my true love, you are my forever love! Thank you for loving me whole heartedly! Simply thank you!

To my children, thank you for continuing to believe in your mother and my dreams. Thank you for continuing to be such amazing children! You are truly a blessing to me that I thank God for every day! Thank you all for being uniquely you!

Acknowledgments

To my family and friends, I thank you for your continued support. For every book purchased, for every share and spoken word about my books to others, I thank you! You all are very dear to my heart and very much appreciated. I don't take what you do for me for granted. I am blessed to be surrounded by an amazing family and such amazing friends. I thank you from the bottom of my heart!

To my girl Keisha (Johnson) Lawrence. You are such an amazing friend and I appreciate you so much for everything that you have done to support me in my journey following my dreams. You always seem to show up when I need it the most with your inspiration, pushing me, reading and editing and giving me your honest advice. You have kept me on my toes with every call and text message making sure I am doing or done what I said I was. I pray that God blesses you with every adventure you take on your journey to success. You are one of God's angels and I am glad he allowed us to meet so many many years ago when we were kids. Thank you!

If you can dream it you can do it – those words were written on the front of a journal giving to me for Christmas last year by my daughter Asha. It wasn't extravagant, expensive, wasn't in a big box or a small box, I didn't even ask for it. But what it was to me was special. I cried when I opened that gift. To me it said momma I believe in you, momma I believe in your dreams, momma I see you, momma you are going to do it. It is a constant reminder for me to keep going, never give up on my dreams and never give up on myself. I have a dream, I have big dreams. Sometimes I overwhelm myself but I do know that, if you have a dream no matter what that dream is, you can make it your reality! All it takes is time and consistent dedication. That journal is one of many that I have but my favorite. It is my reminder that I have a family that see me, believe in my dreams and believe in me! So, thank you my darling Asha for giving me such a meaningful gift that speaks volumes to my heart.

Thank you, cousin Duane, for my pictures! Thank you for your advice and your support!

Tim Dawson, again thank you my friend for my cover. I appreciate you for continuously supporting me. Thank you for everything!

Mrs. Carolyn Vaughn, thank you for your advice! Everything that you do for me when I ask has been greatly needed and appreciated!

Without support from family and friends, following your dreams can be harder to do. Not impossible, but harder when those you love can't see your vision and because of that are unable to support your dreams. Your dreams are yours. Your dreams are real! To all my dreamers, don't ever allow anyone to keep you from making your dreams come true. You only need one believer in your dreams, one supporter and that one person is YOU. Paint your masterpiece and make your dreams your reality! Yes, you can do it!

Be free to be you. Live your life, follow your dreams, find your happiness. Pray for God's guidance and live your life the way God intended for you and I to live, happy!

This world is a canvas waiting for each of us to paint our masterpiece and change the world one dream at a time.

Momma, I love you!

Books by Donna Christopher

Love Never Fails Series – Book 1 and 2
Love Never Fails
Naked Truth of Love

When God created Adam and Eve they were created in their nakedness. No clothes, no money, no material things. Just two people created in his perfect image. Two perfect people loving one another for who they were as people and not for what things they possessed. This nakedness allowed them to fall in love and experience what God intended to be true love.

~ Naked Truth of Love

Naked Truth of Love

Prologue
How it All began

Wait just a moment please, before we jump back in...

Momma Mathews has a few things to say before the story continues. Love Never Fails stands true to what it means, love never fails. But before we get deep into the Naked Truth of Love, I have a few things to catch you up on.

I had a dream last night.

Fish.

I know Jewel is pregnant, I don't think the dream was about her. Something tells me she is not the only one. That leaves Chantae and Brielle. I guess in due time I will find out if I'm having a grandchild. Maybe two if Jewel is pregnant by one of my sons.

Yeap, Love Never Fails was full of twists, turns and surprises. If one of my boys is having a baby I will know soon enough. Momma always knows.

These fish were swimming freely. A group of happy fish. They appeared to be talking to me. However, I don't speak fish. But these fish have me excited. I'm not too thrilled about Jewel being pregnant. Her scandalous ways, sleeping around. My son was about to marry her and Bradon getting caught up in her scandal...

Lord have Mercy.

Well I am sure you are very familiar with what happened with that story.

I know in my heart this baby is a Mathews and a Mathews will always be a Mathews.

When Bryson told me about Jewel calling him from jail informing me she was pregnant, my heart dropped. I taught him well to know when a snake is a snake and not to just trust the word of a snake. Lies are all she ever told. She good at it too, telling lies. Sometimes I think she starts to believe her lies to be true in her own mind. Her life growing up couldn't have been filled with love. Love does not act the way she did.

Love does not hurt.

My Bryson is doing the right thing having a DNA test done. My baby Bradon has to get tested as well. After that scandalous stunt Jewel pulled he has no choice but to get tested.

My Bradon finally found happiness with Chantae. Not sure how she would take news of him being a father to another woman's child. I am going to pray on that one. She a sweet girl though, pretty too. Her butt, well I ain't ever seen a butt that big. Bradon loves her I can tell. If that baby is his, well I don't think being a mother is Chantae's calling right now. But family sticks together and we will work it out. When we find out the results we will deal with that situation then. I know that baby is a Mathews. My heart tells me so. Although it would be nice to have a baby around.

I am so proud of my Bradon finding happiness. He is finally walking in his own shoes. Sometimes a woman can make you act right for sure. That Chantae is good for him and has my baby all in love and focused on his future. I like Chantae. I need to spend more time with her to really get to know her but so far so good. Sometimes my boys think I am too hard on their lady friends and they keep them away from me until they are sure. That's what happened with that Jewel. When I finally met her, I knew she was not for my Bryson. My spirit would not allow me to accept her. Something just wasn't right and we all found out about her sooner than later. Too bad she has a sex addiction. I hear that's a real addiction, a real serious addiction. I love having sex myself, with my husband of course, but never could I imagine being addicted wanting other men. All I can do is pray for her.

Bryson sure is happy. I tell you, God really blessed him with Brielle and those kids. She met him in his purest form as a man portrayed to have nothing but his God-fearing character and his Naked Truth as a man.

True love was destined for them both.

It's rare that a woman would take interest in a man that was homeless or in Bryson's case appeared to be homeless. He had nothing but himself to give her. All she saw was Bryson the man and not his worth. But her trust and faith in God brought her a priceless blessing that only God himself can give.

True Ordained Love.

When that Jewel broke my baby's heart I can't say that I wasn't happy she was out of the picture because I was. But knowing that God had someone better for him beyond his imagination gave me peace in the midst of his pain. Brielle is a sweet, loving girl. I knew she was for my Bryson the night I met her at Bradon's party, before it was even revealed to me that she was the one who captured Bryson's heart. Her time spent with me was enough reassurance from God that my son would be alright! Brielle is perfect for my Bryson. I received a double blessing knowing that both my boys found happiness.

You never know how God will package your blessing.

Now Kenneth is not my biological son but he is just as much mine. He stubborn when it comes to love, but that man knows exactly what he wants. He does not play any games or allow his heart to be toyed with. He has not accepted God's blessing just yet but he is right to be patient. He doesn't see it yet, but he has true love right in front of him.

I have some wonderful men in my life. My husband and his love for our family is so amazing. Our foundation was built upon God, faith, family and love. That's the way a man is supposed to build his family foundation, God, Faith and Love. If you have that you have everything. I wouldn't trade it for anything in this world.

Even with all our past struggles. Yes, we weren't always perfect, but our past, prayer and God front and center made us stronger.

I still worry about my Bradon. Not one hundred percent sure his foundation of love is solid. He has some obstacles he must get through first. His past is not too far behind him and his future will be tested. I pray his teachings from his father and I have prepared him for his journey of love, planting his feet to ensure his foundation will be solid. I pray all the time for my Bradon.

One thing is for sure a constant belief for me and my husband is that Bryson and Brielle, these two love birds are protected by God's favor. They both went through journeys in their life that prepared them for their forever love. I don't have to worry about their foundation being built solid on God, faith and love…God has them both.

I know God is up to something more.

There are going to be some trying times, maybe some heart breaks. I know some storms are coming that are going to cause major chaos. I don't question God. I know he won't put more on us than we can bear.

My God.

I can only keep praying that God knows best and He has us all covered for the good of His glory. Praise God for all things! Praise God for keeping us, protecting us and loving us unconditional. Praise God!

God bless my family and the people who are around them. Continue to cover them in all that they do. Thank you Jesus, for your love, forgiveness and for saving us. Thank you for always being so good to us all. We don't know what the future hold but we know your Will shall be done. Lord have Mercy on those that deserve mercy and protect your children from the evil in the world. Whatever storms are coming Lord shield us from the harm that will come, protecting our hearts and minds. Allow us to walk freely and confidently in our Naked Truth of Love. In Jesus name, Amen!

Chapter 1
Jewel, I made a mistake
August 15

"Girl you are finer than a mother fucker. What the hell did you do to end up in this shit hole?" The guard on duty watched as Jewel wrapped herself in a towel fresh from the shower. He was not supposed to be near where the women showered and dressed, but still he was watching Jewel shower and had been sneaking in since he rotated his shift to work her unit.

"You are a guard, you should know," she said in a feisty voice. She watched as he scanned her body with his eyes. She loosened her grip on her towel dropping it half way exposing more of her naked body. He was handsome and sexy eye candy for any woman that was locked up and deprived from having sex with a man. His body was built just like the type of man she was used to. Seductively she said, "You like what you see?"

"Yes indeed," he said, turning to look over his shoulder. "You that girl who ran a car into a building. The one they say has a sex addiction. I hear you been letting women eat your pussy and finger fuck you." There were no secrets in prison. Everyone knew everyone's business and the guards pumped the inmates for information. Some simply just ran their mouth.

"Fuck you. I don't need you judging me. What I do is none of your business," she said feeling like he was judging her. She wrapped her towel tight around her body still exposing her curves. She wasn't into girls but her addiction drove her to having sex by any means necessary.

"Naw ma, I ain't judging you. That shit is sexy as hell to me. Wish I could watch that shit," he said licking his lips slowly stopping to bite his bottom lip as he scanned Jewel's body with his eyes. He was admiring her curves and all her sexiness that her half naked body revealed.

She smirked looking him up and down before responding, "Come into my cell tonight and watch, them hoes be lined up to get a taste of this pregnant pussy."

"Oh yeah, you are pregnant," he said in a matter of fact tone. "They test all you hoe's for STD's so I know you clean. Why don't you let me fuck you instead of watching them hoes eat your pussy? I can make you feel better than those bitches do. I know you want some real dick." He grabbed his crotch rubbing his hand up and down his hard erection in his pants. He was playing on the fact that she did have a sex addiction and hoping she would take the bait and become his sex slave prisoner.

"You got some nerve coming in here calling me a hoe then wanting to fuck me," she said pausing as she looked down at his erection. "How you gon fuck me in prison anyway? I am an inmate and your ass will get fired." Jewel was irritated with him but turned on at the same time hoping he could and would get away with putting out her burning fire between her thighs. He was right; there was only so much a woman could do for her.

"You let me worry about that. I will be back to get you from your cell in about an hour. Have your pretty ass ready for this dick."

"What the hell is in it for me to let you fuck me?" She thought not wanting to give her sex away to this man for free.

"What the fuck you mean? You get the real thing instead of them bitches fingering your ass."

"Those hoes are good at what they do. They give me shit I need just to fuck me and make me cum. I give them orders on how to make me cum. I need to benefit somehow from you fucking me?" She was locked up but still had the sex addict mentality. Gaining something when giving up sex.

Bryson gave her everything she wanted. He had unlimited money and she knew she needed nothing more from a man besides sex when she was with him. Even though she could have paid for every workout session with Michael Anderson, the highest paid sought-after trainer, she still made him give her free sessions and cater to her demanding schedule just to keep having amazing sex with her.

"What you want extra food or some shit with your meals? I am a married man with five kids I ain't got no money to be given for no jail house pussy," he said irritated. He knew Jewel wasn't going to deny having sex with him because of her addiction but he also knew the game she was playing.

"You funny. Married men ain't shit. How many women you fuck in this prison?"

"I'm just gon be fucking you tonight. So, you want extra food or what? We doing this or not?"

She thought for a moment about her life being turned upside down and the fact that she was craving sex and the only benefit she could receive by letting a man fuck her was extra food with her meals. She laughed out loud before saying, "Aight I will take extra whole fresh fruit. This is funny as hell."

"Aight fresh fruit. Be ready. You gon love daddy's big dick."

"Yeah we will see." Jewel dressed and the female guard was back at her post ready to take her to her cell.

"Lights out." The guards announced over the intercom. An hour had passed since she had her shower and she was anticipating having orgasms from real penetration from a man.

The guard from earlier approached her cell. "Taylor, let's go. You have orders from the doctor," he lied for the sake of the other inmates.

"Orders from the doctor sound suspect this late. Jewel, you alright going with him? We can scream and get the other guards attention. Although they all up to no damn good," her cell mate said aloud. She had been there for a long time and knew how shady the guards can be.

"Yeah I'm good girl." Jewel parted her lips licking her tongue all around. Her mouth watered with the anticipation of having sex with the fine guard. "I will be back hopefully later than sooner."

"Don't you mean sooner than later?" Her cell mate asked knowing now that Jewel welcomed this guard doing whatever he had planned to do to her.

"Naw, I hope not," Jewel said winking at her cell mate.

"Let's go Taylor." He escorted her down an empty hallway into a cell with a solid door and a small window that he earlier taped paper over. He walked her inside the room closing the door behind them. After taking her handcuffs off he asked, "You ready for this big ass dick?"

"Just fuck me already. It's been too long since I had some good penetration."

"Slow down ma. We don't have all night but we won't be interrupted no time soon. Get on your knees and suck me."

"What? I am not sucking your dick. I just need you to fuck me."

"Naw, you got to suck my dick first, get me up."

"I don't suck dick and I am not sucking yours. Your wife can suck your dick when you get home just fuck me."

"Turn around," he said jerking her by her pants to turn her. "Bend over."

"I like the roughness but you are acting like you mad," she said calmly. Her attitude was toned down a bit knowing that she did not have full control of the situation.

"You don't like sucking dick so I'm just gon fuck the shit out of you." He pulled her pants down aggressively and rammed his semi hard manhood inside her. Once he was fully erect, he pushed inside her wet walls harder and faster not caring about pleasing her at all. He was only trying to please himself. Her entire body was jerking so fast as if he was rushing to his orgasm.

"Slow down you gon hurt my baby!" She used the baby as an excuse to get him to slow his pace.

He didn't listen to her and kept going fast. She turned her body to make him pull out afraid he was going to hurt her and the baby making her body bounce back and forth so fast and hard. She turned and sat down on the bed facing him. "You are going too fast," she said looking up at him. As she was talking he forced his manhood into her mouth before she could pull back he grabbed the back of her head to keep it in her mouth as he started cumming. He shot cum inside her mouth and all on her face. "What the fuck," she said spitting on the floor. She was upset and pissed off at what he did to her so much that she didn't enjoy the sex at all as she hoped she would.

That moment took her back to her teenage years. The one moment in her life she tried to forget. The one moment in her life where she felt used. Degraded. Worthless. Uncared for. Abandoned.

"Oh damn, I'm sorry. Here. Take this rag," the guard said. He had a smirk on his face. His sorry wasn't sincere and it showed in his actions.

"Where the fuck this rag been?" she was pissed off and felt disgusted and degraded at that moment. She knew she couldn't do anything to gain control over the situation. The feelings she felt brought back her childhood memories and a flood of emotions she buried inside for a long time. She felt so uncomfortable, used and ashamed.

"Nothing is wrong with the rag. I brought it with me to clean up, its clean."

Jewel took the rag wiped out her mouth and cleaned her face best she could. "What's wrong with you? You act like you ain't never had no pussy."

"Sorry, your pussy felt so good and I was about to cum when you moved."

"I told your ass I don't suck dick."

"I'm used to these bitches letting me do whatever I want."

"Fuck. You didn't use a damn condom," she screamed out in frustration. Her mind immediately raced to possibly catching a STD after he admitted to fucking multiple women in that prison and she was almost positive he didn't use a condom with any of them.

"You pregnant ain't nothing gonna happen."

"You fuck random bitches in here and you just bare fucked me, what the fuck was you thinking, what the fuck was I thinking?" It was clear that she was upset and disappointed.

"Sorry. Look, my wife doesn't have sex with me so when I can get some pussy in here I get excited and take it. Let me fuck you again and I will go slow this time, make you cum before I take you back."

"Yeah right. I don't think your ass know what slow is."

"Come on. Let me taste your pussy, make you cum that way then fuck you, make you cum again," he said softly trying to charm her.

Jewel desired to have multiple orgasms and knew once she got back to her cell she would smell like sex and no one would be up or able to come make her cum. She thought about it for a split second, allowing her desires to win, then agreed to his terms. "Don't use your damn teeth and stop if I tell you to stop."

"Aight. Promise." He did exactly what he said he was going to do. He sucked and licked her clit until he made her cum, then stroked her as slow or as fast as she wanted him to. She felt so amazingly good to him and he told her he would take care of her as long as she kept giving him sex. After another hour of making her cum he took her back to her cell. Her roommate was sleep and she slipped right into bed after taking a hoe bath in her sink. She was sexually satisfied but still felt degraded and humiliated that he treated her like she was nothing. She knew he only went another round to make her cum to keep her coming back and to keep her mouth closed. Before going to sleep she vowed to herself to get help for her addiction. Sleeping with married men who fucked random bitches was a low point for even her. She would have sex with him to conquer her urge to cum but knew she needed to consider getting some professional help so she could be better.

Chapter 2
Love Conquers All
August 15

"Good morning my Queen," Bryson said greeting his wife. He held her close as they lay in their king size bed. His nights were filled with holding her in his arms tight, feeling as if he was living in a dream. From the moment he laid eyes on Brielle he knew he wanted to wake up next to her every morning and hold her in his arms every night. He was sure of his happiness and he was sure of his forever with Brielle.

"Good morning my King." She stretched her body turning to face him. "That was an amazing night we had," she whispered, kissing his sexy thick awaiting lips before laying her head on his bare chest.

"Yes it was. What about a repeat this morning?" he said caressing her back and running his hands through her flowing hair.

"Umm that sounds good, I'm still sleepy but will wake up for that."

With eyes closed enjoying the sensual touches of her new husband, Brielle reached down underneath the covers to find Bryson's hard erection waiting to be caressed. Her face lit up with a smile. "I think he loves me," she said speaking of the long thick hardness of his nakedness under the sheets.

Bryson reposition himself to face Brielle kissing her full lips, pulling her closer to him in one motion. "He does love you, and so do I," he said. He proceeded to turn Brielle over on her back, lying on top of her holding his weight up on his arms. He did not want to press down on her belly. He kissed her passionately and aggressively. She grabbed the back of his head caressing and holding on to his shoulders, wrapping her legs around his waist. He stopped kissing her for a moment saying, "I love you so much Brielle."

"I love you Bryson," she said before he indulged in her lips again kissing her with intensity, wanting to make love to her entire body.

He slid her panties down to her ankles and she helped to remove them completely. He lifted her legs in the air never leaving her lips and he started teasing her clit with his fingers. The wetness of her honey pot turned him on even more and he couldn't wait to feel the warmth of her insides. He raised her gown up and over her head covering her sensitive breast with his mouth. Her pregnancy made her breast very tender but she welcomed Bryson's soft kissable lips. His sucking and kissing on her nipples aroused her more, making her clit throb and her g-spot pulsate creating the onset of her first orgasm of the morning. He made his way down to suck on her clit licking her lower lips as he placed a finger inside pressing against her g-spot. He kissed and sucked until he felt her pulsating again and the orgasm flooding his mouth with her sweet honey.

"I love your lips on me babe," she said breathing hard from the back to back orgasms.

He ventured back up to her breast grabbing them aggressively and kissing her neck as he guided his long, thick, hard manhood inside her. In and out he slowly guided himself deeper inside until he could feel her open and welcoming him. She moaned and he met her moans with thrust of pleasure. Her honey pot was tight and gripping his in out motion. She held on to his shoulders and allowed him to have his way loving her. His kisses were passionate, his touch was magical and his loving was incredible.

"This is the best feeling in the world Brie," he said before kissing her neck again.

"This is the best feeling," she said moaning agreeing with him. "I love you forever," she said with her eyes closed and legs up in the air. Bryson was pushing deep inside her enjoying every second of their love making.

Their passion in the bedroom was hot and sexy. They couldn't keep their hands off one another. Every chance they had Bryson was making love to Brielle. They were learning each other's pleasure points, teasing and pleasing one another, satisfying their sexual desires for one another. Brielle being three months pregnant, her hormones were raging. She was not your normal pregnant woman not wanting to be touched, she was always horny and she was horny for Bryson's sensual loving. He made sure he was fulfilling her desires, putting out her sexual fire just as she was satisfying all his sexual needs.

Brielle and the kids moved in with Bryson a couple months ago and the change was still new to them all. Having children in his home was a joy. He felt they were just as much his children as they were Brielle's. They had help adjusting to the change with their parents staying off and on. They even had help from their live-in maid Maria who also took on the role of being a Nanny. She was great with the children and stepped right in to help, giving Bryson and Brielle some alone time together as newlyweds.

Bryson was truly in love. Getting the news from Jewel about her pregnancy made him panic briefly. He just married Brielle and she was for sure having his baby. The possibility of Jewel having his baby was not what he wanted to hear or tell his new wife. He immediately told Brielle after receiving the call. He didn't want to keep any secrets from his wife. Her reaction was not what he expected. She told him she accepted him and anything that came with him. If the baby ended up being his, they would address it at that time together. Either way she was his wife and he was her husband, and that would never change.

Bryson was making love to Brielle all morning enjoying every moan and orgasm she released. True love was an amazing feeling that they both embraced and felt for the other. It reflected in their words and actions towards one another. They made love and took advantage of every second they could to do so.

Their moans were quickly hushed when they heard a knock at the door followed by a soft-spoken voice.

"Momma, can I come in with you and Bryson?" Jayla said in a soft whimper through the closed locked door.

Panic came over Bryson. He didn't know what to do. "What do we do? Should I go in the bathroom?" Bryson asked Brielle as he rolled over off her naked body. He was covered in Brielle's orgasms. With the covers still on him, he reaches for his pajama pants at the end of the bed.

"Hold on a moment Jayla sweetie," Brielle said to her daughter. Turning to Bryson she said, "She sounds like something is wrong. You don't have to go into the bathroom we will just put on some clothes and let her in. Where are my panties?" she asked in a whisper.

Bryson pulled the covers back rushing to put on his clothes and help Brielle find her panties. He was nervous. He never had to deal with having sex, or in this case making love, and have a child to knock on the door. "Here sweetie, your panties," he said smiling handing over her sexy lace panties.

She smiled back at him and as soon as she was dressed, she walked towards the door to let Jayla inside. She noticed Bryson getting back in the bed putting his arms behind his back then under the cover. "Relax. It's ok," she said smiling amused at his nervousness.

When she opened the door, she was greeted with Jayla's sad face and the housekeeper arriving trying to see what was wrong with Jayla. "I am so sorry. I was in the kitchen cooking. I didn't even know she was awake," Maria said.

"It's okay Maria. What's wrong Jayla?" she asked picking Jayla up into her arms.

"You took a long time to open the door momma," Jayla said.

Bryson sat up on his elbow looking towards Jayla as Brielle sat on the side of the bed with her. "Hey baby girl what's wrong? Are you scared of something? Did anything happen to you?" he asked.

"I had a bad dream," she said burying her face in her mom's chest.

"A bad dream about what sweetheart?" Brielle asked.

"The bad man came back to get us and I don't want him to come back and get us," Jayla said with her face still against her mother's chest.

Brielle looked at Bryson with fear on her face. She knew who her daughter was referring to. She felt so protected with Bryson and thought her kids did as well. "Baby he is not coming back ever. He will never hurt us again. You don't have to be afraid of anything. Nothing is going to happen to you."

"But he is coming back. I saw him out of jail in my dream and he was coming to get me," Jayla said whining wrapping her arms around her mother's waist holding her tight.

"Jayla can I hold you for a moment?" Bryson said touching her arm gently. Jayla turned looking at him pausing for a second before turning and reaching for him. Holding her tight in his arms he spoke softly, "Jayla, I promise I won't let anything bad happen to you. You, your sister and brother and your mom are surrounded by love and people who care for you and will protect you no matter what. No one here will ever hurt you and we will never let anyone else hurt you or your mom or any one. Feel my muscle," he said making a muscle and leaning Jayla back to see and feel.

Jayla giggled and said, "You have a really big muscle." She started squeezing his arm saying, "I can't break it, it's too hard."

"This muscle will knock down any threat that tries to come our way. And there are plenty more muscles just as big and strong as mine that will also protect this family," he explained in a way she would understand.

"I'm your family?" Jayla asked looking him in his eyes anticipating his response.

"Yes, all of you are my family. We are one big happy family," he said squeezing her tight in his arms.

"I love you Bryson. Can I call you dad?" she said looking up at him.

Bryson looked at Brielle for her approval. When she nodded yes with a smile, Bryson turned to Jayla saying, "Yes you can call me dad if you want to my daughter." He held her tight feeling a sense of completion. He was a father times three before he even experienced the birth of his own children. He was continuously reminded how blessed he was and how happy he had become. He wanted to make sure that none of them ever felt threatened by anyone and especially not the man who was supposed to be their protector, their biological father.

"How about we go see if breakfast is ready?" Brielle said placing her house coat on wrapping it tight.

"Okay mommy. Do we have pancakes?" Jayla said.

"Maria will make you whatever you want baby girl. Just tell her you want pancakes and she will make pancakes. Tell her to make them for all of us," Bryson said to Jayla as she jumped down out of his arms.

"Ok daddy," Jayla said.

Brielle turned towards Bryson bending over to kiss his lips. "I love you so much, daddy," she said with a big smile on her face biting her bottom lip. She leaned in to kiss him again slowly as he kissed both sides of her lips before sticking his tongue inside her mouth to taste her tongue.

"Daddy loves you so much. Jayla is gone we could finish…"

And before he could get his words out they heard Jayla yelling from the hallway, "Come on momma."

"We will finish after breakfast," Brielle said to Bryson kissing him again before heading to the kitchen.

Bryson laid there in the bed a few moments longer with his hands behind his head smiling. This was the life he dreamed of having. He had great success. More money than he could ever spend, and now he had the family he always dreamed of having. Nothing could erase or replace the happiness he was feeling. He quickly got up heading to the shower so he could join his family for breakfast.

The aroma from the kitchen smelled amazing, awakening the other kids as well. They all gathered in the kitchen waiting on Bryson. Carter was wiping his eyes looking towards the stove. He turned to his momma and said, "Momma, Mrs. Maria's cooking is just as good as yours and smells good like yours too."

"It does smell good, doesn't it?" she said looking towards the stove. She enjoyed having a break from cooking every now and then, but refused to be replaced in the kitchen. She cooked dinner during the week and Maria cooked breakfast most days during the week and on Saturday mornings

Maria worked Tuesday morning through Saturday afternoons and her presence and hard work was much appreciated. Maria took care of Bryson and Bradon for years and had become good friends with their mother. She appreciated having Brielle there with Bryson. She didn't care too much for Jewel but was happy with and loved Brielle. Working for Jewel was like night to Brielle's day.

"Are we ready to eat yet?" Bryson said walking into the kitchen.

"Daddy, Maria was already cooking pancakes." Jayla said.

"I can smell them." Ummmm.

Olivia looked at Jayla then at Bryson and at her mom a bit confused. "Did she call him daddy?" she asked her brother in a whisper.

"Yeap, she did," Carter said looking up waiting for someone to respond to her calling him daddy.

"What's wrong?" Jayla asked noticing them looking funny.

"You just called him daddy?" Olivia said.

"He said I could. You can too Olivia if you want to, he doesn't care. He said he is our daddy and we his kids," Jayla said. "Daddy, can Olivia and Carter call you daddy too?" Jayla spoke out loud.

"You guys can call me daddy if you want to or Bryson or Matt," he said to the kids looking at Brielle smiling. "It's up to you all, no pressure."

"Well, you take care of us and love us like your kids so we can call you dad too like Jayla." Olivia said.

"Sounds good to me Olivia," Bryson said. He noticed Carter pondering his thoughts before speaking. No one would pressure him to call him dad. It was an honor to him that the kids even thought to call him dad. Carter and the girls were good kids and he loved them regardless if they called him dad or not. They were his kids and he would always be their dad.

"Breakfast is ready," Maria said bringing a platter of food to the table. She had turkey bacon and turkey sausage, pancakes, oatmeal, fried potatoes with onions, a platter of fruit and some Orange Juice. She also made Brielle an omelet full of veggies.

"This is enough to feed an army," Bryson said looking up at Maria.

Just then Bradon walked into the kitchen saying, "I'm that army. Don't worry brother I will eat what you all don't. What's up kids?" Bradon said all chipper.

"Hey uncle Bradon," Jayla said jumping down from the table to give him a hug.

"What's up brother?" Bryson said giving him his brotherly hand shake.

"Hey Bradon," Brielle said.

"Hey sis. You are looking beautiful as ever," Bradon said kissing Brielle on the cheek. "Thanks Maria," he said as she placed a plate on the table for him.

"What brings you by this morning?" Bryson asked filling his plate with food. Everyone was grabbing food from all angles of the table, placing it on their plates.

"I wanted to see my new family," he said tickling Olivia. She grabbed the piece of bacon he was about to grab and started playing tug of war over the bacon with him.

She giggled and he let the bacon go. "I won," she said.

Turning his attention back to his brother he said, "I wanted to chat with you for a minute after breakfast if that's cool."

"Sure thing. Maria this breakfast is good. Thank you for everything." Bryson was grateful to have her there with his new family.

"I love Maria, I miss her too. Maria when you get tired of working for them you come work for me okay."

"Your brother my family. I love him and his new family. Not like before. This is good. I'm good Bradon. Not leaving here. But you come over and I cook for you anytime," she said in as good of English as she could.

"Thank you, Maria. Bradon you can't be coming over here trying to take people who are loyal to me away. Not gonna happen," Bryson said.

"Where is Chantae this morning Bradon?" Brielle asked.

"She didn't want to come with me this morning. She was up all night working on more designs for her upcoming fashion show she is planning. And she said she needs to finish packing a few things for the move today."

"She has been working hard on her business. She is going to be famous for her designs one day. My girl has some real talent," Brielle said.

"Yes, she's good at what she does," Bradon said.

"Tell her we said hello and we missed seeing her face this morning. And congratulations again on the house."

"Thanks Brielle. We are excited about the move. It's a big step for me."

"But you will be fine brother once you get your balance," Bryson said.

Avoiding any more conversations about them moving, Bradon stuffed his mouth with food and directed his attention to the kids. He was very fond of them. "Um this food is good. You kids sure are lucky having two people to cook for you all the time," Bradon said reaching over and tickling Olivia who was sitting on the other side of him. She laughed giving him the escape he needed.

The questions stopped and they all sat around the table enjoying family time.

After breakfast Bradon and Bryson went into the living room to talk. Bradon wanted updates about Jewel and the paternity testing. When his brother called him with the news he was devastated at the thought of Jewel's baby possibly being his. "Hey, any updates on when our DNA test for the baby will happen? I know you are handling things."

"Yeah, Sharese is working on that for me right now. I was planning to give her a call first thing Monday morning when I got into the office. I can let you know more then but it should be any day now," Bryson said. He noticed Bradon's facial expression change and he looked worried. "Are you worried about the results?"

"Just a little bit. You do understand why. I mean she was your girl not mine. There was no protection, so of course I'm worried, scared as hell is more like it." Bradon stood to his feet pacing back and forth.

"Would you feel better if momma raised the baby or me, if Brielle agrees?"

"Wait, I didn't even think this through to the point that she is in jail and can't raise a baby in jail. This situation gets worse every second I think about the 'what if's'." Bradon sat back down across from his brother putting his head in his palms looking towards the floor.

"Stop worrying so much. The baby may not even be either of ours. We don't know how many men she was really with. So, let's just panic after the results and only if the baby is a Mathews," Bryson said trying to calm Bradon.

"You right. I just know Chantae does not want kids, at least not any time soon."

"We will figure out the best solution when that time comes little brother. In the meantime, you and Chantae are moving in together. You have some adjusting to do there. So, balance that first." Bryson watched Bradon quietly thinking to himself. "You are nervous about moving in together. I know you all too well."

"I am nervous. I only had to deal with living with a neat freak, well groomed, clean and quiet nerd basically."

"I know you are not calling me a nerd. I mean, I am smooth, have some swag about myself and yes of course style. Brilliant and business minded but not a nerd," Bryson said and they both laughed.

"Okay then, business minded. You were always in books and contemplating your next move. I had to pry you away to play basketball or to come hang out. Now I have to share my space twenty-four seven and to have someone constantly in my space does make me a bit nervous." He looked at his brother for guidance.

"Well the best part of it all is that you are in love and you acknowledge that. Once it happens you will know that it was a good decision. She is used to having her own space too. So, you both will understand the need to be alone. And then you will come together when you need one another. You both will establish a common ground. But you still need to make an honest woman out of her and not just shack up."

"That's on my to-do list. You know Kenneth is sweet on that girl and trying to hide it," Bradon said changing the subject.

"I think everyone can see that he has fallen for Ameila. You know how secretive he is and I think her divorce is almost final. Her ex put her and the kids in a bad situation. He couldn't even be a man and stand up to protect his family. He doesn't deserve the option to sign off on their divorce. But you know Kenneth has to do things the right way. He is definitely about his business."

"Right he is definitely about his business. Well thanks for letting me crash breakfast and for the advice bro." Bradon stood up to give his brother some love. "It's moving time."

"No problem. Bradon you are still welcome here anytime. I will keep you updated on the testing. Good luck with the move. I would volunteer my time but you got money to pay for all the help you need," he said with a smile walking Bradon out to say goodbye to Brielle and the kids.

"Exactly. We don't have to lift a finger. But I sure hope your right about everything else." Walking in the living room with the kids, Bradon changed his demeanor to say good bye. "Come here my favorite little people. Uncle B about to leave."

"Hey Bradon, when are you coming back so I can beat you in Madden again." Carter asked.

"Ah it's on now. I got to show you who the real king of Madden is." He watched as Carter laughed.

"So you think! I can show you better than I can tell you unc," he said shaking Bradon's hand.

"Ok, I'm coming for dinner Sunday. It's on," Bradon said.

"Okay bring your A game, I am not showing you any mercy," Carter said laughing.

"I'm actually scared of your brother," he said picking Jayla up in the air and tickling her at the same time.

He grabbed Olivia and done the same with her. He loved those kids and loved being around them. One day he wanted to have kids of his own with his wife, but didn't want Jewel's baby to be confirmed as his. He was happy for his brother and his new family. Bryson gave Bradon another reason to look up to his big brother.

Bryson and Brielle walked Bradon to the door saying their good-byes. Bryson picked Brielle up in his arms swinging her around. "I love you with my whole heart Brielle Mathews."

Smiling she kissed his lips saying, "I love you too Bryson Mathews."

Placing her on her feet and watching as Bradon pulled out of the driveway he confided in Brielle. "Bradon is worried about the DNA testing. He doesn't think Chantae will be able to handle the baby being his." He searched Brielle's eyes. He wanted a suggestion they both would agree on. "I told him that we would have his back. And maybe momma would raise the baby or…"

Before he got the rest of his sentence out, she interrupted saying, "If the baby is yours we will raise him as ours. If the baby is Bradon's the decision is ultimately yours and Bradon's but we can still raise the baby as ours. I'm ok with that as well," Brielle said looking in Bryson's eyes.

"We will have our own babies. You don't think that will be too much?" He wanted to be sure she was sure.

"I love kids as you can tell. And I am sure your mom, my mom and plenty of other people will be willing to help and we could always hire someone to come in for the first year. I am sure. So, you both decide and you make the decision for us."

"We are hoping the baby is neither of ours," Bryson said.

"I hope that as well. But, if the baby is your family, the baby is our family. I don't think Chantae will be able to deal with the news

if Bradon is the father. So, we can protect them both if needed."
She tiptoed up to kiss his lips.

"You are truly and angel you know," Bryson said kissing
Brielle heading back to the living room with the kids.

"Are you ready to tell the kids about our babies? This is as
good of a time as any." Brielle whispered to Bryson.

"Yeah, let's do it," he said wrapping his arms around her
pregnant belly.

"Alright! Kids we have something we want to share with you.
But you got to keep it a secret for now," Brielle said to the
children.

"But momma I thought secrets were bad," Jayla said.

"Not all secrets baby girl. This one will be a secret that our
family knows until we share with everyone else. So, a secret
between us five," Brielle said pointing around the room.

"Yes. As a family, you don't share what is said or happens in
your home to others. You keep it to yourself and use best
judgment. But if one of us tells you to keep it within the family
that means us here in this room. Got it?" Bryson said.

"Got it," Olivia said.

"Got it," Carter said.

"I think I got it. That means don't tell anybody else outside of
mommy daddy and our sisters and brothers, right?" Jayla said.

"That's right Jay Jay," Brielle said.

"Okay mommy and daddy. I got it," Jayla said.

"Well we wanted to share with you the news of mommy being
pregnant. You all will have a new sister or brother in about six
more months. Or both," Brielle said as she grabbed Bryson hand
and squeezed it. Olivia was happy in the background saying yes,
she knew it.

Carter had a confused look on his face. "Why you say both
momma? Are you having twins or something?" he asked waiting
for his mom to respond.

"Yes, we are having twins. I see Olivia is excited what about
you two?" she said looking at Jayla and Carter.

"I think it will be pretty cool especially if I get two brothers,"
Carter said nodding his head.

"Jayla what about you sweetheart?" she said reaching for her to
sit in her lap.

"I guess I'm happy, but I won't be the baby anymore." Her lips were poked out with a sad expression on her face.

"You will always be our baby Jayla. Nothing will change about that. You will be a big sister and can help with the babies," Bryson said to Jayla rubbing her back.

"Can I change their diapers too like I do with my baby dolls and feed them?" she asked excited.

"We will teach you how to help in all those ways. You may not want to change their diapers though. They can be extremely messy and stinky," Brielle said hugging her tight.

"You can change their diapers when it's my turn. I'm not looking forward to double dodo diapers," Bryson said.

They all chuckled. The kids were okay with their mom having the babies. They asked her and Bryson all kinds of questions. They explained why they wanted them to keep the secret until after the wedding ceremony when they announced to everyone. This gave Bryson and Brielle the opportunity to discuss some of the wedding details and figure out when they would announce the news of their pregnancy.

"Let's go out for dinner and drinks tonight, virgin drinks for you of course. And we can tell our closest friends the baby news," Bryson said to Brielle.

That sounds like a great plan. Let's do it. You can call Bradon and have him tell Chantae. That way I won't get bombarded with questions ahead of time."

"Sounds like a plan to me. I am on it sweetheart!"

"I will invite Isaiah too so he won't feel left out," Brielle said.

Bryson and Brielle were in love and happy together. Family was important to them both. Bryson had his best friend Kenneth running the business and he worked behind the scenes helping where he needed. Life for him was great just as he imagined.

Chapter 3
More Than Friends
August 15

Sunday evening, Ameila was in the office working. She didn't expect anyone else to be there but was pleasantly surprised when she realized Kenneth was there. Trying to conceal her enormous smile, she took a moment before walking towards his office to say hello. Approaching his slightly opened door she knocked before sticking her head inside. "Hey you! What are you doing here on a Saturday evening?" she said with a slight smile. "Hey Ameila. I could be asking you the same question. Come in, have a seat," he said stopping what he was doing to talk with her. "I'm going over the details for the release of the book and the movie. I wanted to be sure everything would be perfect."

"Same reason I'm here," she said smiling, walking towards the seat in front of Kenneth's desk. "I assumed I would be here by myself and figured I could get a jump start on Monday."

"I see we are thinking alike yet again," he said as his eyes drifted over her body when Ameila was taking a seat. He quickly looked back up to her face when she returned her eyes to his. Ameila was a very pretty girl. He couldn't help but to be attracted to her. Working so close with Ameila, he got to know her well. Her inner beauty is what made the attraction undeniably strong.

"Well they do say great minds think alike and you do possess that greatness," she said catching him smile making her smile herself. "So how long will you be working?" She was trying not to get caught up in his mesmerizing eyes and his beautiful smile showing his pearly white teeth. She changed the subject back to business keeping the conversation safe for her.

"Just a couple hours. Where are the kids?" he asked curious if they were alone.

"The babysitter is with them this evening. She has been great for us and the kids love her."

"Oh, well that's good. Great help is always a wonderful thing to have. Speaking of great help, you want to work on this together since we are both here? We can put our great minds together?"

"Yes, I agree. Two minds are better than one. I will go gather my files and be right back," she said getting up from her seat nervously to walk out the door.

"Awesome, do you need any help?" he asked. He was excited she agreed to come back and work with him. He watched as she was walking away. She didn't have on her normal work attire. She was wearing fitted jeans and a cute short sleeve buttoned up top and sandals exposing her manicured feet. Her hair was pulled back in a ponytail and she wore very little makeup showing curves and natural beauty.

"Oh no, I got it. I will be right back," she said smiling catching his eyes admiring her body. She enjoyed working with Kenneth but majority of the time other people were always around. She knew that there was an attraction between them but she also knew Kenneth was not going to approach her because she was still legally married. His values were strong and he always played by the books. She didn't know if it was a policy in place that said co-workers couldn't date but she didn't want to inquire either. But he was the boss, at least one of them and he could change any policy he wanted. She decided to follow his lead and leave any gestures of them having any type of relationship up to him.

She stood in her office smiling thinking about Kenneth. She was about to be alone with this man for the first time since working for him. *"Lord give me strength to be professional and not high school giggly around this man. I know I'm technically still married and my marriage is almost final but I really like Kenneth, I mean who wouldn't. He is good looking, charming, sweet, kind and so giving. Okay Lord I know you know that but please help me to get through this evening and don't allow me to make a fool out of myself. Besides I am only assuming he likes me,"* she said a quick prayer before gathering her things to work in Kenneth's office.

Kenneth couldn't believe that he was about to be alone with Ameila and he was nervous. Looking out in the hall way he made sure she was gone. "What is wrong with me? I have never in my life been nervous around any female before ever. Shoot I'm the man! Get it together Kenny man you trippin," he said talking to his self. He looked in the mirror at his reflection to make sure he didn't have anything in his nose and to be sure he was picture perfect sharp. "Be professional Kenny, be professional. The girl is still married. You will get your chance soon enough." In the middle of having a conversation with his self, his cell phone rang. He quickly answered without looking at the caller ID. "Hello."

"Hey Kenny man what you up too? You sound a bit startled," Bryson said on the other end.

"Hey man, I didn't check the caller ID before answering is all. What's up man?" Kenneth said walking over towards his desk to sit in his chair.

"Hanging out with my beautiful family. Enjoying this Saturday relaxing, being normal for a change," he said.

"Oh yeah, well I'm on your old schedule. I'm here at the office working," Kenneth said flipping through some files.

"What you working on? Is something going on? Do I need to come in with you?" Bryson asked.

"No, no no," Kenneth said trying to change the desperateness in his voice from the first no. He didn't want Bryson coming into the office messing up his alone time with Ameila.

"Ohh ok, that's a definite no I'm assuming. Are you okay man? You sound a bit strange."

"Naw just working man, I won't be here too long. Just going over all the information we have for the release of the book and the movie. Making sure I didn't miss anything."

Just then Ameila walked through the door looking down at her files. "I think I have all the information we should need to discuss both the book and the movie details but I couldn't find..." She looked up stopping mid-sentence realizing Kenneth was on the phone. She mouthed the word, "Sorry", before taking her seat at the table in his office.

"Was that Ameila's voice I heard?" Bryson asked Kenneth curiously.

"Oh, yeah. We are going to work for a couple hours and then we will be done. No need to worry. We were both on the same page, didn't even know the other was coming. So when realized we both were here we decided to work together, we shouldn't be too long. Did you need something or just calling my friend?" Kenneth said. He was extremely nervous trying to fix the lie he was just caught in by Bryson.

Bryson was on the other end laughing at the way Kenneth was talking. He has never seen Kenneth so nervous when it involved a girl. "Kenny man, I was calling to see what your evening looked like. Brielle and I are going to the club tonight for dinner and we wanted to invite some friends out. We were going to call Ameila but you can just bring her with you seeing as how you two are together," Bryson said laughing at Kenneth knowing he was busted even if it wasn't planned.

"Well not together, together but yeah okay cool." Kenneth said trying to whisper.

Ameila was consumed in her files but knew that the conversation being had was about her, or at least the together part. She chuckled a bit quietly in her space.

"Yeah I hear you man. So, can you be there tonight?" Bryson asked.

"Yeah I will be there what time?" Kenneth said knowing he was not getting out of the obvious.

"We should be there at eight. That gives you two a few hours," Bryson said laughing.

"You got jokes," Kenneth said.

"Hand Ameila the phone so I can ask her myself. We don't want her to think it's a date but that she was officially invited. We want you both to be there," Bryson said still teasing Kenneth trying to let him off the hook at the same time. He didn't want to put him in an awkward position to ask Ameila for them as if it was a date.

"Of course, hold on a second." Kenneth walked over to hand Ameila the phone. "Hey Ameila, Bryson wants to speak to you for a moment. He recognized your voice and yeah I will let him tell you," Kenneth said still nervous.

"Oh okay, thank you," she said grabbing the phone from him. "Hey Bryson, how are you?"

"Hey Ameila," he said stretching out her name. "Just wanted to invite you out for dinner and a few drinks tonight at the club. If you are not busy, Brielle and I would love for you to join us. It will be several of our friends there and we wanted to make sure that you were there as well my friend. So, if you are not busy we will be getting together about eight. So, what do you say?"

"Oh, it will be an honor. I wouldn't miss it for anything. My sitter already planned an evening with the kids so I will be free," she said excited that she was about to have some adult fun without the kids.

"Perfect! It will be fun. We will expect to see you soon."

"Thanks Bryson. Here is Kenneth." She passed the phone back to Kenneth. At that moment, she knew the together comment was about them coming to the dinner together. She didn't know if Kenneth didn't want to be seen with her or not. Or if he just didn't want people thinking they were a couple. She told herself to put her game face on and concentrate on the work they were doing. She was done assuming.

"Alright man, we will see you this evening. Drinks are all on you and you know I'm not a cheap date," Kenneth said to Bryson. He knew this was not the end of Bryson teasing him about Ameila.

"You know I had the tab anyways. We boys so, real talk. I know she is sitting right there and you can't speak like you want too…"

"Right, right. Exactly." Kenneth said glad they were both on the same page.

"But seriously, I have never seen you react towards any female like you are with Ameila. Maybe it's the fact that she works so close with you but everyone that knows you can tell you have a thing for her. We know your values and we all know she is not yet divorced, but we all know and God knows that her marriage is over. It's ok to express yourself around your friend's man. We know you and we all know the truth behind everything that has happened. Ameila is great and she is great for you so just follow your heart and stop running from what God has right in front of you brother." Bryson wanted his friend to be just as happy as he was with Brielle.

"I hear you man. We can talk about that tonight when I see you but thanks my friend. You are always on point."

"No doubt. We will talk later finish your work."

"Yeah we shouldn't be here too long. I'll catch up with you tonight Brys." He ended the call with Bryson and walked over to join Ameila sitting at the table.

They went straight to talking about work. They were already completed with everything they had to do. This was more so a final check to make sure what was perfect was still perfect from two different perspectives. They worked for an hour going over their files comparing notes and consolidating their data.

When they realized they were at a stopping point, they both knew the time to leave was quickly approaching.

Ameila's hormones were raging over this man and she was not ready for their time to end even if it was just sitting beside him. She had not been with a man since her last encounter with her husband. Even that had been a while due to his cheating and him having no desire to have sex with her. She wanted to know more about Kenneth and why he was not or if he was in a relationship that no one knew about.

"I think we are done here. All we need to do at this point is execute our plans," Ameila said.

"I believe you are right. We have plenty of time to change before tonight's gathering with Bryson. You want me to pick you up? I'm taking the car service so there won't be any drinking and driving."

"Oh yeah, I didn't think about that. Sure, I will take you up on the ride."

"Awesome I can pick you up about seven thirty. That gives you a little over an hour to get ready," he said looking at his watch.

"That should be plenty of time." She paused, looking up at Kenneth. "I have a question for you. If it is not too personal," she said nervously.

"Anything. Ask away," he said looking at Ameila. He could tell she was nervous, but he didn't mind her asking him anything.

"Well, to be straight to the point, do you have a girlfriend? I mean, I never hear anything about you having one, nor have I seen you with a girl before, and you are a very handsome man. I know women are attracted to you," she said feeling like she was rambling.

Kenneth went over and sat in the chair next to her before he responded. "Well I have been with plenty of women in my past but I am not the type of man to publicly display any type of relationship that is not intended to last. Most of my relationships have been short lived because I'm not into wasting my time or anyone else's time. So, you wouldn't see anyone because I have never brought anyone around my family or friends. But to answer your question no, I do not have a girlfriend," he said looking at her for a response.

"Well that is a great way to be I guess. Not wasting anyone's time. I'm afraid to get out there and date again. I was married for so long and even though the last couple years were bad I guess I'm just scared. My husband, well soon to be ex-husband tried to break me down saying things like no other man would want me with kids and put me down. Sometimes I think those things stuck with me and scares me." Just then she felt Kenneth's hands on her face.

His hand caressed her face until she looked up at his awaiting eyes. "Any man that tries to break a woman down is a selfish, insecure man that knows he lacks qualities as a man that you as a woman need. He didn't say those awful things to you because they were true. He said those things to hurt you because even though he acted like an asshole, cheating or whatever he did, he couldn't stand the thought of you with another man. Ameila, you are beautiful! You are talented and smart! Your personality and kind heart is irreplaceable and lovable. And having children that you love and take care of adds to the beautiful woman you already are. That alone shows your passion for love and proves that you do indeed have a caring heart. You are beautiful and you won't have any problems dating and finding someone to love you," he said still looking into her now crying eyes.

"You are the sweetest you know that," she said noticing Kenneth now reaching for her hand.

"I really hope you don't start dating anyone else." He paused looking at her, studying her face. "When your divorce is final I would love to take you out on a date, spend some real quality time with you outside the office. Treat you like the Queen that you are," he said squeezing her hands in his.

Realizing that everything she thought about him being attracted to her was indeed true she started smiling. "Yes, I would love that but do you mean out in public where people can see us together?"

"Yes, out in public where people can see us together. I have been falling for you since you got here. You have been a great friend to me and someone I can see as being a part of my life forever," he said smiling back. They both knew what that meant that he was serious in his choice about Ameila being with him.

"Are you sure?"

Going against his values of having any type of affection with a woman who was legally still married he reached for Ameila pulling her closer to him and softly kissed her lips. "Yes, I am sure," he said pulling back for a moment to study her face for approval. "I have wanted to taste your lips for a long time now."

The burning desire that the two of them suppressed for so long for one another was raging at that moment. Ameila reached for his lips again grabbing at the back of his head, giving him all the approval he needed. Their bodies were reacting in a horny, I want to make love to you, take me right now kind of way.

In one quick swoop, Kenneth grabbed Ameila up out of the chair and onto his solid oak conference table pushing the files back out of his way. Her legs were spread open and wrapped around his waist. Her hands were wrapped around his neck caressing his broad shoulders. His hands grabbed her bottom squeezing, pulling her closer to him so she could feel the large erection in his pants. She was running her hands under his shirt feeling the solid glorified perfect abs underneath. Everything was fast paced. They were anxious to be closer to one another.

Their lips were locked and their tongues tasted the sweetness of their kisses they both yearned for. He grabbed at her shirt popping the buttons revealing her yellow lacey bra filled with her voluptuous full breast. Her nipples were erect poking through her bra. He left her mouth and headed for her neck grabbing and squeezing her breast until he could no longer resist and his mouth was covering her nipples sucking, flicking his tongue back and forth.

She held on to his back caressing and scratching wanting this man in the most fulfilling way. The feelings he gave her made her release orgasms without him even being inside her honey pot. He went back to kissing her lips and she grabbed at his belt in an attempt to release the hardness inside his pants. His hands ventured inside her now unzipped jeans feeling the wetness building up in her panties and between her warm lips below. Their bodies were on fire and there was no stopping what was about to happen right there in his office on his table.

Until they heard the door open and saw the intrusion of the janitor coming into the office to clean. With head phones in his ears and music blazing he was unaware of what was happening with Ameila and Kenneth.

"Oh shit," Kenneth said. He never thought about the janitor who worked weekends. All they could do was quickly button and zip their clothes trying to compose themselves. The janitors back were to them. When they finished with their clothes, wiping their faces and skin with their hands from all the wet kisses, they gathered the files and sat at the table as if nothing happened before the janitor turned around realizing someone was in the office.

"Oh, pardon me sir, I had no idea anyone was here today. I'm so sorry sir I can come back." The janitor said to Kenneth knowing exactly who he was.

"It's ok. We were just finishing up Clyde. You can continue and we will get out of your way." Kenneth said gathering the files from the table.

"Yes sir, thank you!" Clyde was shocked that he knew his name but was glad to know that he did. Made him realize even more that not only did they pay well and reward their workers with bonuses but that he mattered.

Walking behind Kenneth, Ameila was quiet until they were in the lobby area outside their offices. "You want to put the files in my office for now? I can lock them up until Monday morning."

"Yes, that will work," he said walking behind her. "That was close."

"Yes it was. If he didn't have those head phones on we would have been caught like a couple of sneaking teenagers," she said walking into her office.

"Yeah we would have. I guess I meant more so close to going all the way when we shouldn't be. At least not right now." Kenneth said looking at Ameila.

"Oh." Was all she could say. She didn't know if he meant he made a mistake or if something was wrong with her kisses or the way she felt when he was caressing her. She was confused. Horny for him and confused.

"Wait! Please don't think anything was wrong. Trust me, if Clyde would not have walked in we would still be in there doing way more than kissing and touching. But afterwards I wouldn't' have been happy with myself."

"I get it," Ameila said with a half-smile on her face turning to put the files away. She had been hurt by her husband so many times that she couldn't see how Kenneth was trying to honor her in the right way.

"I don't think you are following me Ameila. Come here. Pretty please!" he said watching her try to hide the smile on her face. She stood in front of him and he caressed her face before reaching for her hands. "I was raised under the covering of Bryson's mom. One of the things we were taught was to never dishonor another man's marriage, even if it was having problems and headed towards divorce. We were taught God's timing. That's why I would have felt bad. I can wait two more weeks to have you forever, if that's where God wants us to be. Besides I don't want our first time to be on a desk in an office. I would want it to be special for you," he said looking in her eyes watching her smile spread across her face.

"You are a great man Kenneth and believe me when I say I want the same thing you want. I'm just afraid that I might not be perfect for you."

"You are perfect. I am about to sound like Momma Mathews but here goes. God didn't make any imperfect people. Everything that happens in our lives happens according to God's purpose for our life. God has perfect timing. That dude was just a placeholder. You have two beautiful children that gave you the love you lacked. They were also a part of your blessing when Bryson met you. Who's to say he would have broken his cover pretending to be homeless to help you if your babies were not there. It's all part of God's perfect plan. His plan to bring you here pulling out your gifts he gave you. You are so happy working here, your kids are happy, and you make me happy. This was all in God's plan. I believe that and you should believe that as well. When your divorce is final, I will show you how perfect you are for me and how perfect I am for you," he said brushing a piece of her hair back off her face with his fingers.

"I believe that as well. I know and knew from the beginning when you brought me here that I was in good hands and under God's covering! Thank you Kenneth!" she said grabbing at his hand before it left her face holding it to her lips to kiss.

He leaned down kissing her forehead, pulling her closer to him in a loving embrace. "So, I should pick you up at seven thirty?"

Smiling she answered, "yes that should be plenty of time."

"Alright then. I will be there my friend. Come on I will walk you out." He released her from his embrace and headed out the door.

"So, what do we do until my divorce? Just be friends?"

"Try to appear to be friends but we are so much more than just friends!"

Chapter 4
Moving In Together
August 15

Bradon looked up to his big brother Bryson. After seeing how happy he was with Brielle and the kids he wanted to make sure he was positioning himself to be able to raise a family with Chantae. He was still not ready to be a father. He enjoyed being single and free for so long without focusing on his future, that he decided now was time for him to dedicate his energy towards his business, not having kids.

When his brother called with the news about Jewel being pregnant, his happiness with Chantae flashed in front of his eyes and fear of losing it all evaded his thoughts. The morning Jewel came into his room while he was in a drunken sleepy state brought him nothing but pain. Every time he thinks about his brother's girl seducing him it brings sadness. He would never intentionally hurt his brother, and the fact that it happened hurts even if his brother did know the truth of what happened that morning. Now, to find out her baby could possibly be his was devastating to him. He didn't want Chantae to know anything about the possibility. He would only tell her if the test results came back that he was the father.

Two weeks ago, Chantae put in her notice at work to leave the company when she realized Bradon was supporting her dreams one hundred percent. Once they were moved into their new home she wanted to focus on nothing more than her clothing line. Bradon built her a studio large enough to work and have a boutique inside. With the unlimited budget he gave her, she started ordering material to arrive at their new home on their move in day.

Bradon thought about his morning visit at Bryson's home. He loved the family vibe that he received when he was with him and his new family. It's the same vibe he wants in a few years once he was ready to start a family. He couldn't stop thinking about the DNA testing. Brielle already knew not to mention it to Chantae even though they were friends. He didn't want to be sneaking on the phone or texting about the situation risking being overheard or Chantae looking at his text. He needed to be face to face with his brother to discuss Jewel and to get reassurance from his brother he was not making a mistake moving in with Chantae. Going from being single and having fun for years to a serious relationship was a huge step for Bradon but being with Chantae was worth it, even if he didn't know how things would be.

"Babe the movers are here, you need me to get the door?" Chante yelled from the upstairs bathroom of their apartment.

"No, I got it sweetheart. You keep doing your hair. Although I'm going to mess it up when the movers leave," Bradon said walking towards the door.

"Well in that case I might as well put it up in a ponytail until afterwards," she said laughing. "I don't even know why I work so hard on my hair its always messed up after all the great sex we be having," she said not knowing if Bradon could still hear her. She continued to straighten her hair despite his comment.

"Hey come on in, I'm Bradon. Glad you all are here to help with the move," he said shaking the men hands as they walked through the door.

"How are you doing man. Good to see you again," the last gentleman said walking through the door.

"What's up Mike? Glad you all are here. We are actually all ready to go."

"Then we are ready to roll," he said seeing all the boxes packed.

"Go for it. Everything is labeled and we will be upstairs if you need me," Bradon said.

"Yes sir. You and your wife being here is not a problem. No need to worry about anything. We will protect all of your items and take good care of everything."

"I appreciate that sir. Thank you!" Bradon said before heading up stairs. "Wife," he said out loud. Hearing the man call Chantae his wife didn't sound bad to him and a smile appeared across his face.

"Hey beautiful," he said coming up behind Chantae. He wrapped his arms around her waist and planted a kiss on her neck.

He avoided the hot flat irons she had curling her hair. "I thought you were putting it in a ponytail?"

"I was until I thought about all the people that would be here moving us and didn't think you were really trying to have sex here." She looked back at him through the mirror to study his face.

"We look great together don't you think?" he said with his arms still wrapped around her waist and his head leaning up against hers.

"We do babe. We are a beautiful couple and I love you so much!" Chantae said placing the hot irons down turning around to face Bradon wrapping her arms around his neck to kiss him.

His hands were still wrapped around her waist keeping her close to him. "Umm keep kissing me like this and you are going to make me lock this door and take you right now," Bradon said looking towards the door then back at her smiling face.

"You wouldn't, not with all these people in the house working," she said looking down seeing that he now had a large bulge in his pants. She then knew he was serious. She seductively kissed his lips again calling his bluff.

Bradon dropped his hands from her waist, walked over to lock the bathroom door. He turns to see her reaction making sure she wasn't protesting. Chantae was smiling not believing how bold he was to have sex with her with a house full of people, strangers at that. "You down?" he asked.

"Baby I 'm down with you so hell yeah I'm down." Chantae started to undress. She did a quick strip tease taking her shirt off swinging it to throw to the ground. Then she turned her back to Bradon as she slipped out of her pants and panties at the same time bending over so he could see the roundness of her butt staring him in the face.

Bradon got down on his knees behind her as she pulled her feet from the pants. With one leg up, he was under her butt sucking and licking her lips. He licked his tongue back and forth over her clitoris grabbing at her ass until she had her first orgasm. Sweet honey cum was dripping into his mouth and he enjoyed how she taste. She was gripping the counter with a slight moan not wanting anyone to hear her. Bradon leaned her over the bathroom counter propped one leg up and was inside her wetness quickly pushing in and out slowly until his thickness was all the way inside her honey pot.

"Ohh baby, that feels good," Chantae said, moaning softly. She grabbed at her breast with one hand bracing herself with the other. Bradon started to go faster pushing in and out. He leaned over grabbing her face to kiss her sharing the sweetness of her honey. He was pushing deep inside hitting her spot. "Umm baby don't stop. You are hitting the pussy right. Just like that. Yes, B that's my spot. Ohh yesss." Chantae was cumming back to back.

"You like that. You like daddy dick?" Bradon said turned on by Chantae's moans and words of satisfaction. His pumps started to get faster and deeper. Her small but perky breasts were bouncing and her moans became louder. He heard something fall to the floor from outside the door and realized someone was listening to the love making on the other side of the wall. He slowed his pumps and hushed Chantae. He was not ready to stop regardless of who was listening. That turned him on even more. For a moment, he was fucking her like his 'single I don't care' days and had to quickly remember that he was with the woman of his dreams. The woman he planned to live the rest of his life with. He slowed his grind grabbing Chantae's breast, kissing her all at the same time. He was attempting to silence the love making without ending the love making.

Slowly Chantae started moving her hips back and forth on Bradon. She had them both in a love zone. Bradon couldn't wait to christen their new home together. The sounds of an amazing orgasm escaped Chantae's mouth, moaning loudly not able to hold it in. She gripped the sink holding on tight, holding her position to feel every inch of Bradon pushing inside her. He knew she was cumming and kept his pace pushing inside her, hitting her spot over and over as she released her sweet honey all over his manhood. The pulsating from her warm walls contracting around his penis gave Bradon a feel-good sensation making him erupt in orgasm. He pulled out quickly and shot cum all on her butt.

"Damn baby that was good spontaneous love making!" Chantae said trying to catch her breath.

"Yes, it was. I almost forgot I didn't have on a condom. It was a quick thought to pull out," Bradon said. He didn't want kids right now and had to be sure not to be so careless. Thoughts of his carelessness with Jewel and her being pregnant flashed in his mind.

"Yeah this spontaneous sex is great but we need to be sure we have condoms close by as double protection with the pill. We have our five-year plans to accomplish before we start having babies," Chantae said as they were cleaning themselves up, putting their clothes back on.

"At the pace we are going, staying consistent with our dedication and commitment, we should have our five-year plan completed in three years or less. Oh yeah, the front gate called said you had several packages delivered this morning."

"That's perfect timing. I ordered everything two weeks ago when I put in my notice. Friday was my last day and once we get the house in order, I can jump straight into working on my clothing line. I am so excited about everything Bradon." She turned to him half-dressed wrapping her arms around his neck. She kissed him on his neck before reaching his lips.

He pulled her closer kissing her passionately. "You are going to make me bend you over the sink again woman," he said holding her tight.

"We will have all the wild sex you want tonight when we celebrate being in our new home together." She pulled away from him grabbing her pants slipping them on.

"Tonight we are going to have some freaky fun all over the house with your sexy ass." He watched as she giggled loving his compliments. "Are the jeans you have on some that you designed?" he asked noticing how well and comfortable they fit her.

"You are always so observant with me. Yes they are. I had to test a pair out and see what adjustments are needed. They fit great and feel great," she said as she was running her hands over her hips feeling the texture of the material.

"You are the perfect model to test fit your designs," he said watching her smile.

"Thanks babe you are so sweet. We are the perfect couple and we are going to be a beast in business, we are like Will and Jada," she said turning towards the mirror. "Loving, fun and go getters.

Bradon had a moment thinking about being smothered with someone always around. "Yeah working all the time, we will have to make time for one another. You will be buried in your work creating designs and working with the clothing industry, doing shows and whatnot and me with the architectural business," he said waiting for a response.

"I promise not to neglect you babe. If I am too busy for you or you get to missing me, just let me know. I will probably be in my shop majority of the time so you will know where to find me. You know I am used to living alone but we will adjust and know when to give each other space and when we need to be together. We will help each other until we have a system in place," she said looking in the mirror doing her hair.

"You right. We will adjust," he said relieved that they were on the same page. "I'm going to check on the movers so we can say our goodbyes to this place and hello to our new home," Bradon said.

"Okay babe, I will be finished with my hair in a moment."

Just then Bradon's phone started ringing and he realized his phone was on the floor. He picked it up answering seeing that it was Bryson. "Hey Bryson," he said before exiting the bathroom. Bryson invited them out for dinner and drinks. After confirming with Chantae, he told him they would be there. Bradon was hoping no one would get drunk and say anything about Jewel. He wanted to spare Chantae any pain that she didn't have to experience. They had a promising future and he didn't want anything to interfere with his happiness, especially not anything concerning Jewel.

Bradon was taking a huge step moving in with Chantae but he felt in his heart that he was doing the right thing. He just wasn't ready to make an honest woman out of her as his brother says. He wanted to make sure he was ready to say I do when the time came. To him, moving in together was a big commitment and he would work on future commitments in due time.

When they arrived at their new home, the movers were quickly unpacking and placing furniture where it needed to go. This was the first time Chantae saw the house in person. Her excitement was not what Bradon expected. She was more excited about her material for her clothing line than the home he thought.

"Do you like our home? You don't seem too excited," Bradon asked Chantae.

"Yeah I do. It's ok for a starter home. I mean you go from having me in Bryson's home to anything else it's just average not extraordinaire. But I do like it and appreciate you for this boo. I love you for loving me," Chantae said.

"Wow, so will you compare Bryson's home to every home we will ever live in?" he asked Chantae.

"No not compare babe. I love our home. But you do have to understand my point of view. I invited friends over told them that Bryson's home would be my home soon thinking it was yours. I felt like a Queen and like I was the shit! I mean I still do but it's different," she said.

"You are a Queen. My Queen. What we have is ours and no one else's opinion should matter. I am sure it's still more than they have," he said not sure how he felt about her comment.

"You right babe. I love you and I love the house. I love my space and we are going to do great things together and get what we want together. And, we are going to break in every room in this house," she said kissing his lips.

"That's my girl," Bradon said kissing her. "That's what our night time plans are but first. let's get ready for my brother's dinner."

"I wonder why Brielle didn't call me and tell me about the party tonight?" she wondered, feeling left out.

"Well, they know we are together and we were moving. I'm sure she was right there with him when he told me."

"I guess," she said dropping it.

When the movers left their home they quickly found something to wear for the evening. They got ready and headed to the club.

Chapter 5
New Love Interest
August 15

"Hello," Melissa said answering the phone.

"Hey beautiful are you up?" Isaiah asked. He spent the night before hanging out with his new love interest.

"Yeah I'm up. I'm still tired from hanging out with you all night. It was after six this morning before I went to sleep."

"But we had a great time though, well worth it."

"Yeah we did have a great time. You sound like you are wide awake."

"I just left the gym. I slept a few hours and had to get up and get my day started," Isaiah said.

"Well, I could sleep a few more hours. But like you said, I need to get up and get my day started. Don't want to sleep the day away."

"Well how about you get ready and I come over to pick you up, take you to get some lunch." Isaiah suggested.

"Sounds like a plan. I will be ready in twenty minutes."

"Okay, I will see you in twenty minutes then."

"I will be ready."

Melissa hung up the phone to get ready for lunch with Isaiah. He was so sweet to her the night before and such a gentleman. She was not use to that type of treatment. She was used to men taking her home the first night to have sex with her. She let them use her for sex so she could use them for money. Isaiah was different from what she was used to but she was excited to try something different.

Isaiah pulled up to her home, walked to the door wearing his slacks and button-down baby blue dress shirt, looking business casual with swag waiting on her to answer. He arrived in exactly twenty minutes. But he was not ready for what was waiting behind closed doors. When she opened the door Isaiah's eyes widened and his mouth dropped.

"Hey sexy. I thought you may want some dessert before the main course," Melissa said with her hands on her hips holding her silk robe open exposing her lacey pink bra and panties.

"Uhm, uhm, uhm, you are wearing, uhm, you are wearing that to lunch?" Isaiah managed to get out. He was stunned that she was standing their practically naked ready to give him her candy. He was used to dating a woman and working towards getting the goodies just as his father taught him. His dad said anything that is given too easily may need to be questioned of its quality. Isaiah liked this girl and didn't want to stop seeing her because she didn't respect herself enough to wait. He wanted to show her a different way.

"No silly, I figured we would have hot steamy wild sex before we went for lunch. Don't you want that? All men want sex," she said looking a bit confused as to why Isaiah was still standing outside the door.

"Yeah, yes, I do, hell yeah I do. No, no, I mean yes, I do but I am hungry and we have plenty of time for this so hurry up and put some clothes on girl. I'll wait for you in the car," Isaiah nervously said.

"What? Eat first?"

"Yes, eat first. I can't perform on an empty stomach especially not after an intense workout. Hurry up girl." Isaiah said with a smile backing up towards the car still enjoying the sexy view she gave him.

"Okay, if you say so," she said closing her robe watching him walk to the car. She was shocked that he turned down having sex with her. Her feelings were a bit hurt and she did not know how to respond to him rejecting sex but she decided to dress and go out to have lunch first instead. She was confused by him. he was not like the men she was used to dealing with.

Isaiah was sitting in his car hitting the steering wheel talking to his self out loud. "Dude are you stupid? She was basically giving you the ass. It was all up in your face ready to be taken. Isaiah no, no your parents taught you better than that. Fuck! Is something wrong with her? Why she giving it up so easily? I should probably run but damn I like this girl. I mean I have had sex with a girl after two weeks but never after two days. Damn." Isaiah was talking to himself as the good and the bad angel trying to decide his next move. "Okay I'm going to take her to lunch, play it cool and decide then what to do. Yeah that's what I am going to do. Get it together man here she comes." Isaiah tried to compose his self. He jumped out of the car to open her door. "Hey, you look beautiful all dressed in clothes. Not that you didn't before. I mean, you were beautiful then too," he mumbles as she got into the car. Melissa smiled and said, "Thank you."

After Isaiah closed the door he walked around the back of the car. "I am a fucking idiot. Yeah that's what I am. All dressed in clothes, really? That was stupid." Isaiah was beating himself up over what just happened. He wasn't prepared to handle the situation. He got in the car and turned to see Melissa looking uncomfortable and nervous.

Melissa started talking to him looking down at her hands placed in her lap. "I am sorry I came on so strong. I assumed you were like all other men wanting sex from me."

"Oh no, no need to apologize to me for anything. No not at all. You are a beautiful lady, a desirable lady. My parents just taught me to respect a woman and treat her better than just a piece of…" he paused to rephrase his words. "My father and mother have been together since before I was born, so they are old school. You know court a woman, treat her like a Queen. Let her know you value her without her giving of herself, her body."

"Your parents must be good people. Wise in their words," she said half smiling still looking down at her hands.

Isaiah had one hand on the steering wheel driving and reached over to hold her hand with the other. "Girl for a moment you had me about to go against my parent's teachings. Your body is beautiful. I'm probably one of the biggest idiots but I hope one day after we get to know each other more I will be given the opportunity to redeem myself."

She smiled and bit her bottom lip. Looking up at him she said, "You really are a nice guy. Thank you for honoring me. My feelings were hurt but I understand now. You are not like most guys I have dealt with. So thank you for that!" she said squeezing his hand.

"I didn't mean to hurt your feelings at all. You are such a beautiful lady and you are worth the wait. Any man that doesn't see that is not the man for you."

She smiled and was now okay that he didn't take advantage of her giving up sex two days after meeting. "I am starving where are we going?"

"It's a surprise but I am sure you will love it." Isaiah was ok now that they talked. He still decided he liked Melissa and would keep seeing her. He hoped that the relationship would blossom into something good for him. He held on to that hope and enjoyed his afternoon with her. Their time together didn't end after lunch. They hung out longer after lunch, not wanting to leave one another. Melissa enjoyed having a man pay attention to her and not just her body. Isaiah was hoping this was the start of a promising future. He got the call from Brielle inviting him to dinner that evening and he was excited to bring his new girl around positive real relationships of true love.

Chapter 6
Wedding Plans
August 15

Sitting in their living room with the wedding planner, Bryson and Brielle finalized the remaining details for their wedding. Tulips and roses in her bouquet. A variety of wedding flowers on tables and decorating the aisles. When to announce the news of her pregnancy. What flavors of cake and the final cake design. They finalized all details down to the garter belt and their first dance. Bryson wanted Brielle to have the perfect wedding even if she wanted it to be simple. She was his Queen and he wanted her to feel like his Queen in every way possible.

"Thank you for making me feel so special Bryson. From the moment we met you have taken care of me and the kids and that has not changed."

"You are my Queen and I want you to always feel that way. God blessed me when he brought you into my life. I am going to make sure I take care of my gift. Well, my gifts. You and the kids have made me a family man and I love every moment of being a father and a husband," he said pulling her closer in his arms rubbing her belly.

"You are a great father to the kids and will be a great father to our twins as well. My King forever!" she said turning her head to kiss him.

"Oh momma I saw that. You kissed daddy," Jayla said walking into the living room just as Bryson kissed Brielle. She was always giggly when she saw the affection her mom received, more so because she still had memories of the abuse her mom endured by Jayla's own father and she enjoyed seeing her happy and in love with Bryson.

"Hey baby girl. You see me kissing your momma?" Bryson said kissing Brielle again as they both giggled.

"That's because you in love with her. That's what Carter say is the reason you kiss momma all the time," Jayla said.

"Carter is a very smart young man. I am in love with your momma and I love you kids very much," Bryson said to Jayla.

"You in love with momma and you just love us. So, what's the difference?" Jayla said asking a more detailed question neither Bryson nor Brielle was expecting.

"Well honey. It's different when you are in a relationship. You fall in love with that person in a different way that you love your children or your parents," Brielle said.

"You still love them the same as God loves us but you show more 'in love' affection when you find your soul mate like me and your mom," Bryson said.

"Like granddaddy and grand momma? Are they in love? Cause granddaddy always kissing grand momma," Jayla said.

"Yes, like granddaddy and grand momma," Brielle said. "Speaking of them, they will be here tonight to watch you, your sister and brother. We are going out for a little while this evening."

"Are y'all going somewhere for grown folks only momma?"

"Yes, for grown folk's baby," Brielle said.

Jayla was excited that her grandparents were coming over. She ran out of the living room to tell her siblings. "Carter, Olivia, grand momma and granddaddy coming over," she said excited.

"They love their momma and their grandparents," Bryson said squeezing Brielle tight.

"Lots of love going around and I love every bit of it," she said laying her head up against Bryson's chest as he held her.

"We need to get both our parents together for dinner or something and tell them about the pregnancy at the same time and soon," Bryson said.

"Yes soon, the first chance we get. We don't want them mad at us for not telling them sooner than later," Brielle said.

"Right. First chance we get we will tell them together before the wedding."

Moments later the door bell rung. "That must be my parents," Brielle said.

"I had the limo service on call to pick them up when they were ready," Bryson said as they walked to the door.

"Mom, Dad." Bryson and Brielle said at the same time seeing both of their parents at the door. Brielle leaned in giving her parents hugs and kisses on their cheeks.

"Hi Mrs. Mathews, Mr. Mathews," she said hugging them as well. She did not know they were coming but was pleasantly surprised just as Bryson was.

"How are you my favorite new daughter?" Mrs. Mathews said as she hugged Brielle.

"I'm doing great," she said before hugging Mr. Mathews.

"What are you two doing here? Not that you need a reason it's just a pleasant surprise," Bryson asked.

"Well, we were talking to Marcella and Mitchell and we found out they would be here to watch the kids so we all decided to come watch the kids and hang out. Have us our own old folk party with the kids of course.

"That's great! I'm sure the kids will be so excited to have all of you here," Brielle said as they all walked through the door.

The limo driver brought their bags in asking where he should place both couples' bags.

"All the rooms are nice so whatever empty room you come to first that's where we will rest our heads." Mr. Summers said.

"Up the stairs first door on the right," Bryson instructed the driver.

"And you can place our bags in the downstairs room. I appreciate that sir," Mr. Mathews said.

"There are rooms downstairs too?" Mr. Summers asked Mr. Mathews.

"It's like a whole 'nother home downstairs. Come on I will show you," Mr. Mathews said.

"Before you go dad, Mr. Mathews we wanted to share something with all of you since both of our parents are here," Brielle said looking up at Bryson.

"Oh yeah right. Both of our parents are here. Right," Bryson said nervously.

Brielle was smiling as she reached for her husband's hand. This would be his parent's first grandchildren with the twins. Even though they knew about Jewel, this would be different. This news would be coming from Bryson and his true love, a loving home with a loving relationship having their grandchild. One they didn't have to doubt and would see often to help them raise.

"Well, since you all are here together we wanted you to be among the first to know that we are expecting. We didn't want to tell everyone else until after the wedding but we wanted our immediate family and close friends to know first."

"Wait, are you saying you all are having a baby?" Mrs. Summers asked.

"Yes, momma. We are having twins actually," Brielle said.

"Well that is just some amazing news. Congratulations son. I am going to be a grandfather." Mr. Mathews said reaching to hug his son's neck.

"Thanks dad," Bryson said hugging his father.

"I had a dream about a lot of fish. I should have known it meant twins. I am so happy for you both. We are having twins, thank you Jesus for a double blessing," Mrs. Mathews said.

"This is great news. I am happy for you both," Mr. Summers said hugging her daughter's neck.

Everyone was hugging and congratulating them both, rubbing on Brielle's stomach and making baby talk. The kids came running in when they heard the commotion. "Granny here. Granddaddy here. They both are here." The kids said full of excitement.

"Are all of you watching us?" Jayla asked holding on to her granny's leg.

"Yes, we're all watching you kids. We're going to have fun," Mrs. Summers said.

"Your grandparents know about mommy having twins. So you don't have to keep it a secret from them," Brielle said.

"I'm glad because I wanted grand momma to know so bad," Olivia said. Everyone laughed at her serious and relieved tone.

"I'm hanging out with the men," Carter said standing by his grandfather and Bryson's dad.

"Alright youngster, we are going to head to the man cave."

"Well we are going to leave you all to tend to the kids while we go get ready for tonight. I am so glad all of you are here," Brielle said hugging her and Bryson's mom again.

"You are just as sweet as pie," Mrs. Mathews said.

"Yeap, that's my baby, sweet as pie," Mrs. Summers said.

Brielle and Bryson headed to their bedroom and the mothers headed to the living room to talk. "Twins. Well I'll say that is just awesome news," Mrs. Mathews said.

"It is indeed awesome. We are so blessed to have Bryson in Brielle and those kid's life. He is a great man. You all raised him well." Mrs. Summers said.

"Well thank you. Your Brielle is a wonderful girl too. We don't worry about those two at all. She is the daughter we never had. Now, Bradon and Chantae I worry about." Mrs. Mathews said.

"Oh no, why you worry about those two? I think they are both good kids as well. I mean they are not Bryson and Brielle but they are still good kids." Mrs. Summers said.

"They are honey but my Bradon was wild in them streets before he met her. He always had a different girl but no one ever serious. He never committed to anyone. We never saw them unless we happen to be there in the morning when the girl did her hoe walk out of his room to leave."

Mrs. Summers laughed saying, "Not the hoe walk girl. The walk of shame the morning after."

"Honey yes, he always wanted his freedom. I used to worry about him all the time with all the partying he did."

"I guess you can say Chantae was a bit out there too. After being abandoned by her father when she was a little girl she took it hard and I think she craved attention from men."

"Oh no that's awful."

"But she grew up like overnight. Ended up being a good girl looking for love and I believe that is what she has found with your Bradon, love."

"He obviously loves her."

"I can see it. I guess they are alike in a way and they both finally found love." Mrs. Summers said.

"They are in love. For Bradon to give up living the wild life I know he is in love. I just pray to God they are reminded about that love and not fall backwards to their old familiar ways." Mrs. Mathews said.

"I know what you mean honey. Sin is everywhere and the devil will tempt them with bringing their past to the present. Only true love can withstand temptation."

"Exactly. The Devil is always at work trying to steal God's promise of happiness. God has blessed those two bringing them together and now they need prayer warriors like us to pray for them constantly."

"That is the truth. We need to constantly pray for all of our kids." Mrs. Summers said.

"My friend, I am glad to know you." Mrs. Mathews said reaching to hug Mrs. Summers.

Bryson and Brielle were getting ready for their evening out with their friends. Brielle was flawless even with her belly sticking out. She concealed her belly with a blouse that hung loosely falling to her hips. However, there was no covering her huge breast.

"Are you ready to share the news with everyone tonight?" Brielle asked Bryson. She stood in the mirror looking at him smiling back at her.

"I am ready for the world to know my wife is having my twins," he said looking at Brielle's face light up with a smile. "You look beautiful by the way. You have a beautiful glow to match your natural beauty!"

"You are so sweet to me always and I love it!" Brielle said turning to kiss her husband.

He picked her up and gently sat her down on the sink. He stood in between her opened legs wrapping his arms around her waist. "You are my Queen and I will always be sweet to you. I love you Mrs. Mathews," he said kissing her lips.

"I love you Mr. Mathews." She closed her eyes and allowed him to kiss her face so seductively. He kissed the corners of her mouth sucking on her lips before piercing her lips with his tongue to dance with her tongue. Kissing her lips again he caressed her back as his lips moved down her face. She held on to his shoulders with her eyes still closed and leaned her head backwards as he kissed her chin making his way to her neck. He kissed her neck up to her ear whispering, "I can't wait until we get home tonight. I am going to make love to every inch of your body all night. First, I want you to enjoy dinner and our friends but anticipate the love making when we return home."

"Yes daddy. I will be thinking about you making love to every inch of my body the entire time we are out. You know I will be anticipating our return home." She opened her eyes with him close to her face looking at her. He kissed her lips slowly as her chest was moving up and down. He could have made love to her nonstop and she would have not protested.

"Let's finish getting ready before the hosts of the party are late or no shows," Bryson said still holding on to her.

"But yet you are still holding me tight," she said. He leaned in kissing her lips again. "And you're still kissing me," she said with her eyes closed enjoying the feeling of love.

"It's so hard to break away from you. I love you so much. Words cannot explain how much I love you Brielle," Bryson said holding her, leaning his face against her face with his eyes closed.

"Babe you are about to make me cry. I feel your love for me. God is so amazing to have created such a thing as true unconditional love. I am so blessed to have you," Brielle said with tears in her eyes.

He leaned in kissing both her eyes and her nose before kissing her lips again. "Don't mess up your makeup," he said pulling her close in a tight hug before releasing her. He picked her up to stand in front of him.

With her back to the sink she wrapped her arms around his neck looking into his eyes. "You are my forever Bryson Mathews."

"You are my forever Brielle Mathews."

"Okay, if we don't leave now we are not going anywhere," Brielle said. "Come on let's get ready to go. Our friends are waiting on us."

Slowly releasing her he agreed. They finished getting ready finding the kids before leaving to say their goodbyes. The kids were so occupied hanging out with their grandparents all they managed to say was bye without looking up.

Chapter 7
Night Out on the Town
August 15

Saturday night was one of the busiest at Club Luxe. Bryson and Brielle pulled up in the limo to the front entrance of the club walking straight inside without stopping, bypassing the extremely long line. He was the owner and everyone knew who he was. Sometimes they confused Bradon for Bryson but when Bryson showed up they definitely knew him and made sure he was in without pause and escorted directly to VIP. He didn't come to the club to manage anything. He hired the best team to manage everything for him to ensure the club was a success and to give him and his business partners a prestige place to relax and enjoy the atmosphere.

When they arrived at the VIP area the table was set just as Bryson asked. Appetizers and Wine glasses filled with water were placed. The arrangement was beautiful. He even had roses for all the ladies. When they walked up to the table, Ameila and Kenneth were seated next to where they would be seating. They were so in tune with one another smiling and giggling as if they were two lovebirds they didn't notice them walking up.

"Well don't you two look beautiful and happy I must say," Brielle said walking around to hug Kenneth first.

"Hey beautiful," Kenneth said standing to hug Brielle. "What's up Bryson?" he said giving Bryson a manly hug.

"Ameila how are you girl?" Brielle asked leaning in to hug her.

"I couldn't be better. You are gorgeously glowing tonight. Must be all that true love," Ameila said.

"Thanks girl," she said giving her a wink looking at her, Kenneth and then back to her. "I'm just saying, you do have a similar glow and you look fabulous!"

"Thanks girl," she said smiling trying to avoid the insinuation she gave about her and Kenneth. She had no problem sharing her feelings about Kenneth but she had to keep in mind she was legally still married and wanted to respect Kenneth's wishes. When her divorce was final should would be sure to show her true feelings every chance she could.

"Hey Ameila. You look beautiful. Glad you were able to join us," Bryson said hugging her.

"I wouldn't miss it," she said, taking her seat. She was sitting in between Bryson and Kenneth.

"Babe, here come Isaiah and a he has a girl with him look," Brielle said quietly to Bryson.

"Wow, Isaiah walking in here like he is the man for sure with his new girl," Bryson said laughing. He greeted Isaiah as he walked up. "What's up brother glad you could make it."

"Man, this VIP treatment is amazing thanks for that! This is my girl Melissa. Melissa this is my sister Brielle and her husband Bryson. That's Kenneth and Ameila," he said introducing his girl to everyone. They all greeted and welcomed her.

"I see you little brother," Brielle said motioning for him to come to her.

"How are you doing sis?" Isaiah said squeezing his sister tight.

"I'm great. You look happy and your girl is cute."

"Thanks sis. I'm hoping she is a keeper. I like her a lot." Isaiah said talking into his sister's ear soft enough that only she could hear him. The music was playing just loud enough in their area that a soft-spoken voice would go unheard. "Give me another hug sis I miss you."

He surprised Brielle by picking her up off her feet and he noticed her baby bump. "Put me down boy," she said straightening out her clothes realizing that he now knew.

He whispered, "Wait, is this what I think it is? Are you..." He looked her in her eyes with his brotherly vibe waiting for her response.

"You do know me well but can you not say anything until we announce it to everyone please."

"I knew it. And of course." He hugged his sister again tightly. "I am so happy for you sis. I love you so much."

"I love you too now go keep your girl company she looks nervous."

"Aight sis," he said releasing her before walking to his seat still smiling.

They all took their seats and indulged in the Wine as they waited for Bradon and Chantae. Bryson checked his phone for any messages from Bradon.

Bradon Mathews
6:55 pm
Hey Brys, we just left the house headed that way. We will be about 15 minutes behind.

Bryson Mathews
7:05pm
All good. See you in a sec.

"That was Bradon. They should be here any minute now," Bryson said to everyone. Turning to Brielle he asked, "Are you okay? You need to eat now don't wait," he said reaching for the Salad and Bruschetta topped with shrimp.

"Okay yes, I am ready to eat but you eat with me okay until we tell everyone the news," she said whispering.

"I sure will my Queen," he said picking up a piece of Bruschetta and feeding it to her before placing the other piece in his mouth. "You all indulge. We can order dinner when the other two arrive," Bryson said turning to Kenneth and Ameila.

"Oh, this is so good!" Brielle said. "I could eat this as my meal."

"We can order more. They are a favorite of mine," he said with his arm around the back of Brielle's chair.

"This is good," Ameila said eating the bruschetta with shrimp. "Taste it Kenneth." She picked up another piece stuffing it in his mouth.

Bryson caught the look he gave her and knew that Kenneth was really feeling Ameila for him to show any type of affection in public, even if he was trying to be discreet. "They are cute together," he said to Brielle.

"They are cute together. Are they in a relationship now or still in denial?" Brielle asked Bryson.

"They are waiting until her divorce is final I believe. He knows everyone is picking up on it though."

"That's understandable. I love all this love around us." She ran her hand down the side of his face.

He grabbed her hand pulling it closer to his mouth to kiss. "True love is so beautiful," he said putting his arms around her to kiss her awaiting lips.

"Bryson and Brielle sitting in the tree K I S S I N G," Bradon said walking up behind them with Chantae on his arms.

"What's up brother?" Bryson said as he stood from his seat to embrace Bradon.

"Hey girlfriend," Brielle said embracing Chantae. "You are looking beautiful as always.

"Hey Brielle. You are looking beautiful yourself. Your makeup is flawless and you are glowing too anything you want to tell me?" Chantae asked still hugging her.

"You always did know me well. We have not announced it yet only to our parents and the kids. That's why we wanted you all to meet us. Keep it to yourself for now until we tell everyone else," she said quietly to Chantae.

"I knew it." Chantae whispered with excitement in her voice. She hugged her again. "Girl I have missed you!"

"I have missed you too," Brielle said before taking her seat.

"I will be back let me say hello to everyone else." Chantae headed for Bryson, Kenneth, Ameila, Isaiah and his girl to speak before taking her seat. Bradon set in between the two friends but Chantae still managed to talk with Brielle.

They ordered dinner and everyone engaged in great friendly conversation. Bryson and Brielle announced the news about the baby and everyone was excited for them.

Bryson stood up to give a speech, "I want to thank everyone here for coming tonight but more importantly thank you all for your friendship, your love, and your support you gave in my journey that led to me having and holding my Queen Brielle. Finding her and the children has been the best thing that has ever happened to me. And now she is carrying my children and I couldn't be any happier than I am right now in my life. You all have played a major part in our life and that's the reason we wanted to share the news of the pregnancy with you all first. Our happiness is a gift from God and he blessed us with true love and the love of family and true genuine friends around us. We want to thank you Bradon and Chantae for agreeing to be the Maid of Honor and the Best Man in our wedding ceremony. We love you both dearly. So, with that said we thank you all. And Brielle thank you for taking my last name, making me the happiest man alive. God truly blessed me and showed out when he gave me you. I love you sweetheart." He leaned over and kissed Brielle on her lips, wiping her tears from her eyes.

"That was beautiful babe," Brielle said.

"There is no denying his love for her," Chantae said to Bradon.

"It is a beautiful thing and he deserves this happiness," Bradon said.

It wasn't what Chantae expected him to say right after hearing something as beautiful and romantic. Her mind was racing with thoughts, some good some not so good. Between the wine and other drinks she consumed, she was not thinking clearly and her thoughts were not at all pleasant. After another moment, she excused herself for the bathroom. "I will be back babe. I'm going to the ladies' room," she said to Bradon.

"Come on I will go with you," Bradon said getting up to walk with her. He didn't want to leave her to the vultures waiting to attack any beautiful lady they thought was available. He caught Melissa eyes staring at him and thought for a second she looked familiar but quickly dismissed the thought and followed Chantae.

Chantae loved the fact that he wanted to go with her, even if it was for his selfish reasons. "I will be right back babe." She said walking into the lady's room.

"I will be right here when you come out beautiful," he said watching her walk away. Standing there he realized being in the openness of the club may have been a mistake. He spotted several girls that he had slept with. He received some evil looks, eyes rolling at him and even some smiles and winks. He was approached by one girl he didn't even see walk up to him until she was in his face.

"What's up Bradon? Long time no see," she said caressing his chest. It was obvious she had a few drinks.

He grabbed her hand letting her know not to touch him. "Hey what's up?" he said turning to see if Chantae was coming. Turning back to the girl, he was engaged in conversation and didn't see Chantae come out walking towards him.

"You must be here with your next victim. You have never turned this pussy down. You may have gone behind my back and fucked my best friend and that hoe Mel that was pretending to be my friend to get to you, but you have never turned down this pussy. You remember Mel, right? You stood me up for that bitch." The girl was intoxicated and rambling her truth to Bradon.

"I guess. Look I can't talk to you right now. I'm here with my girl," he said not knowing Chantae was right behind him. She had a smile on her face hearing him say that to the beautiful girl talking to him. Until she heard her next words.

"Well you go on with your girl," she slurred. "I'm sure she can't do what I did for you." She turned to walk away but quickly turned back to Bradon. "Oh yeah, you might want to call Mel. Yeah, the bitch you stood me up for that tried to get you for your money. She pregnant or was. She might have had the baby by now I haven't seen her in over a year but she said the baby was yours," the girl said before turning to walk away.

Bradon remembered the night she was speaking of. She was one of the girls he had a threesome with that gave him head until he came, then ran into the bathroom. Later the other girl told him she put his sperm in a Ziploc bag to try to impregnate herself. She wanted to have his baby hoping she could put him on child support. He was supposed to be her big payday. He was deep in thought and was startled by Chantae's touch when he realized she was behind him. He was hoping she didn't hear any of that conversation.

Chantae pretended she didn't hear what the girl said. "You ready babe?" she said putting her hand in his.

"Yes, I'm ready. You good?" he said putting his arm around her neck.

"Yes babe. I'm ready to leave if you are. I'm tired," she said wrapping her arm around his waist.

"For sure. Let's go tell everyone good bye."

Chantae's mind was wandering all over the place. She loved Bradon. Her heart was all into loving him. But she couldn't stop thinking about the possibility of him having a baby. She knew girls who trapped men into paying child support by stealing their sperm. Most of the time it was men who were famous so they could get paid in child support never having to work again. Then she thought about Brielle's happiness with Bryson, living in the house she thought she would be living in with Bradon. And without thinking she was now comparing her life to Brielle's life. She was having a baby by a man who gave her his last name. Her life was picture perfect. Sure, she deserves to be happy, everyone does. But her happiness was now threatened. Bradon's past and lack of what she thought was his life was bothering her more than she thought. It appeared as if his past was catching up with him. She held her composure long enough to say good bye to everyone and leave the club.

As she hugged Brielle to say good bye Brielle grabbed her by the hand holding on a little longer. "Are you ok? You look like something is wrong."

"Oh yeah girl, just tired from moving today. It just hit me I guess. I'll call you tomorrow and congratulations on the babies. I am so happy for you."

"Ok girl. Call me tomorrow okay," she said releasing her hand.

After Chantae and Bradon left the other six stayed for a while longer enjoying one another's company. Kenneth knew that Bryson knew about his feelings for Ameila. With the liquor in his system he became more affectionate with Ameila not caring who witnessed him flirting with her, touching her and saying sweet things to her. There was no doubting the love Kenneth was feeling for Ameila. She also reciprocated that love back to him. They may both be in denial but everyone around them could see what was obvious.

Isaiah and Melissa looked cozy together. They were hugged up, even kissing. Isaiah wasn't a drinker and only had a glass of Wine to celebrate the news. He was contemplating his next move with Melissa. She was all over him and he knew she wanted to have sex with him. He was torn between honoring her or having sex with the beautiful woman knowing he would regret it later.

It was time for everyone to be heading home. Bryson signaled for them all to leave. He made sure Ameila and Kenneth had a car service waiting outside before he and Brielle left for home. Kenneth and Ameila both had more than enough to drink. He knew Isaiah drove and he watched as they got in their car. They all pulled off about the same time.

Chapter.8
Regretfully in Jail
August 24

All you could hear were keys jingling and footsteps walking towards the door. There was only a small window but nothing could be seen through it. Jewel ended up in a dark cold cell because she wanted to have sex with the handsome married security officer. He took her to holding in the basement and she was ready to have some fun with him. She flirted with him insinuating that she could fuck him better than his wife. She knew that the officers were having sex with inmates so she flirted until he decided to give her what she wanted. Once he put her in the cell behind the closed door it was nothing as she imagined. The space was small and confined to four walls that were six feet from the other. No mattress on the concrete frame of a bed, it was cold, smelled like a stale wet basement and dirty.

The encounter she had with him before relieved her pent up sexual frustration. Even though she said she would not go back, she found herself sexually frustrated and desperate to be penetrated by a man. So she agreed again but this time it wasn't as pleasant as she had hoped.

The officer made Jewel strip down to nothing and he proceeded to pull his pants to his knees. He grabbed her by her hair forcing her to her knees telling her to suck on his manhood. She played the role of bad girl and got him hard but refused to suck him. He then forcefully turned her around onto the hard concrete bed like he was mad and about to punish her. After putting on a condom he pushed his manhood hard inside her. He grabbed her by her breast squeezing them hard and he pounded her pussy as fast as he could. He didn't care about giving her any pleasure or making her have an orgasm as she hoped. She told him to stop she felt sick from moving too fast. He told her to shut up and kept going. She vomited everywhere and he kept going until he had an orgasm.

She was pissed off and cursed him out. He told her she wasn't better than his wife because she was just some jail house pussy with a pretty face. She didn't deserve to have an orgasm. He threatened her telling her if she said anything to anyone she would be forced to have sex with every guard there even if it meant they each took a turn all day long. He heard from one of the inmates that she told someone she had sex with him and he was pissed off. He decided he wanted to teach her a lesson about running her mouth.

She had never felt like this. Not even when she was raped as a teenager. This was a feeling she never felt before and one she didn't want to ever feel again. He told her he would be back with a change of clothes since she puked all over herself. She told him to hurry so she could shower asking if he would take her to the nurse because she felt so sick. He told her he would be right back. It was an hour later before he came back. But it wasn't the same guard.

"Who are you? Where is the other guard?" She had a bad feeling when she saw a different guard return with no clothes and closing the door behind him.

The guard opened the holding cell door and entered closing the door quickly. "Oh he will be back later. It's my turn to taste the sugar," he said walking towards her.

"Sugar. What are you doing? Why are you in here?" she said watching him undo his belt to loosen his pants. He pulled his pants down enough to expose his full erection as he walked towards her aggressively grabbing her. "Get off me. I'm not having sex with your fat disgusting ass."

Jewel tried to fight the guard off but she was too weak to go up against him. "Consider this a little extra insurance to keep your fucking mouth closed bitch." He cuffed her hands to the iron frame of the bed. He stuffed a wash cloth in her mouth and he had his way with her for over an hour. Her screams went unheard. Her cries were merely wet drops falling with no one to rescue her.

She went from being horny wanting to have sex with a fine handsome officer to being forced to have sex with a fat ugly officer. She felt humiliated, violated and disrespected in the worse ways. She was being raped repeatedly by the same two officers for three days straight. She barely ate the food they brought her but had to force food down because she was sick from being pregnant.

They handcuffed her every time they entered the cell and her screams fell on deaf ears and cold empty walls. The married officer was always quick. The other officer was single and he took pleasure in having sex with a beautiful woman like Jewel. Both men had a bright idea that she couldn't get pregnant and they both were STD free so they stopped using condoms and started releasing their orgasm all over her body washing her with soap and water when they were done to wash away the evidence. They degraded her in every way possible using their power to get away with what they did repeatedly.

Jewel had served two months of her sentence in jail for destruction of property and endangerment from running her car into Bryson's building. Her sex addiction caused her to miss out on a great life with Bryson and she was now regretting every bad decision she made to jeopardize her happiness. She cheated on him, seduced and tricked his brother, having sex with him and manipulated and deceived Bryson. When he caught her in the act of cheating she knew her life was forever changed. It hurt her knowing that she had hurt him. She knew things between them would never be the same. The one man that made her feel unconditionally loved and cared for completely was now out of her reach. She regretted ever hurting him and needed him more than ever to rescue her now.

She made every attempt to call Bryson from jail but he never accepted her call. Her sexual addiction led her to a place that she could not control. The evening she thought she had the upper hand convincing a married officer to have sex with her was a mistake she wish she would have never made. The evening he came to get her was after final count when the other inmates were loud and no one would miss her. Her cell mate tried to tell her she was making a big mistake but she assured her she knew what she was doing. He took her to the holding cell where he took advantage of her not caring that she was pregnant. She regretted her decision and knew she needed help to get out of that place.

For three days her screams were unheard. Her pleads for them to stop went in one ear and out the other. They raped her for what seemed like forever. They threatened her to keep her mouth closed. Scaring her that if she told anyone all the horrible things they would do to her. The rapes were repeated until they had to take her to see the doctor.

She didn't care about any of their threats she just wanted help, wanted to never feel like that, be treated like that ever again. She told the doctor what happened and begged to make a call. After a thorough examination confirming her story she granted her all the time she needed feeling sorry for what happened to her. In the past, the doctor heard stories of rape in the jail but never had the proof she needed. Nothing ever was done so people stopped talking about it but she knew it still happened. She never had the evidence she needed that said rape and not consensus sex until now.

The doctor knew Jewel had been raped but also knew proving it would be hard even with the proof she had. She knew Jewel had a sexual addiction. She also knew Jewel flirted with the guards. Her condition would be used against her in proving she was actually raped. But the rape kit could confirm the guards were having sex with inmates, which was against policy and considered a crime. She advised her to do all she could to get moved to a different facility. She put in a transfer request to have her moved herself to a facility that provided medical and psychological support for her condition. But she also knew that wouldn't happen overnight.

She kept her in the infirmary longer than normal trying to prevent any more attacks until she could get her moved. Her reasoning for keeping her was based on her being dehydrated and lacked nutrition needed for her and her developing baby. She classified her as a risk to herself and unborn child.

When Bryson continuously did not answer, she called her father. He may have left her when she was a little girl and needed him the most in her life but now he continuously tried hard to get his little girl back. She figured it was time to put aside being mad about the past and lean on the one man who will never stop loving her. She picked up the phone and quickly dialed her father's number.

It was early that morning but he answered on the first ring. "Hello."

"Daddy it's Jewel," she said into the receiver happy he picked up.

"Hey baby girl. What's wrong? You sound like you are crying?"

"Daddy I need you to call Bryson for me on three-way. He won't answer my calls," she said with tears in her eyes.

Her father's heart was breaking. He knew what she did to Bryson and that he did not want to hear from her. "Baby I know you are hurting but Bryson does not want to talk to you sweetheart."

"I know daddy. I need him to help me. I know he still has some type of love for me and don't want to see anything bad happen to me. I am carrying his child."

"Something bad like what sweetheart what's going on?"

"Daddy the guards are raping me. I know you might not believe me no one does because of that stupid sex addiction. But I am telling you the truth they are raping me and I don't want them touching me and hurting me. Those fat disgusting ugly nasty fuckers are raping me. I scream but no one comes and no one is doing anything about it. Please call Bryson he can have me moved right now. He has power to have anything he wants done. Please daddy you got to believe me."

Furious and hurt her dad closed his eyes clinching his fist. "I do believe you sweetheart. Where are you now? How are you calling me?"

"I'm in the doctor office. She is keeping me in here in the hospital trying to help me get moved but they don't want to move me."

"Hold on let me call Bryson. Don't hang up," he said before clicking over to call Bryson.

"Hello?" Bryson answered on the first ring.

"Bryson please don't hang up on me son. I know things ended really bad between you and my daughter but I need your help."

"Mr. Taylor, I respect you but Jewel put herself in jail and I don't want to help her get out. Maybe that's what she needs to get better."

"Bryson all I am asking is for you to pull some strings to have her moved. The doctor there has already put in a request for her transfer but they are not moving her. I just need you to make some phone calls," Mr. Taylor said with desperation in his voice.

"Sir, I am sure if the request is in they will move her soon. Now if you will excuse me…" he said before he was interrupted.

Mr. Taylor's voice got louder. "Those motherfuckers are in there raping my daughter who is possibly carrying your child. I know she has done some terrible things but dammit she doesn't deserve what they are doing to her. You once loved her and all I need you to do is make a few damn phone calls, use your influence and have her moved, today." Mr. Taylor's tone was direct but full of frustration.

Bryson was silent for a moment hearing about her being raped. He didn't want to have anything to do with Jewel but he didn't want any harm coming to her either and especially not to the baby. He knew Brielle could hear the conversation and she could see the look on his face. She reached for his hands and whispered "Please, help her if you can babe, it's ok."

Bryson then told Mr. Taylor, "I will take care of it sir."

"Thank you so much Bryson. Thank you so much son! I really appreciate you. Please get my baby out of there as quick as possible." Mr. Taylor was grateful and relieved Bryson would help Jewel despite all the pain she caused him.

Mr. Taylor ended the call with Bryson before merging his call back to Jewel. "Sweetheart he is going to help."

"Is he on the phone? Bryson are you there?" Jewel asked hoping to hear Bryson's voice.

"No sweetheart I talked to him alone man to man but he agreed to help get you out of that place today."

Sadness was in Jewel's voice. She was hurting because of what was happening to her inside the prison, hurting because she was regretful for hurting Bryson, hurting because all the bad things she has ever done was flooding her mind and she couldn't take any of it back. She could only ask for forgiveness. "Daddy, thank you. I am so sorry for disappointing you. I am so sorry for everything I have ever done to cause you and mommy pain. I need help and I am going to get better. I will make you proud of me. I'm sorry daddy. Please forgive me. God forgive me." She cried releasing tears of hurt and sorrow.

"I forgave you a long time ago sweetheart and God has already forgiven you. First step to healing is admitting and acknowledging your wrongs and asking God for forgiveness. We are going to get you out of that place and get you some help. Don't you worry sweetheart."

"Thank you daddy. I love you so much. Thank you for never giving up on me," she said still crying. The doctor came in the room giving her some tissues and checking on her. "Thank you. I don't have to leave do I?" She asked her.

"No, you stay here and talk to your father as long as you need." The doctor said leaving the room closing the door behind her.

"Don't leave sweetheart stay here with me on the phone. I want to pray with you."

"I'm here daddy. She said I can stay as long as I want."

"That's good." Her father said relieved that he could ensure she was safe for a little while longer. "Can I pray for you my child?"

"I would love that daddy."

"Alright baby girl. I need you to receive the words and be in agreeance in asking God to help you and heal you. Believe in your heart and trust and know that God is a forgiving God. That God is a healing God. That God loves you and will never leave you or forsake you. God will get you through what seems like a difficult time for you. He will use your situation to make you stronger. Father God, we are coming to you right now with a heavy heart full of hurt, pain, sorrow and regret. Father God, I am asking you as a Father to wrap your loving arms around our daughter. Squeeze her tight, hold her tight and deliver her from the evilness around her, from those who are out to harm her. Father God, protect her unborn child so that he or she may grow up to walk in the greatness you have planned for him. Father God, Jewel needs you. She has confessed her wrongs and asked for your forgiveness. Forgive her Father and deliver her from evil ways. Deliver her from the sex addiction that has a hold on her. Deliver her from any hold that is not meant for her good. Father God, provide her with the help she needs to help her along the journey of healing. Surround her with love and people who care about her wellbeing, her health and healing. Bless my child, bless your child and deliver Jewel from the holds that have her bound. Satan, we rebuke you in the name of Jesus you have no place here, you have no place in

Jewels heart, in her life. In the name of Jesus, I command you are no longer welcome to dwell where God is now present."

Mr. Taylor continued to pray for Jewel as she cried and released all the built-up anger, resentment and regret. Her Father abandoned her when she was a little girl and she never forgave him for that until now. Her healing process was starting and she had hope that everything would be alright. They stayed on the phone for another hour or so cherishing the father daughter moments. Jewel's healing process had started and she now had her father back in her life and he had his daughter back.

The door opened to the office where Jewel was and there stood the Dr. and a few officers. "Oh no please don't take me back. Daddy help me."

"What's happening Jewel." Her father screamed in panic.

"Jewel this is Dr. Monroe, she is the Psychiatrist that has been appointed to care for you during the remainder of your imprisonment. You are being transferred to a secure and safe hospital."

"I am." She asked watching the Doctor smile and shake her head yes. "Daddy Bryson did it. They are moving me."

"Praise God! Thank you Jesus! Let me know where so I can come see you, see your face and wrap my arms around you."

"Can you tell my Father where we are going?" she asked the doctor that took care of her, the one person that she knew cared in that jail.

"Yes, I will fill him in with the details."

"Daddy I love you come see me soon please."

"I love you too daughter and I am on my way to wherever she tells me you are going."

"Thank you daddy." She handed the phone to the Doctor and headed towards the Psychiatrist. As they walked out of the facility she saw police officers approaching the security guards who raped her.

The Psychiatrist had her arm around her saying, "You worry about getting well. There will be a full investigation and repercussions for what they did to you. We already have the rape kits completed which is the evidence needed to punish them and I am sure it won't be long before they are dealt with. Your treatment has been paid for. You will receive the best care possible and I will make sure you are comfortable and you feel safe at all times. We will monitor your pregnancy and make sure your baby is healthy as well."

Jewel started crying, relieved and thankful for Bryson. She knew he didn't stop caring about her. She didn't know how she could ever repay him. After everything she did to hurt him he still found love in his heart to help her. She still hoped in her heart she could have him and the life they had back. She wouldn't give up on that hope but for now she would try to heal and get help for her addiction. Healing and taking care of the unborn baby growing inside her was all she needed and wanted to focus on for now.

Chapter 9
Business As Usual
August 24

Monday morning Bryson was up getting ready for work when he unexpectedly received the call from Jewel's father. He previously blocked all calls from the jail facility where Jewel was calling. With Brielle by his side he placed the call on speaker phone so they both could hear the discussion. Brielle had a heart of gold and being a victim of rape herself by her kid's father, she insisted that Bryson help Jewel. She knew about what she did to Bryson and blackmailing Bradon. But in her mind and her heart, wrong doings do not justify wrong being done against anyone intentionally. And no woman should ever be violated by rape. Bryson immediately called Kenneth to take care of the situation for him.

"I am so proud to call you my husband! You are an amazing man," Brielle said to Bryson.

"Me? You are the amazing one. Knowing that she was my ex and I was about to marry her you still have a heart full of love and compassion. I am so grateful to have you and your loving heart. You are my greatest blessing Brielle!"

"Well you married the right one. God made sure of that! Even if God doesn't do anything else for us I think we are thankful enough to keep on being a blessing to others."

"You're right my beautiful Queen." He kissed her lips seductively feeling her smile beneath his lips. He kissed the corners of her mouth before indulging in her tongue. Pausing he held her close to him saying, "I will see you and the kids when I return this evening my love."

"You have a great day at work babe. I love you," she said tiptoeing to kiss his lips again.

"I love you to. Call me if you need anything even if you just want to talk."

"I won't bother you. Just call me when you take a break."

Bryson headed out the door to the awaiting car service and headed to his office. He started his day calling Kenneth from the car. "Good morning Kenny man, I am heading to the office but just wanted to follow up on the Jewel situation. Were you able to take care of that?"

"Yes, I called in favors and they are removing her from the situation now."

"Did they say where they would take her?" Bryson asked.

"Bryson, I thought the reason you asked me to do this for you was so that you were not involved at all. Please tell me you are not trying to go see her?" Kenneth asked concerned.

"Kenny. You know me better than that. I would never do that to Brielle or do anything to jeopardize what we have. Jewel is not worth it."

"Aight man. I know. Just didn't want you having a relapse for any reason."

"Naw, never that man. I am one hundred percent good. I promised Brielle I would follow up to make sure Jewel was moved and safe, getting the help she needs."

"Ok well they are taking her to the Women's Psychiatric Hospital. They are going to get her some help and let her do the remainder of her time there. It's secured and locked down and they can monitor her and the baby until she gives birth."

"That's what I needed to know. It's crazy that stuff like that is allowed to happen in jail. I was shocked when her father called me. He damn near cursed me out."

"Crazy. You just can't get her out of your life huh?"

"Don't seem that way."

"Brielle was cool with you helping her out?"

"Yeah, she is amazing always surprising me. She insisted. I mean I don't want anything bad to happen to her either, she just not my responsibility anymore."

"I feel you."

"I'm about to pull up. I will meet you in your office."

"I will be here."

Bryson parked in his private garage and came up the back elevators headed to Kenneth's office. "Knock, knock," he said before entering.

"Come on Bryson." Kenneth said signaling for Bryson to come in as he finished up his call. "Yes sir. Okay I will relay the message. Thank you so much!" He ended his call and headed to greet Bryson with a hand shake showing him love. "That was Consuela. She said the book will drop Friday, September 4th and the movie premier will be October 16th."

"Those dates sound good. How are they going to add the ceremony in, I know they have majority of the work completed except the wedding scene."

"They do. Everything is looking great on that part. The book is complete and the movie is done except the wedding scene. They are going to add it in the extra footage as 3 months later. They will add pieces from the wedding before closing it out."

"So, do we still agree that Ameila should be the face to promote the book since she wrote it and be the person to talk about the movie and do interviews?"

"Yes, I mentioned it to her. She was hesitant at first but she agreed. The PR team has been coaching her and preparing her. She is actually excited now and I trust that she will do a great job."

"I know she will be great. Have her sit in on the Board meeting this morning. It will be good for her to get a bit of insight from everyone," Bryson said looking up at Kenneth as he cut his eyes at him. "What? Is that a problem?"

"Not a problem. But I know you are up to something so spill it," Kenneth said curious as to what Bryson had planned.

"I know you feeling the girl man and you two seem to work great together."

"That's not it. Something else is going on in that never-ending mind of yours. Are you planning to leave the company or what?"

"I will never leave the company man you know that. Ok, I want to take off for a while when the baby is born to be daddy and enjoy my family. I can work maybe twice a month. I figured Ameila could be your work help mate and you could run the business while I am taking an extended vacation."

"Okay I feel you. But you know we are not together right? I mean her divorce is not even final yet."

"I hear you."

"No seriously. I do like her a lot but I'm trying to wait until she is divorced before really pursuing her."

"I know Kenny man. You my boy. You know I don't judge you regarding anything. But think about it, even if you did get with Ameila now I don't think there was ever a chance for her husband to come back in the picture to be with her."

"I know. But what would your mom say?"

"You right, never dishonor another man's marriage even if problems existed and they were sure to be divorced. You are doing the right thing. Everything happens in God's perfect timing. But the attraction is there and has been there no matter how much you try to deny it. God has already created your destiny. So embrace that fact and when the time is right don't hesitate to completely embrace the love."

"You are your mother's child, more business savvy than anything but definitely your mother's son!"

They both laughed because they knew Kenneth was right. Bryson had a lot of his mother in him but he also had a way with words and speaking what he believed as the truth. He knew Kenneth had finally met someone he felt strongly about. Someone that he was in love with before even sleeping with her. He was in love with a woman knowing her situation before coming to them. He fell in love with her naked truth and not her nakedness. He learned a lot about Ameila the day he met her, picking her and her kids up off the street wounded from brokenness. But her heart and her strength were not broken and her God caring spirit never left. He admired Ameila and he was also in love with her.

Chapter 10
Documentary Book Release
September 4

Ameila was on board to be in the spot light discussing the release of the book to Bryson's upcoming movie. Advertisement was up everywhere online, social media, bulletin boards and commercials playing on several major television networks. There was a lot of buzz going around and a lot of questions wanting to be asked. Ameila was setup to interview on several radio stations and talk shows about the book and the movie. She had a very busy weekend ahead of her but Kenneth would be right by her side helping to get through.

Her divorce was final. She was so wrapped up in work that it wasn't a topic of discussion between her and Kenneth. Since her divorce was final everything had been fast paced with long hours and days getting ready for the release. Bryson worked in the office that morning so Kenneth could be with Ameila to handle business outside the office.

Kenneth arrived in a limo to pick up Ameila early that Friday morning. Stepping out of the car to greet her, he walked over to hug her as the driver took her bags.

"Thank you Kenneth," she said with a smile. She stepped into the limo with Kenneth right behind her. "You are such a gentleman," she said once inside the limo.

"Always for you Ameila. This has been one crazy week leading up to today," Kenneth said attempting to ease the nervousness they both seem to be experiencing.

"Yes, it has been very eventful but exciting." Ameila looked towards him then quickly away.

"You have worked really hard on this and you know how much we appreciate everything that you have done and still doing. Being in front of the camera is not easy at all but you are a natural."

"I sure hope so Kenny. I hope I don't mess up any words or worse, freeze when asked a question."

Kenneth laughed. "All you have to do is sit there and look pretty and it will still be a great interview."

"Ahhh how sweet. I am flattered."

"Don't be nervous at all. I have seen your practice interviews and you handled yourself like a pro then and I know you will work your beautiful magic in front of the camera now."

"My divorce is final. I just thought I would let you know that," she said nervously. She wanted to be sure he knew he didn't have to hide his feelings with her anymore.

"I figured it was. I remember the day you said you were coming in late due to court and we were so busy after that I didn't want to bring it up. Are you okay with everything?"

"I am actually. We still need to work out visitation but the divorce is final. He didn't seem to care about visitation. I thought I would be nervous to see him. I didn't really know how I would feel. But I was great. I guess he expected me to come in there looking broke down because he kept staring at me as if he was trying to figure out how I look so fabulous." She smiled thinking about his reaction." I told the judge I didn't want anything from him and he was shocked. He tried to talk to me afterwards but his new girlfriend started going off on him. It was the funniest thing ever. And for the first time since being thrown out of our home I feel completely free."

"That is a great feeling to have Ameila!" he said looking into her eyes.

She turned to look at him seeing he was still staring at her. "What's wrong?"

"Now I can love you like I have desired to love you. I can treat you like the royalty you are. Ameila, will you be my girl?"

"That depends on one thing?" she said surprising him? Her face had a serious expression before her smile appeared putting him at ease.

"What's that? I will do anything," he said.

"Love me forever!" She whispered waiting for his response.

At that moment he grabbed her pulling her closer to him, leaning in so that her face was close to his. She wrapped her arms around him as he whispered! "I promise to love you forever Ameila!" He immediately indulged in her lips, kissing her aggressively and squeezing her tight. He kissed her passionately wanting more than the sensual sweet taste of her lips.

The limo slowed down and they both realized they reached their destination when the limo driver cracked the window in between them saying, "Mr. Cartwright we have arrived."

"Thank you give us just a moment please."

"Take your time sir. Press the call button when you are ready," he said rolling the window up.

"Well, we are here but I don't want to stop tasting your lips," Kenneth said still holding Ameila close to him kissing her face.

"What do you want to do? The interview starts soon," she said

"I'm going to kiss you in between the interviews on into a late-night dinner in hopes that you will be my dessert. I want to make love to you with a passion Ameila!" he said all in between kissing her running his fingers through her long flowing hair."

"Kenneth, you are making my hormones rage with excitement and my panties wet," she said panting. "If you don't stop we might miss the interviews." She was enjoying Kenneth's hands all over her body and his lips kissing her so passionately with a burning desire to feel his loving all over her body.

"Maybe just one interview," he said jokingly.

"You are the boss. Whatever you say." With her eyes closed she was enjoying every second of passion between them.

Kenneth's phone started to ring startling the both of them. The moment of passion stopped as he answered his phone. Ameila tried to compose herself, straightening out her clothes, fixing her hair and wiping the wetness from Kenneth's kisses from her neck. Kenneth was talking with the radio station confirming that they had arrived and would be up in a moment. He kept his eyes on Ameila the entire time admiring her beauty. "You are beautiful," he said to her.

Ameila turned to see that his eyes were fixed on her. "Is that right?" she said with an uncontrollable smile on her face.

"Yes, you are more than your beauty and I will show you better than I can tell you. You will see." He leaned in kissing her lips again. "Now let's get you upstairs so these interviews can begin."

They headed in the building and up the elevator. There were several radio stations and talk shows in the same building and on the same street. They hopped from show to show starting with the

Steve Harvey radio morning show. Kenneth grabbed her hands before entering the room and said, "You are going to be great and I am right here when you need me. I am not going anywhere until we are ready to go."

"Thank you Kenneth! I appreciate you for being with me."

"Forever as I promised," he said reminding her that his words were true. She smiled entering the room and the staff immediately approached to get her ready.

"Are you nervous?" the employee attaching her mic asked.

She looked up at Kenneth smiling and said, "Not anymore."

"Ladies and gentlemen, we have a very special guest in the building with us today. She is the author of 'Escapades of Love from Riches to Rags to Riches' the book of the most talked about and anticipated movie this year featuring the one and only Bryson Mathews himself. Please welcome to the show Ms. Ameila Daniels." Steve Harvey announced and everyone on his show welcomed her.

"Thank you, Steve, it is such an honor to be here talking with you and the morning crew."

"We are happy to have you here with us. I am going to jump right in Ameila and ask the question that everyone wants to know. Did Bryson Mathews really play himself and really pretend to be homeless?" His co-host asked.

"Yes, he played himself the entire time," Ameila said.

"Bryson is such a handsome man and seeing the previews to the movie with him looking scruffy and in those old dirty clothes made me have a renewed respect for him knowing that he really played the role."

"Yes, he is a very humbled man with great character. I was so blessed meeting him," Ameila said.

"The book was released today and I must say it is surely a page turner. I received an early copy and read the book in one day," the host said.

"Wow, one day?" Steve said.

"I know right. Now Ameila, you were in the book and you will be in the movie as well."

"Yes, that is correct."

"We see you in the movie previews playing yourself so were you really homeless? Was that live footage of you and your children?"

"Yes, the footage was live and yes I was homeless briefly. Bryson is an amazing man. I met him on his first day of his journey. You will see how that plays out in the movie but he saved me and my two children. My ex-husband literally put us out of the house with nowhere to go and for three months I struggled and I prayed every day for God's blessing. You don't see much of my story in the movie but will see a bit more in the book. I didn't want to accept that situation to be the life for me and my children. I knew that wasn't my truth and God answered my prayers and He sent me Bryson. His amazing partner and best friend Kenneth, after talking to me discovered my talents as a writer and he gave me a job. After I started working for the company, I would watch the footage of Bryson with Kenneth and that's how I started writing the story that led to the amazing book about the movie," Ameila said.

"Wow you have a great story. Everything about the book was great. I admire your strength as a woman. Your story will help women around the world I am sure. God truly has a calling on your life," his co-host said.

The interview went on for a few minutes more. Her name was being mentioned on the radio to be heard across the world. This was an amazing dream for Ameila. She went from one interview to another from radio interviews and talk show interviews. They had to travel by private jet to get to different interviews and tapings. Some interviews were even done by phone.

Later that evening, Ameila attended a live taping on Steve Harvey's talk show. "Welcome to the show Ms. Ameila Daniels author of the sky rocketing Best Seller Book Escapades of Love from Riches to Rags to Riches," Steve said welcoming Ameila to the show as the crowd applauded.

"Thank you for that warm welcome Steve. I am so honored and happy to be here."

He played the trailer for the movie and talked about the book release. Steve was really engaged in conversation with Ameila asking questions. "The movie is scheduled to be released in about a month and the book hit the shelves this Friday. How does it feel to know that your book sells in pre-orders alone are well over a half million books sold?"

"I was honored to be able to write the book for the movie so to know that the sales are climbing so quickly is an amazing feeling. Mr. Mathews and Mr. Cartwright are two awesome men to work for so when the idea for the book was presented it was an absolute dream to see it through."

"How does the book compare to the movie itself? Is it exact to what will be seen on the screen?"

"Yes and no. You will get to know the characters and their story that is portrayed in the movie but the ending in the book will leave you wanting more and the movie has the more that you will crave," Ameila said. She was not nervous at all and made Bryson and Kenneth so very proud of her representation of the book, movie and of their company.

"Great job today Ameila you were amazing," Kenneth said with his arm around Ameila walking back to the limo.

"Thank you. That was an amazing feeling and I really enjoyed today. I mean being on the radio and television was amazing. But the best part was being with you all day outside of the office. Your kisses in between gave me life and motivation, like a treat in between doing a good job." She was startled at the sudden stop and Kenneth pulling her closer to him.

"What about kisses just because you're an amazing woman," he said kissing her lips. "I want to make love to you Ameila."

"You have my permission to have your way with me. Make love to me Kenneth," she said looking up in his eyes waiting for his response.

"Where are the kids tonight?"

"The sitter has them all weekend while we are traveling."

"Well in that case you are staying with me tonight. We don't need two rooms, one will do. I promise not to keep you up too long."

"That sounds like a great plan to me," she said nervously and excited at the same time.

"Let's go, shall we?" he said as the limo driver held the door open for them both. Kenneth held her in his arms the entire ride back to the hotel and they talked about any and everything.

They arrived at the hotel in no time and she was in awe of how beautiful the place was. Kenneth made sure to stay in the best five-star hotels. "This is a beautiful place Kenneth."

"Thank you. Make yourself comfortable. I'm going to pour us a glass of champagne to celebrate today's success. Well it's really ginger ale that's we have in here," he said walking into the kitchen area of their suite with Ameila right behind him. "But I can order something more if you like."

Giggling she replied, "Oh no, Ginger ale will be fine."

Kenneth fixed their drinks and they headed into the living room. "A toast to your success," he said as their glasses met.

"A toast to success, to our success!" Ameila said with a smile.

After a few moments of talking and drinking their ginger ale Kenneth started kissing her. As their tongues tasted the awaited sweetness of their mouths, he caressed Ameila's back embracing her, squeezing her in his arms. He couldn't wait to make love to her so he picked her up in his arms carrying her to the bedroom.

He placed her on the king size bed. "I am going to light some candles and then we can shower together unless you prefer to take one alone," Kenneth whispered standing over her kissing her lips before walking away.

"Ok," Ameila said. She craved to make love to Kenneth but was nervous at the same time. She had confidence in herself and knew that she was a beautiful attractive woman. Kenneth made her feel beautiful but the hurtful words of her husband telling her no other man would want her still haunted her in the back of her mind. She didn't know how Kenneth would react to her afterwards.

"You don't need to be nervous Ameila. We don't have to do anything if you are not ready. I'm okay with lying here holding you. We can even remain fully dressed if you want," he said hoping she didn't want that.

"No. I am a bit nervous. But I'm ok. I want this. I want you." She stood up and took her top off, then her skirt. Standing there in her bra and panties she watched as Kenneth's eyes scanned her body "Let's shower together." Her desire to be with him outweighed her nervousness. She was sure she wanted to make love to him that night.

"Your body is beautiful Ameila." He walked up to her running his hands down her arms. He placed his hand on her lower back pulling her closer to him. "I am going to make love to every inch of your body pretty lady."

She blushed. "I am anticipating every moment."

Kenneth kissed her passionately. He held on to her body as she clung to his every move walking into the bathroom. Ameila didn't worry about anything, she walked backwards kissing Kenneth with him holding her and guiding her. She trusted the man he was and felt completely safe.

In the bathroom, he released her briefly to take off his shirt exposing his bare chest, his smooth chocolate skin. His muscles were well defined and sexy. Ameila took her hand and ran it down his chest touching the sexiness of every crease, of every muscle in his abs. His muscular body was adding to her arousal creating more panting and more wetness in between her thighs.

"Are you still okay Ameila?" he asked giving her one last chance to stop his passionate love making from exploding all over her body giving them both pure satisfactions.

Breathing heavily, she replied, "yes, I'm better than ok." Her hands were still on his abs as his pants dropped to the floor exposing his well-endowed package protruding from his boxer shorts. She gasped. He guided his hard penis up and out of his boxers and it extended well above his navel. The length and size of his penis was unreal, and nothing close to average. "He is huge," she said with her eyes wide opened looking as he stood half naked in front of her.

"Bigger than normal I guess but I promise I won't hurt you," he said grabbing her hand to place on his penis. "He will make you have many orgasms and I will be sure to stimulate every erogenous zone your body has for me to explore." Kenneth was a very sensual and passionate person who loved sex with the right woman.

This was a side of him that was surprising to Ameila. "Wow, your words are making me quiver with anticipation. Your, uhm, this, uhm…" She didn't know how to say what she wanted to say and was stumbling over her words. She looked up at Kenneth's smiling face and suddenly became flustered knowing that she was now with a man who had the largest penis she could never imagine. "Ok you are smiling and tickled at my amazement. But you have a damn anaconda for a penis. I'm not sure this thing will fit inside me," she said smiling back at him.

"If you want me to stop I will stop, you just say the word," he said as he leaned down towards her kissing her on the neck. He gently bit her in between his kisses then slowly rubbed his thick soft lips over her neck kissing and licking his tongue down the nape of her neck then back up to her ear. He nibbled on her ear as her panting increased. Every touch was with a desire and a passion to love her.

"Please don't stop," she whispered enjoying his hands on her body squeezing and caressing her soft skin up against his. Kenneth unbuttoned her bra then turned her back to him still kissing her neck. Her bra fell to the floor. He pulled her panties down helping her slide out of them. He reached over to turn the shower on never skipping a second of making Ameila feel good.

She stood there naked in his arms as the steam from the shower started to fog the mirror adding to the steaminess already in the atmosphere. His penis was pressed up against her back as he held her tight to his body. He placed one hand on her breast and the other hand he placed in between her legs spreading her lips to massage her clit. He could feel the extreme wetness and he slipped his fingers inside her vagina moving them in and out hitting her g-spot. With his lips on her neck, one hand on her breast and the other inside her honey pot she had one of the most amazing orgasms in her life.

"How does that feel?"

"Oh that was simplyyyyy aaamazzinggg," she said breathing hard stretching her words.

In one swoop Kenneth picked her up and stepped into the shower. "Let's shower so I can make love to every inch of your body. Their lips locked as he stepped in the shower under the running water. Anticipating making love to her inside and out, he washed their bodies sensually with urgency. After rinsing their bodies, he dried her off slowly caressing every part of her body. "You are perfect Ameila," he said standing in front of her.

"Are you sure Kenneth?" she asked as he stared into her eyes.

"You are perfect in every way Ameila. I'm going to love you now, tomorrow and forever. You are my Eve, my God sent perfection."

"You are so amazing. Make love to me right now," Ameila said wrapping her arms around his neck.

At that very moment, Kenneth picked her up and carried her to the bed. Gently laying her down he ran his hands over her body touching her, arousing her desires for him to make love to her. He kissed her soft skin licking her all over making her relax to receive his large penis. He played with her honey pot sucking on her clit making her cum once more with his fingers inside her honey pot to loosen her up, making it easier for him to push inside. She was extremely wet and she was ready to receive Kenneth.

He kissed her face as he guided his penis inside. "Ahh," she started to moan. She held on to his shoulders. He kissed her aggressively to keep her focused on him and not the tight feeling of him pushing his large penis inside her. Her moans became louder. Her grip on his shoulders became tighter. He was inside her pushing deeper and deeper until he was hitting bottom and could go no further. He kissed her through her moans, sucking on her lips. Her moans turned into screams loudly bouncing off the walls. "Ohh, Kenneth this feels amazing. Ohh, ohhh, ohhh."

Kenneth kept his promise to make her feel good and have multiple orgasms. He was not a selfish lover and took pleasure in giving her pleasure. After hours of making love to one another they were exhausted.

"That was an amazing first time," Ameila said laying in Kenneth's arms.

"It was amazing. Are you ok? I didn't hurt you, did I?" he asked kissing her forehead, squeezing her tighter in his arms.

"No hurt, at least not in a bad painful way. That was the best orgasms I have ever had in my life. I thought it would be uncomfortable you know with you being so anaconda'ish and all but the orgasms were incredible the moment you were inside me," she said still feeling amazing.

"That is what I was aiming for to give you unbelievable pleasure. I like your word you created too, anaconda'ish," he said laughing.

"It fits darling. Besides writers can create any word their creative mind desires," she said smiling snuggling closer to his warm body.

"And you are very creative. I'm glad we are spending the weekend together. Today was a great start."

"Yes, indeed it was."

Silence fell over their exhausted bodies and Ameila was fast asleep in Kenneth's arms as he held her tight until morning. Saturday was the start of another busy day with more interviews and travel all over again. Having each other made the trip feel more like pleasure than business. They were in love. Ameila felt like a new woman after Kenneth made love to her entire body. She didn't think she would be able to handle his large package and now she was addicted, thinking about the pleasure, anticipating him loving her body all over again.

Chapter 11
Bachelor Life
September 4

Charles Churchwell was living the single life. He had different women coming in and out of his home. He started drinking heavy after the woman he left his wife for left him. She realized he didn't make enough money and he wasn't worth her time anymore. The relationship was fun when he was cheating on his wife sneaking around with her. But after he left his wife, putting her and their children out, the thrill and the respect for him left. Charles planned to replace his wife with his secretary, but that plan back fired when his secretary quit her job leaving him for another man making more money than him. When she left, he was left alone feeling stupid for destroying his family for what he thought would be a better life. He quickly realized his wife built him up, made their family better by taking care of home, their children and helping with his now failing business.

After his wife was gone, he tried to manage his business alone. When he realized he was starting to lose money he tried to gain help from his Secretary but she refused to play wifey and perform any duties that didn't benefit her. She took anything she could from him and when his money and gifts ran out so did she. After she left, Charles ventured out to bars, clubs and strip joints bringing home random girls. Some would stay for a few days partying at his expense before moving on to the next man. It was clear that Charles was only looking for a good time. He talked about his wife a lot to these women but he was clueless as to where she was.

For a couple weeks after he put her and their children out she tried to come back to the house until one day she stopped. She was degraded and disrespected by him and the women he brought into their home and he refused to allow her to come back into the home they built together. After she stopped attempting to come home, he had no contact with her. His pride wouldn't allow him to go find her begging her to come home even though he needed her. How can a man apologize and expect forgiveness for what he had done to his family, he thought. All for the sake of some new pussy that didn't want him past his money and sneaky sex.

Charles struggled keeping his magazine business afloat. He barely made enough to pay his bills and eat. He started searching for a regular job. His selection in women became poor as his funds became low. He found women with low self-esteem that he could sell a dream just to sleep with them. The women didn't stay around very long. His last victim enjoyed being there with him playing house. She was a young girl who was fascinated with the idea of living in his home, which was more than what she had. She did whatever he wanted her to do but was of no value to help financially. She was a high school dropout who barely knew how to read so helping him with his business was out of the question.

His marriage was over. When Ameila filed for a divorce she didn't ask him for anything. He noticed she looked amazing but assumed it was for show and maybe she was given clothes for court by some homeless shelter or some place that helped women in need. She looked amazing and he wanted to be with her again but when she refused to even speak to him he kept his pride and kept quiet. His young girlfriend was furious but quickly forgave him. He was just happy and surprised she didn't want anything from him, not even alimony or child support.

One Friday afternoon, he was sitting on his sofa with a beer in one hand and the remote in the other. The young lady staying with him was in between his legs performing oral sex. As she was sucking him, he started to moan throwing his head back enjoying the sexual pleasure. The young lady was working him over good and had him at his peak ready to have an orgasm until he heard Ameila's name and heard her voice blaring from the television. She wasn't going by her married name but by her maiden name and a knot formed in his throat. He thought she was somewhere struggling without him and to see her on television looking great and doing great gave him a sickening regretful feeling.

"Welcome to the show Ms. Ameila Daniels author of the sky rocketing Best Seller book 'Escapades of Love from Riches to Rags to Riches.'" The host said welcoming Ameila to the show.

"Thank you for that warm welcome Steve. I am so honored and happy to be here." Ameila's voice was unmistakable for Charles and he knew it was her on the TV screen.

He immediately jumped up pushing the girl off him. "Move," he said to her as she fell backwards trying to catch herself.

"What did I do wrong?" she shouted with a confused look on her face.

"Nothing shut up," he said to her as he turned the volume up on the television to hear clearly.

"What do you know her or something? Wait, that's the lady from court," the girl said with her hands on her hip still talking to him.

"Bitch shut up," he shouted.

"Whatever," the girl said heading towards the kitchen.

"The movie is scheduled to be released in about a month and the book hit the shelves on Friday. How does it feel to know that your book sells in pre-orders alone are well over a half million books sold?"

"I was honored to be able to write the book for the movie so to know that the sales are climbing so quickly is an amazing feeling. Mr. Mathews and Mr. Cartwright are two awesome men to work for so when the idea for the book was presented it was an absolute dream to see it through."

"How does the book compare to the movie itself? Is it…"

Charles tuned everything else they were saying out and crunched numbers in his head. "Damn! She worth a whole lot of money. Shit, I fucked up," he said out loud.

"Who worth a lot of money? Fucked up how?" the girl said from the kitchen taking a bite of the sandwich she made.

"Shut the fuck up, I'm thinking. I got to figure out how to get in touch with her. Fuck."

"Her Instagram and twitter info on the screen. You would have seen it if you weren't cursing me out and talking to your damn self. You call me stupid, can't you see?" the girl said irritated by how he was talking to her.

Charles ignored her last comment. He tried to remember what it said before it left the screen. He reached for his remote to rewind and pause the screen so he could write down the information.

"How do I get on Instagram or whatever this is?" he asked the young girl.

"Oh, now you want me to talk and help your ass?" she said sarcastically rolling her eyes.

"Get your ass over here and help me," he said and she quickly ran over to him.

After she set him up an account and showed him how to work it, he was determined he had no further use for her. Seeing Ameila and his kids all over her Instagram account looking so happy and rich, he knew he had to try to get them back. He had sex with the young girl one more time and afterwards told her she had to leave. Putting her out of the house was easy for him. He had no feelings for her and didn't care one way or another how she felt or where she would go. All he had on his mind was to get his wife and kids back.

Chapter 12
DNA Test
September 8

Bradon arrived at Bryson's home early Tuesday morning to ride with him for their DNA testing. Jewel was now six and a half months pregnant and Bryson wanted to know the results so they could put the situation behind them or plan for what is to come.

"Hey Bradon," Bryson said opening the door to greet him. Bradon followed his brother through his home to the kitchen.

"What's up bro, are we ready to roll? The quicker we get this over with the better." Bradon was so nervous about having the test done. It was five o'clock that morning and everyone else was asleep in Bryson's home except Maria who got up to make him breakfast.

"Thank you Maria for breakfast," Bryson said to her before responding to Bradon.

"You are welcome sir. I will be in my room if you need me," she said before walking away.

"Thank you. Bradon sit down and have breakfast with me and then we will be on our way." He motioned for his brother to have a seat. "Ok sure. You know I don't turn down good cooking." Bradon sat down and started to eat. The room was quiet nothing but forks hitting plates and the sounds of them both eating. Occasionally they would look up at one another until Bradon couldn't take it any longer. "Why the hell are we sitting here in silence? Is something going on that I need to know about?" He placed his fork on his almost empty plate curiously questioning Bryson.

"It is quiet huh. I was just eating and thinking," he said and fell silent.

"Thinking about what? You over here playing, messing with my head while I'm stressing about this test," Bradon said looking at his brother with a frown.

Bryson laughed knowing that he was messing with Bradon. "ok seriously, I know you stressed about the test and all but try not to stress. I talked to Brielle and it's ultimately up to you and me how we deal with the situation. She doesn't mind raising the baby as ours if that's something you want."

"Man, I can't do that to you all, she already having your twins adding another baby won't be a good idea especially if..." He paused getting choked up at the thought of the baby being his.

"You don't have to go through with this if you don't want to Bradon. But we need to know for sure. I mean it could be either of our babies according to the calculations of when she was impregnated. As bad as it sounds we both were with her on the same day within hours of one another." Bryson didn't mention to his brother that he was pretty sure he had a condom on. But he couldn't remember if it was one of those days he penetrated her bare before putting a condom on. He made sure to always wear a condom, even if he started without one.

"Yeah, that sounds bad. Can we not say that again? I mean damn, it is what it is but that was some foul shit she did and I'm just ready to know and get this behind us. You know I would never intentionally hurt you. But hell this hurts me and to hear you say it, damn this is fucked up."

"Bro, we already discussed this and I know you wouldn't do anything to hurt me or betray me come on now. We are brothers who have each other's back and loyal to one another. Me, you and Kenneth grew up together knowing the code and always honoring the code. No need to dwell on that situation again."

"What up, what up, I heard my name." Kenneth said walking in to the kitchen.

"Hey Kenny man. I didn't know you were coming through," Bradon said.

"What's up man? Yeah, I asked Kenny to come by so we could have someone there for moral support. Besides, we have some business to handle," Bryson said.

"Are we ready or what? Look like y'all in here having a moment," Kenneth said looking back and forth at the both of them.

"Naw we good. Let's get this over with," Bradon said getting up from the table.

"Let's go, let's get it over with," Bryson said following behind him.

The gentlemen headed to the doctor office where the DNA testing was to be performed. When they arrived, all three men were nervous. Bryson and Bradon looked at Kenneth fidgeting and just as nervous as they were.

"Kenny man, what is wrong with you? Why are you over here fidgeting?" Bradon asked.

"Man, I'm nervous for the both of y'all. What if they can't tell which brother is the father? I mean, assuming that one of you are?"

Just then a nurse walked up to them asking, "Are all three of you being tested this morning?" she asked with one foot in the door and the other out.

"Hell no I'm not being tested. I'm not that baby daddy and I'm one hundred percent sure I'm not," Kenneth said nervously.

"Ok, well then. What about the two of you?" she asked Bryson and Bradon.

"Yes, it is us that will be tested," Bryson said to the nurse looking back at Kenneth with raised eye brows. "You ok man?"

"Yeah, I'm cool. Good luck to you both."

"Ok. Follow me please. The both of you. He can come too if he thinks he will be alright." She looked at Kenneth and smiled.

They laughed at Kenneth how direct he was in saying the baby was not his. He didn't have any kids and he didn't plan to have any no time soon. He was there simply for moral support and clearly didn't want any confusion regarding that fact.

When they were back in the testing area Bryson started to ask questions. "When will the mother be tested?" Bryson asked.

"Well her doctor can speak more to you about that. But you do know that testing the baby before birth could be risky and lead to complications even early delivery and possibly miscarriage. After the trauma Miss. Taylor endured from the rapes, I'm not sure that is the best route to go for her or the baby if it is preventable."

"Oh no I didn't know that," Bryson said.

Bradon looked over at Bryson confused trying to figure out what his next move would be. "We wouldn't want anything to happen to the baby. So, what now do we still get tested and wait to test the baby? I mean it's less than three months away." Bradon was nervous but didn't mind waiting. He felt that gave him a little more time to not know the truth and not be obligated to tell Chantae if the baby was his.

"Could we still test and use the results of our test for when the baby is tested or should we wait too?" Bryson asked the nurse.

"You all can test now if you want and if all parties want to wait to test the baby, yes we can still use today's testing. That way you won't have to come back. So do you want to test and wait to test the baby?" the nurse asked Bryson.

"Yes that's what we will do. I think me and my brother agree." Bryson turned to look at Bradon.

The nurse looked at them both. She knew there were two men coming in to be tested but didn't realize they were brothers. She just figured they were cool with one another. She looked back and forth confused but now seeing that they looked so much alike they had to be brothers. She wasn't trying to judge nor ask any questions, but she was curious about their story.

"Yes, I agree. Let's get our testing over with, test the baby when born."

"Alrighty then. I will let the doctor know of your decision and we will go ahead and test you both today." She turned to gather her materials to start the test. "Are you their brother too?" she asked Kenneth.

"I'm close enough to their brother. I know this sounds bizarre two brothers being tested but it's nothing that was intentional trust me," he said seeing the confused look on the nurse face.

"No need to explain anything to me sir. I am merely doing my job. Trust me I see some pretty bizarre situations come through here. I am just enjoying being here with three fine young men who are not fighting but actually getting along and making my job less stressful and more enjoyable. Curious, yes but none of my business," she said walking towards Bryson to start his test.

"Well we have a movie coming out that touches on what happened so hopefully you and your friends will go see the movie," Bryson told her.

"I thought you looked familiar. I have seen the movie trailers. Oh wow. Oh wow. I really feel honored to be in your presence and yes, of course we will support the film.

Bryson and Bradon were tested. They could not wait to leave. The nurse arranged with the doctor to postpone Jewels testing until after the baby's birth. Once Jewel found out she was upset until she found out they were calling Bryson the baby father. She held onto that and agreed to postpone the testing.

After the guys were tested, Bryson stayed behind to chat with the doctor and Bradon and Kenneth headed to the waiting area where they met their father waiting for them.

"Hey Mr. Mathews," Kenneth greeted him shaking his hand.

"Hey Kenny, what's up son."

"Dad what are you doing here?" Bradon asked.

"Thought I would come support my boys. I was hoping to get here before you went back but there was a wreck on the way here that held me up. How was it?"

"We just tested but they won't test the baby until after it is born," Bradon said.

"Oh ok. Where is your brother?"

"He is in the back with the doctor."

"Ok. Just know that everything will be alright son no matter the results. I love you."

"Love you too dad. Glad you came down to support us. I have been a nervous wreck."

"I can imagine son."

Bryson walked out greeting his father. The men sat there chatting for a moment before leaving. Their father headed home and the other three headed to the gym to play a quick game of basketball before going to work. Andre met them there and they chatted about the testing briefly.

"So, which one of you is the baby daddy?" Andre asked.

"We won't know until after the baby is born. Too risky to test the baby right now," Bradon said.

"Damn. So y'all have to wait until the baby is born before knowing?"

"Yeap," Bradon said taking a shot.

"Talking about extended stress," Andre said rebounding the ball after Bradon's missed shot.

"I know. But if it is one of ours then we want the baby to be ok. So a few more months won't hurt anyone," Bryson said.

"I wouldn't want to be either of you right now," Andre said.

"It's going to work out the way it is intended to work out. I believe this is all a part of some plan God has for us," Bryson said.

"This is one fucked up plan for sure," Andre said.

"Can't question God's plan now can we?" Kenneth said.

They continued to play basketball for the next hour before heading to work. Bryson mentioned to Kenneth that Brielle agreed to say the baby was his and not tell Bradon if it was indeed Bradon's. He told him he paid the doctor a pretty penny to switch the test if needed. Andre over heard what he said but didn't say a word. They said their good byes and all went their separate ways. Bryson and Kenneth were in the same car headed to work together.

The DNA testing for the brothers were done. Now they were playing the waiting game and Bradon had a little more time to build his relationship solid with Chantae. He knew he wanted to be with her and eventually marry her. The fear of the unknown future and the haunting of his pass kept him from being excited about what the future possibilities were. Instead, he felt his happy world could come tumbling down that he was being punished from all the past hurt with all the girl's hearts he had broken. He was content until he received a text from an anonymous caller.

Anonymous
8:49 AM
I saw you and your girl at the club the other night. You two look real cozy together. I wonder how she will feel about you having a baby. Don't worry you will find out who had your baby real soon. Your little girl has your eyes. Pay back is a mother fucker.
Signed... Wouldn't you like to know...

Bradon was spooked not knowing who this could be. He had changed his number so many times that he thought for a moment it could be someone who had the wrong number. But the fact that they said saw him and his girl at the club was true. This wasn't the first time he has heard someone say he had a baby by some girl. It had to be the same girl who set him up, taking his sperm to impregnate her own self. He wondered if the accusations could be true. Things were not looking good for Bradon one way or another. Now he was hit with the realization that he could possibly be the father of two kids.

Bryson always saved him from situations but this time Bryson couldn't save him. He had to be his own man and face his truth. He had to deal with the cards life dealt due to his careless ways and past lifestyle. Bradon was raised right and he knew what he had to do.

Chapter 13
Confiding in The Dr.
September 10

Dr. Vanessa Carols walks into the occupied patient room to see Brielle sitting on the table. She didn't expect to see her there but could tell she needed a friend. "Hey Brielle. Are you here as a patient? They have a chart in the door for you."

"Yes, I am here as a patient. That's the only way I could get a moment to talk with you."

"I am due a break here in a few if you want to grab a bite to eat and talk."

"Don't worry, I am paying for the time. They had a cancellation and I took that slot. They told me you were really busy today so that was the only way I could get back here."

"Well as a paying patient you have my undivided attention. Give me some love girlfriend," she said embracing Brielle in her arms.

Brielle hugged her back squeezing her tight as tears rolled down her face. "I miss talking to you like we use to as kids."

"Yeah girl me too," Vanessa said pulling back. "How is the baby? Wait, Brielle why are you crying sweetheart? What's wrong?" she said grabbing some tissue to hand her.

"I just need a familiar friend to talk to. Chantae is living her life with Bradon. My parents and everyone around me are so happy that I am happy. They are happy for me and Bryson and don't get me wrong, I am happy too, very happy. The kids are good, the baby is good. I just have my moments where I wonder if I am really enough for Bryson."

"Oh sweetie you are more than enough. You know that and he knows that. Girl we all know that."

"Everything feels wonderful but I saw videos of his ex and they look so happy together. She is pregnant too you know but no one knows who is the father of her baby since she was cheating with multiple men. But what if the baby is Bryson's? Oh and did I tell you she is beautiful. What if the baby is his and he want her back? What if he wants to be with his first child and the mother. After all, he is a family man."

"Brielle, listen sweetie. You are having his twins. You are his family and Bryson loves you. Everyone can see that," she said in a soft tone.

"I don't doubt in my mind that he loves me. But he has history with her. Everything happened so fast with me and him and me being pregnant. I just pray that the happiness we have right now will always be, even if we find out the baby is his."

"Alright. I see. Woman to woman as your friend I need you to listen to me ok."

"Like I always do. You have always given me great advice and always been nonjudgmental. That's why I came to you."

"You know I never judge and will never steer you wrong. So since this visit is paid for you lay back on the table and let me be your shrink for about five minutes and the next five we will pull it together before I have to see more patients." They both laughed.

"Yes ma'am Dr. Carols." Brielle laid back on the table smiling as her friend sat beside her squeezing her hand.

"Now listen. Men are simple. One thing I know for sure is when a woman hurts a man the way that girl hurt Bryson, un doing that hurt is almost always impossible. You have to analyze that situation and ask yourself if what she did was something he could live with even if his friends knew what that situation was. And I know some of the facts to their story and I know that his brother was involved. Without knowing any other fact, I know that what she did to his brother was the ultimate betrayal for Bryson. He is a family man and his brother is one of the most important people in his life.

"Yes he does love his brother. He is always around and Bradon is great with my kids too," Brielle said smiling.

"Which brings me to another point. His momma and his brother didn't care for Jewel as they do for you, especially his mom. Just as Bryson knows how perfect you are for him, everyone around you two can see just how perfect you two are for one another."

"Well what about the sex part, you think he would miss the sex they had? I mean she was very flexible and freaky on a whole 'nother level. I was even enthralled in what I was watching and shame to say but turned on watching the videos," Brielle said with her eyes open wide.

"I see. So, do you think when a man puts his penis inside a woman he loves, he is thinking about the tricks she can do? I mean, I know you not no boring lover and you too have a few tricks yourself. I'm sure over time the both of you will learn and know what to do to please one another. When God unites two together in true love I know he makes sure that their love making is perfect for one another as well."

"We do have great sex. He is definitely a pleaser."

"And I am sure you allow him to please you. That's where his pleasure from sex comes from, pleasing his woman. Not from the tricks she can do. If the baby is his, he will be more so concerned with how you feel than he will be about Jewel. He won't be thinking about getting back with a woman he does not love and he knows is not perfect for him. True love was the only thing Bryson was missing and he has that with you Brielle. What you two have found is priceless and only God himself can bless you with that type of love. There is no letting that go. Now, I think I have said enough but I want to say one more thing. All you need to do is love that man with all your heart and let him love you. Don't bring in your past or his and deal with what life brings you. God has you, you all are favored. I believe that in my heart to be true."

"Thank you so much Vanessa. I really missed you! I am so glad you are back," Brielle said and started to rise from the table.

"Not yet. Lay back down. Since you are here let's listen to the baby's heartbeat. That will cheer even a non-pregnant woman up."

"That would be wonderful! You are coming to the wedding, right?"

"You know I won't miss it for anything in the world. September nineteenth is etched in my brain, marked on my calendar and I even have a reminder on my phone." She placed the Doppler on her belly and the sounds of both heartbeats echoed through the air.

Brielle felt better after her visit with her friend. Bryson was in the waiting room when she was done waiting on her. It warmed her heart to see him and she knew that nothing would come between them, not even Jewel having his baby.

Brielle and Bryson met with the wedding planner to finalize more details of the wedding day. They met the designer for her dress and gathered for the fitting of everyone in the wedding party. Everyone looked happy. Bryson's parents and her parents were close and got along so well. Everything was perfect. Bryson noticed her observing everyone's behavior and he came and stood right behind her wrapping his arms around her waist.

"It's a beautiful sight to see everyone so happy," he said kissing her on the cheek.

"It is a beautiful sight to see," she said leaning her head against his face squeezing his arms.

"What about you Brielle? Are you happy?" he asked wanting to be sure that she was the happiest of all.

She turned to face him wrapping her arms around his waist with him still holding her. "I am so happy. I must be the luckiest woman alive to be loved by you," she said tiptoeing up to kiss his lips.

He rested his head on her forehead holding her tight. "I am the luckiest man in the world to have the perfection of you as my wife. It amazes me how much God loves me to bless me with the greatest love imaginable," he said watching her blush. Their lips locked and their embrace tightened. Bryson wanted to make love to her and his bulge in his pants made that evident to Brielle.

"Well look at these two love birds. Can't keep their hands off one another." The wedding planner said out loud causing everyone to look in their direction.

Brielle started to pull away but Bryson pulled her back whispering in her ear. "Sweetheart, there is no hiding this bulge in my pants. Stay right here."

"I got you babe." Brielle kissed his lips and turned her body to face everyone still holding on to Bryson who never released his grasp from her waist.

"That right there is that God ordained love for sure. Reminds me of me and my husband at that stage. You just know that's a love sent and blessed by God," Mrs. Mathews said to Mrs. Summers.

Mrs. Summers leaned in closer whispering, "That is a beautiful feeling of love. Good thing they already married because they wouldn't make it to the honeymoon." The women laughed.

Brielle and Bryson were happy and being surrounded by love from their family made it even sweeter for them being together. They were prepared for whatever life dealt them and prepared to spend the rest of their life together.

Brielle was glad she went to visit Vanessa that morning, she confirmed everything Brielle already knew to be true.

Chapter 14
Night Before Wedding
September 18

Bryson was getting ready for his bachelor party his brother and friends were having for him. He dressed down in some jeans and tennis shoes but still wore a dressy shirt. He was about to marry the woman of his dreams all over again the very next day. "This will be my first night away from you sweetheart. Since you have been my wife. Keep your phone close by so I can call and check in ok," Bryson said to Brielle as she buttoned up his shirt.

"I will but babe you enjoy your friends and have fun. Knowing your brother I already know you all will have strippers so behave," she said tiptoeing up to kiss his lips.

"Sweetheart you have nothing to worry about. I will be on my best behavior and I will see you at the altar tomorrow."

"I can't wait to reclaim my King again."

"You have a good time with the ladies tonight. And I told Chantae and your girls no strippers in my house," he said looking at her with squinted eyes.

"Babe you know there will not be any strippers in here with our parent's present."

"I'm just checking. Come here," he said pulling her closer to him. "Why don't we skip the parties and go get us a room," he said smiling feeling the beat of her heart up against his chest.

"That sounds like a great plan but you know I have a schedule of events tonight and in the morning. But part of tonight includes getting my nails and feet done for tomorrow. Babe, you go have fun seriously. Enjoy your friends." She held his hands in hers and pulled him towards the door. "Wait before you leave I have one question," she said thinking.

"Anything," he said still holding on to her hand tightly in his.

"When you were pretending to be homeless, why did you stay in my place and give up living like a king when you didn't have to?"

"I live as a King wherever my Queen will be. It doesn't matter the place. Even if we were truly homeless together I would still feel as if I was a King having you by my side. Now, as the man that God has ordained me to be and as my father raised me to be, I could never allow you or our family to be homeless. As far as the home you purchased and I stayed in, that was a beautiful home. If that is where we were living I would be content. I don't have these lavish things because I need them but because I can afford them. Now you on the other hand I do need," he said holding her tight in his arms.

"Thank you babe. That was beautiful." She laid her head on his chest as he embraced her.

"That was truth sweetheart." He loved making Brielle smile and giving her the feeling of happiness. "You call me when you are done and I will come rescue you if you change your mind."

"You are the best babe," she said standing with him by the door. She tiptoed up meeting his awaiting lips, kissing her husband just as the door bell rung. There kiss was sweet and meaningful yet quick when reality set in that they needed to part momentarily for the entertaining to begin. "I believe that would be more ladies arriving."

"That's my cue to go. I will have my phone in my pocket if you text or call. I love you sweetheart," he said kissing her once again on the forehead.

"I love you babe."

Bryson headed out the door to the awaiting car headed to Bradon's house.

"It's about time he left," Chantae said walking up behind Brielle. "Now we can get this party started."

"Hey Chantae, I was just about to come find you. You think you could help me finish my hair?" Brielle asked.

"Sure. Of course I can help," she said following behind Brielle heading to her bedroom.

Brielle stopped in her tracks turning to Chantae to ask, "Uh we don't have strippers coming do we?"

"Not anymore. After you dropped the bomb shell on us about the bun in the oven that was cancelled. You know how they do flipping and twirling and yeah you can't be doing all of that now."

Brielle continued walking to her bedroom relieved no strippers were coming laughing at Chantae's remarks. She was ready to enjoy time with her girls and get pampered at the same time relaxing before her big day tomorrow. "Thanks for being here girl. I know we haven't spent much time together lately not working side by side anymore. We had some great times working so close together."

"Yes we did." Chantae was quiet gathering her thoughts looking at Brielle's hair to finish what she started. "I miss our talks. I knew you would always be there the next morning to have girl talk with me. I guess I became spoiled."

"I am still here girlfriend. A call a way or a car ride over. Anytime and you know that," Brielle said sitting in the chair as Chantae curled her hair.

"I know you are. It's still different. Well I might as well tell you. I am sure you will know eventually, if you don't already. I found out about some girl that could be pregnant with Bradon's baby. The news has just devastated me. Apparently, the girl is freely saying he could be her baby father."

Brielle's mind was racing with thoughts and she wished she would have told her about Jewel before now. "Oh wow, I know I heard a mentioning of that but didn't know you knew. I probably should have said something when I heard about it but didn't want to say anything until it was confirmed or not," Brielle said.

"It's cool we are dating brothers so I am sure we are bond to hear things. I hope he is not the father. God knows I am not ready to be a step mom," Chantae said still styling Brielle's hair.

"How did Jewel spread the news from jail? Has she been calling him? When did Bradon tell you?"

"I didn't know her name. I overheard this girl he knew from his past talking to him in the club that night we were all there. And then I saw some papers in his pants pocket where he was tested for DNA. This has really devastated me."

"Oh girl, I am so sorry you had to find out that way. Bryson had to get tested as well. But there are other men involved so it's a possibility the baby could not be either of theirs," Brielle said.

"Bryson was tested too?"

"Yeah Jewel was his ex, so they both were tested. Girl we have not talked in a while. I hope the baby is not either of theirs."

At that moment Chantae was putting everything together that was said by Brielle, what she overheard in the club and the papers she found in Bradon's pockets. She realized that Brielle had just revealed news to her about another possible baby that could be Bradon's. The incident Bradon told her about Jewel coming into his room is why he was being tested. So now there was a possibility that Bradon could be the father to two babies. She was gathering her thoughts trying not to show any emotions nor reveal to Brielle that she didn't know about Jewel. "I hope the baby is not his. I am not sure I can handle being a mother to a child that is not mine. Besides my God children, I don't want to be mommy to anyone else. Not right now." She was trying to be calm but the news was tearing her up inside. She couldn't even tell Brielle that Jewel was new news to her and she was referring to someone else, another possible baby momma.

"Right. I really hope the baby is neither of theirs. Especially not with me and Bryson having twins." Brielle was unaware that she had just told Chantae about something she had no clue of.

"Your hair is all done pretty lady." She turned her towards the mirror so she could see. "Now let's get in here to the party," Chantae said wanting to cry but holding it all inside.

"Thank you girl it looks amazing as always. I am so glad we had this time together." Brielle turned to hug her friend. Noticing she seemed sad she asked, "Are you ok Chantae?"

"Girl yes. just thinking about that mess but I am all good. Everything will work out like it should." Chantae was sad. She didn't know how to digest the news about Bradon possibly having two babies and didn't want Brielle knowing they were talking about two different girls. She decided to keep it inside and enjoy the evening with her best friend. She felt a bit jealous of Brielle at that moment but dismissed the thought and poured herself a strong drink. Once in the kitchen she whispered to Brielle, "Can we keep that conversation between us. You don't tell Bryson and I don't discuss with Bradon?"

"Sure, not a problem at all. You know you my girl."

"Thanks my friend."

"Hey Ameila girl. So glad you are finally here," Brielle said greeting her as she walked into the room to join everyone. Brielle took her seat in a chair to get her nails and feet done for the wedding tomorrow. "You and Chantae did great planning the party. I love everything." She was grateful for the ladies putting together the party. And although she didn't want strippers the half-naked men were pleasing to the eyes for all the ladies there. They were just as good if not better than having strippers.

"I was caught up at the office but wouldn't have missed it for anything. I see the ladies are turning up and enjoying everything," Ameila said looking around the room.

The rest of the ladies were sipping on alcoholic beverages listening to music and enjoy the ambiance of the room. There were men servers walking around half dressed showing off their muscles flexing at every request and the ladies loved the eye candy.

"Girlfriend go get yourself a drink. The waiter announced they would be taking orders soon for dinner," Brielle said to Ameila. They had personal chefs waiting to serve the ladies appetizers and dinner for the evening as they all received nail, foot and spa services.

"Thanks. Are you enjoying yourself so far?"

"Yes. I love every bit of it. The spa treatments, the sexy men..." She looked up at Ameila and laughed.

"Good eye candy for now until the real eye candy comes back to you," Ameila said gazing into nowhere thinking about Kenneth.

"Are we talking about Bryson or some other eye candy?" Brielle asked knowing that she was not talking about Bryson, instead talking about Kenneth. It was obvious she was in love with Kenneth.

"Huh? Oh girl yeah, you know I was talking about you and Bryson. Everyone knows how much you two only have eyes for one another. I am going to get that drink now, excuse me," she said nervously smiling making a quick exit away from Brielle.

"Ok girl," Brielle said smiling. She knew she was feeling Kenneth and that Kenneth was also feeling her. She watched Ameila noticing that her walk was different. She had a walk of a woman who was sure of herself and sure of the man she was claiming to love and she was sure that she was loving him in more ways than from her heart. It also showed in her smile when her phone buzzed.

Ameila looked at her phone realizing she had a text from Kenneth and her face lit up with a smile that she tried to conceal.

Kenneth Cartwright (Boss)
6:47 pm
Hey gorgeous. Just checking to be sure you made it there safe and sound and still smiling...
Hope the party is a success.

"I will be sure to change his title in my phone soon enough." She thought to herself seeing his name in the message. Yes, he was her boss but now he was more than a man that she answered to in the office. She now took orders from him in the bedroom and as her new man. She responds to him letting him know she was ok.

Ameila
6:48 pm
Hello darling, yes, I am still smiling and I am safe and sound. The party is a success, missing you though. Enjoyed our rendezvous at the office. Biting my bottom lip wishing it was you biting instead of me...

Ameila was in love and Brielle picked up on it long before then. "Excuse me, do you have my design and color for my nails? This is for my wedding tomorrow." She asked the nail techs working on her.

"Yes ma'am we do. Miss Chantae gave it all to us. She explained what you wanted for the wedding. See," she said showing her the designs she had.

"Awesome. My girl Chantae is always on top of things. Where is she anyways?" Asking out loud to herself more so than asking the techs.

"I saw her walking towards the bathroom moments ago on her phone." The lady responded.

"Oh ok," Brielle said looking down at her nails. She started to think about Bryson. Seeing Ameila smiling knowing she was texting Kenneth she had an urge to text Bryson. With her free hand she grabbed her phone.

Hubby King Everything

6:57 pm
Hello darling just wanted you to know I was thinking about you. The party is nice. No strippers but we do have half naked sexy men serving us. Hard to miss them but you know I only have eyes for you. Missing you and can't wait to see you when I walk down that aisle tomorrow…

My Forever Love Brielle (Wife)
6:58 pm
HALF NAKED SEXY MEN SERVING MY WIFE… Don't like that at all. First and last time so enjoy your evening sweetheart. I will be the only sexy server you have after tonight for the rest of your life. I miss you more. I rather be with you tonight then hanging with the fellas. You say the word and I will be there so fast to sweep you off your feet.

Brielle was grinning from ear to ear. She was so much in love with Bryson that even a blind man could see their love.

Hubby King Everything
6:59 pm
You swept me off my feet the first day we met my King. Don't worry about the men here they are harmless. I am getting pampered for tomorrow's big day. One night away will make the love making tomorrow night that much better. Enjoy your friends tonight, I love you with my whole heart.

Brielle was grinning. Ameila was grinning. Chantae was in the bathroom fixing her face from crying.

The thought of Bradon having children outside of them was overwhelming for her and the alcohol was making it worse. "How come she gets the man, the house, the money, the baby and I get the man that lives in the shadow of all of that and now he might have two babies' and two baby mommas'. My perfect life seems to be crumbling," she said to herself in the bathroom mirror. Chantae was feeling the pressure of being in love while dealing with issues that she never before had to deal with. She wasn't as strong as her friend and willing to accept what life dealt her. She was used to being free, to choose what she wanted, to deal with what she wanted to and walk away when she chose not to. But this time she was in love and walking away was not something she wanted to do nor was it an easy decision for her to choose.

When she met Bradon she felt everything would be perfect. They would live in the big beautiful house that is now Brielle's. She would have everything a princess wanted from her man. Then she would eventually have all his babies. She loved Brielle as a sister but the pressure of everything happening around her and the distance between the two because of their new men and life was weighing down on Chantae, causing her mind to roam to places of neglect and jealousy.

Just then her phone buzzed.

Bradon Big Daddy
7:02pm
Hello beautiful. Hope you are enjoying the evening you worked so hard to plan. I love you so much and I am so glad you danced with me the night we met and slept the night away in my arms with me holding you. I am the luckiest man in the world because I have you as my beautiful Queen. Can't wait to kiss your beautiful face. Until later I'll be thinking about you...

For the moment she forgot all about her hearts reason to ache. She dried her eyes and touched up her makeup. She downed the rest of her drink, smoothed her clothes and held her head high. She was going to enjoy her evening in preparation for her best friend's wedding and deal with the possibilities of baby momma drama later. She reached for her phone to reply to Bradon.

Chantae
7:04pm
Thanks handsome. I am so glad you sent your love through the phone. Just what I needed. Glad you asked me to dance and I can't wait for many more dances with you. I love you back and yes, the evening is lovely. Can't wait to see you later...

She was now ready to enjoy the evening with her girlfriend and everyone else that came out to celebrate Brielle's big day.

Chapter 15
Bachelor Party Turn Up
September 18

The guys were turning up at Bradon's home and to his surprise they got him a few strippers giving him the full Bachelor party experience. He called Brielle from the bathroom to let her know what was going down to make sure she knew he had no clue but that he could leave right then. She gave him some do's and do not's regarding the strippers and told him to enjoy his night because she had him for a lifetime. The bachelor party went on and the rest of the guys had more fun with the strippers than Bryson. All he could do was think about Brielle and how lucky he was to have her as his wife.

Kenneth was texting Ameila with a smile on his face and Bryson knew exactly who he was texting. Bryson leaned over and whispered in his ear, "I knew you two would end up together she was your blessing from the start."

Kenneth looked up and said, "Yeah, she is something special. Your ass so in love you can't even enjoy these big booty strippers. Guess it's time for me to follow the Boss and get some of what you got."

"I hear you. She is a good woman with a great heart. You two are perfect for one another. You did good my friend. You did good," Bryson said and stood to watch Isaiah enjoy the big booty strippers triple teaming him. The quiet one's were always a target.

Isaiah was trying to resist but when the men started pumping his ego up he gave in and allowed the women to have their way with him. The men were enjoying the show and Bryson was glad someone else could enjoy the fun he avoided. He looked over at Bradon seeing him enthralled in the booty's shaking.

"That's what I'm talking about, shake it fast show me what you working with." Bradon was singing the Mystical song right on beat as the women were dancing on Isaiah. For a moment it seemed he forgot all about Chantae being his girlfriend and he was back in player mode. Two of the girls seeing the stack of money Bradon had gravitated towards him and freaked him down with bare breast in his face and booty shaking on him.

"Damn Bradon you are acting like you ain't got no girl waiting on you after the party." One of the guys joked creating laughter.

Bradon had an 'oh yeah' moment and eased away from the women after placing a couple twenties in each of their G-string panties. "Y'all got jokes I see. Don't hate on a brother having fun for one night. My brother getting married, again. Somebody got to enjoy all this goodness." He headed towards the group of men shaking hands.

They knew Bryson was not going to be caught up in the middle of these women because he was already a married man. But they tried their best to get him to at least enjoy a lap dance. They forced him to sit in the chair in the middle of the room. He caved in knowing that Brielle insisted he enjoy a lap dance. He sat there as the ladies performed their special dance for the groom. He gave them serious instructions nothing too drastic as he was a married man. Strippers were not his thing. Bradon and Kenneth grabbed his hands behind his back and tied them to the chair.

"We know you can get out of this if you wanted to do so but why? Just enjoy the performance," Bradon said.

"Yes sir," Bryson said. He didn't know what to expect but his friends knew him well enough to know he didn't want anything to happen that would totally disrespect his wife or the ladies performing in front of him. Tasteful and sexy was what he preferred and that was what he got.

"Don't hurt him ladies."

"We plan to embrace him with a little bit of pleasure not pain. Sweet and tasty, delicious even with a lot of insatiable hot and horny but nasty bad girl swag. You ready daddy?" the lead girl said to Bryson and all the men in the room.

"I guess I have no choice but to be ready," Bryson said. The men in the room were enthralled by her take charge demeanor. They were quiet as she spoke and after Bryson said he was ready they all were shaking their heads and faintly mumbling yes signaling they too were ready.

The women all performed exotically for Bryson and his friends. Tasteful but sexy and erotic. Everyone was pleased with the performance of these sexy women, including Bryson. He knew he had a wife to go home and make love to. Some of the men would be leaving horny and all alone. After the women left the men stood around talking and toasting too Bryson and true love.

Bradon's phone buzzed and he answered immediately. "Hey sexy," he said into the receiver.

"Hey to you. It sounds like the strippers have done just what I needed, got you all hot and bothered ready to make love to my body."

He laughed. "Woman you funny. Where you at? Still partying with Brielle?" He walked away from the men to talk to Chantae.

"I'm actually leaving, just got in my car heading home. I wanted to be sure no half naked woman would be in our home besides me when I get there," she said letting him know that the Bachelor party should be ending so they could start their own after party with just the two of them. There was no way she was allowing her man to adventure away from home after being teased by strippers leaving him horny.

"I hear you loud and clear sweetheart. I can't wait to make love to you," he said in his sexy voice. He was indeed horny and ready to take it all out on her body.

"I am on my way babe I will see daddy in a few moments," she said in a seductive sexy voice. She was ready to be in Bradon's arms, to feel his love for her.

"Be careful okay." Ending the call he quickly headed back to where the men were gathered. "Fella's. The lady of the house has called announcing she is on her way. I don't need to spell it out for you but it's about to go down in here and yes I am doing this."

"Don't say it. Is he about to say what I think he is?" Kenneth asked.

"Yeap I think he is," Bryson said.

"You don't have to go home but please finish your drink and head towards the exit. Y'all got to get the hell up out of my house. I only need one horny man here when she arrives," Bradon said proudly.

"Bout time you can put somebody out of your own shit." Andre said. "I have some big booty strippers waiting on me so I'm out anyways."

"Andre! You hooking up with the strippers?" Bryson asked? Everyone was looking at Andre as he was downing his drink.

"Hell, don't hate brothers. I will be sure to tell you all about the adventure when I recover from all that booty tomorrow," he said doing his pimp stroll towards the door.

"Damn man really? The strippers?" Bradon asked.

"What? You think I am going to pay for some strippers to come perform and not sweeten the deal for me? I arranged this on the front end," he said laughing.

"Damn. You were always the slickest pimp I knew," Kenneth said acknowledging his game.

"Pimping ain't easy but somebody got to do it. Y'all niggas all booed up in serious relationships and shit. But it's cool. Leaves a better playing field for me to win all the way around. I don't even have to compete with Bradon pretty boy ass no more." The men all laughed at Andre speaking in a pimp voice. "I'm out brothers. Got some horny ass fat booty bitches waiting on me," he said walking out the door as the men laughed at him.

The other men started to head towards the door as well including Bryson. "Thanks for the party fella's. We had a great time tonight as always."

"Yes we did. We don't need to let our relationships take us away from having a little fun together every now and then," Bradon said.

"We brothers, we will make time even if we do have to do couple events just to get together, we will always hang out," Bryson said.

"Good women don't hinder us they enhance just remember that. When you leave the single life for true love she becomes priority and with that comes understanding. So hanging out should never be a problem." Kenneth said.

"I hear a car pulling up so we shall continue this conversation another day. I can't let y'all ruin my plans for tonight. Remember you said it Kenneth, she becomes a priority," Bradon said.

"On that note, I am going home to my wife. I will see you two tomorrow for the wedding bright and early. Thanks again."

Chantae was walking in the house just as Kenneth and Bryson were leaving. They were the last two from the party. They spoke to Chantae saying their goodbyes all at the same time. When they were alone Chantae started to strip down talking nasty to Bradon the entire time. "Were you thinking about me babe when you were watching those fat asses bounce up and down daddy?" she said removing her jeans.

"Nothing but you baby, your ass is the best ass," he replied.

"And when they were shaking their titties, were you thinking about sucking on mine the entire time daddy?" she said removing her bra.

"Sucking all over your titties baby. Putting them in my mouth, sucking on your nipples just how you like it with my tongue moving fast back and forth," he said as he was stripping down to nothing but his socks.

Standing in the middle of the living room where the strippers once stood with the music still playing, Chantae started to move her hips side to side. "Come and sit daddy. Let me perform for you like the strippers couldn't."

Bradon was eager to see what Chantae had up her sleeves for him. "Your wish is my command darling," he said as he sat in the chair where Bryson once sat to enjoy his performance. Now Bradon was enjoying his very own private performance.

Chantae straddled Bradon and his fully erected penis. "Have you been a bad boy Bradon?"

"Yes, very bad. You gonna punish me?" he said feeling her tie his hands up behind the chair.

"Your ass is in some major booty trouble mister," she said kneeling in front of him. She took his penis into her mouth attempting to push it deep down her throat. She wanted to be sure to completely satisfy her man and his every fantasy possible that he had about those strippers. She used her hands to massage twist and grip his penis aggressively wanting to give him the ultimate pleasure. He couldn't do anything but sit there and moan out in pleasure.

"Untie my hands babe. You trying to make me cum sucking daddy so good," he said pleading for more pleasure but to be in control.

"Naw, not yet daddy. You are being punished for being a bad boy!"

"Ah shit that feels so good. Chantae, I'm not ready to cum baby." He was pleading for control but Chantae was not ready to give it to him. She wanted to remain in control and have her way with him.

"No not yet daddy," she said standing to her feet wiping her mouth. She leaned in and started kissing Bradon passionately. She nibbled on his neck working her way down to his chest. She backed away from him turning so he could see her ass in his face. She bends over so he could see her pussy from behind and watch her fingering herself. "You want this pussy daddy?"

"Yes girl. Bring me that pussy. Let me do that," he said watching her play with her clit teasing him.

She faced him and laid back on the floor with her legs opened wide so he could see her pretty legs and the sweet honey goodness in between. She held a bullet in her hand and turned it on full blast placing it on her clit while her other hand pushed her fingers inside her pussy going back and forth.

"Chantae untie me girl. I need to feel that pussy. Damn that pussy is fat. Girl come here untie me." And just then he was amazed at her squirting cum all over the floor. "Damn baby that shit was amazing," he said licking his lips.

"You like that Mr. bad boy?" she said standing to her feet walking towards him.

"Hell yeah I loved that shit. I love you girl." He had no control and was enjoying the aggressiveness Chantae was giving him but he wanted to be inside her at that moment.

She straddled him putting his penis inside her and his head fell back. "Now you are about to take this pussy Mr. You can't go around being bad. Now take this pussy good." She was forcefully riding Bradon, kissing his face and biting his neck. She was biting him hard but he wasn't fazed because she was riding him skillfully giving him ultimate pleasure.

In the middle of her riding him she managed to untie his hands. He wrapped his arms around her tight guiding his penis in and out of her gaining control of her body. With one breast in his mouth and one around her waist he picked her up swiftly and headed towards their bedroom. Bradon was in love and Chantae kept their love life interesting. He laid her on their bed and explored her entire body with his mouth. He made love to her for hours until they both collapsed from exhaustion. They had to be up early the next morning but a night of amazing passion was worth the lack of sleep they both would not get. Bradon held Chantae the entire night. Her sadness realizing Bradon may be a father to another woman's child, possibly two was temporarily dismissed due to a night of passion and her man holding her lovingly in his arms. She felt Bradon's love for her always have. She would remain quiet and hope Brielle would too until Bradon was ready to discuss the news with her. Until then she wanted to love him and receive his love. She committed to trying to keep it together and go on living their lives as if she didn't know anything about the babies or DNA testing.

Chapter 16
Wedding Day
September 19

Today was a beautiful day for the married couple. It was the day of their wedding ceremony. Even though they were already married, they decided to share their special moment with all their family and friends who were not present when they married the day in the park. Everything was perfect. Chantae was there by Brielle's side and she had her parents, her brother and Mr. Floyd. Besides her children, they were the most important people in her life. There was nothing that could ruin her special moment.

"Thank you so much for being here with me, for being my best friend, for being so loving and so supportive," Brielle said to Chantae.

"No need to thank me, that's what best friends are for. To always be there for one another. Especially on their wedding day," Chantae said to Brielle. "You are such a beautiful bride."

"Thank you. I'm so nervous and I don't understand why," Brielle said smoothing down her wedding gown. She wanted to be sure she was beautiful and sexy but not revealing her baby bump all at the same time.

"Maybe it's because all those cameras are about to be in your face. Girl it is cameras everywhere. Hell, they are making me nervous," Chantae said walking up behind her friend placing her hand on her friend's shoulders to help her relax.

"Yes, I know. This is the last piece of Bryson's contract with the producers. Then we don't have to worry about cameras everywhere and we can live a normal life."

"Girl there is nothing normal about your life. Everything is exciting, beautiful and very interesting and very rich and famous. The story is already a huge success with ticket sales through the roof. And it is one of the hottest discussions on social media." Chantae was reflecting on everything that has happened realizing that Brielle was living the life, the life that she had always dreamed she would be living. Her beginning moments with Bradon had her hopeful that the life he introduced her too while he was living in Bryson's home would be hers. Her life was still wonderful but she was not in the spot light as Brielle. Their dreams were totally opposite and right now Brielle was living the life of Chantae's dream.

"Girl I was thinking about how we use to talk about our dreams of being happily married and you use to talk about this lavish life and I would talk about a simple life can you believe this? I wouldn't trade Bryson for anything even if he didn't have all of this." She looked up at Chantae and noticed her facial expression changed. She almost looked sad.

"You deserve all of this Brie. Greg took you through so much drama and you out of everyone I have ever met deserve complete happiness. Yes, your life is what I imagined for me but I will get there. Me and Bradon have big dreams and we are slaying girlfriend." She reached for Brielle and hugged her tight. She was happy for Brielle but she was also overwhelmed with the changes that were happening and possibly could change her life forever.

"Thank you Chantae," she said squeezing her tight. "What would I do without you!"

"Well if I don't get you down this aisle your husband may be coming to get you his self. So let's finish getting you ready and get you out of here." She helped her finish getting ready before the wedding coordinator came telling her it was time.

As the wedding party lined up, cameras were everywhere flashing and recording the entire event. Everything was perfect and the room was full of all their friends and family and some of Bryson's A list clients.

Mr. Summer's walked his daughter down the aisle handing her off to Bryson. "Who will be giving this bride away?"

"I will," he said kissing his daughter on the cheek. "You are beautiful my dear."

"Thank you daddy," she said squeezing his hand.

He placed her hand in Bryson's and firmly shook his other hand. "Thank you son," he said to Bryson.

"Yes sir," Bryson said to Mr. Summers. "Brielle you are breathtaking beautiful as always. I am the luckiest man in the world," he said quietly to his wife as they stood in front of the pastor.

"We are gathered here today to join these two amazing people, Bryson and Brielle, together in holy matrimony to be witnessed by you all that are here today. Family and friends, I know we all agree when I say God's love shows brightly between these two and the journey that brought them together has strengthen their love, strengthen their faith and strengthen their bond that God has ordained as unbreakable. True love that is ordained by God is a love that we all desire to have and is a love that Bryson and Brielle has been blessed to receive from one another." The pastor blessed their marriage and continued with the ceremony until it was time for the two of them to read their vows to one another.

"Bryson, the day we met my spirit was awakened and my soul was jumping for joy. I experienced an amazing feeling that I couldn't explain at that moment because it was something I had never experienced before meeting you. My heart was beating differently, my smile was different and every fear I had ever experienced disappeared and replaced with what I know now as true love. True love that can conquer any fear, true love that brings so much joy in my heart, true love that makes me smile even when you are not near me. My heart beats to a new rhythm that sounds like angels singing a happy song that never ends. You are an amazing man to me and to my children. You took on a role that only a man of God would. I love you with my whole heart and I thank God for you every day. You are one of my greatest gifts from God and because he gave me you I know without a doubt that he loves me and I am favored to be blessed with such an amazing husband to love me in return with his whole heart. I am honored to have you as my husband and I vow to love you forever."

You could hear people sniffling in the audience. Even Chantae and Ameila standing next to her were crying because of her words of loves confirmation. Bryson held her hands tight looking into her eyes and even he was on the verge of tears.

"That was an amazing confirmation of love. Bryson, when you are ready."

"Brielle, you are my answered prayer from God. You are the epitome of what God's angel represent. Your genuine love you give, the kindness in your heart. You have given to me what every man desires but only few acquire, true genuine love that only God himself can create perfectly in His image so perfect just for me. I thank God for blessing me with you and your children. From the moment I saw you my spirit spoke to me with joy and excitement knowing that I was looking at my wife. Before I even knew your name or spoke a word, my heart knew that you were one of God's angels sent here just for me. For me to love you whole heartedly. For me to hold you every night close to my heart and wake up to your smile every morning. To love you and protect you and make you so happy because that's how you make me feel. You are my breath of fresh air. You are my smile. You are my hearts every beat. Because of you my life feels complete, my life feels rich, my life is happy. God is an amazing God and you too are my greatest blessing, my greatest gift, my greatest joy in my life. I promise to always cherish you, to protect your heart and to love you whole heartedly for the rest of our lives. I pray God's love always remain first in our hearts and I know that everything else will be an amazing journey with you by my side. I am honored to have you as my wife and vow to love you and our children forever. You are my joy, you are my true love and I thank God for blessing us with this perfect union."

"And after those words of love's confirmation with Bryson and Brielle's vow to love one another forever. May God protect and bless this union. I know again pronounce you husband and wife. You may kiss your bride." The pastor said holding his bible close to his heart looking at Bryson nodding his approval.

Bryson lifted the veil from Brielle's face, she handed her bouquet to Chantae who was drying her eyes. "Hello my beautiful wife," he said to Brielle as she stood before him smiling biting on her bottom lip. He kissed her lips so passionately lasting what seemed like an eternity of embracing his wife. The cameras were flashing and the television crew was filming the last moments of their kiss before they were done filming.

After they came up for air after their passionate kiss they walked back down the aisle with everyone cheering for them and congratulating them. Bryson spoke with the producer briefly confirming they had enough footage for the release of the movie and his contract has been successfully fulfilled. They went inside to take pictures of them together and their wedding party and family. After they were done they joined their guest at the reception where they were already drinking and partying.

Everyone welcomed them with applause as the coordinator introduced the wedding party and the Bride and groom as they entered. They were in the middle of eating dinner when the best man was ready to give his speech. That was also Chantae's cue to give her speech as Brielle's Maid of Honor.

With the sound of the knife hitting against the glass, Bradon was demanding everyone's attention to be on him and the Bride and Groom. "May I have everyone's attention please. I am Bradon Mathews for those of you who don't know me I am Brys little brother." The crowd laughed at his gesture of not knowing who he was. He looked so much like Bryson that it was obvious they were brothers. "Yeah I know we look a lot alike. I'm the cutest brother though, I am the baby." They laughed again. "Seriously, I want to congratulate my brother on finding true happiness. He has always been a go getter accomplishing everything he set his mind to. He has been the best big brother anyone could ask for and he has always been my best friend. I look up to him for everything and he has now given me something else to admire and strive for." He looked over at Chantae. "True love is hard to find but when you do find true love you know that it is the work of God. It warms my heart to know that my brother has found his true love and I have gained an amazing sister in Brielle and two wonderful nieces and an incredible nephew. Brielle has brought so much joy not only to my brother but for us all. Seeing Bryson happy makes us all happy because we know how genuine of a human being he is and the man that God created him to be is so impeccable that he deserves nothing less than true happiness. Bryson, I love you brother. Thank you for being the best brother I could have ever asked for and such an incredible example of what it means to be a man of God. Brielle, I am honored to call you my sister and welcome you and your children to the family. Thank you for making my brother so extremely happy. I have never seen him so crazy in love as he is with you but it's a great look for him to not be so business serious but to have a balance that only true love can give. So, to happiness and true love forever I toast to my brother Bryson and his beautiful bride Brielle." Everyone raised their glasses and toasted to the bride and groom and they applauded Bradon's speech.

He hugged Bryson, "Thank you Bradon, that was a great speech brother. I love you man!" Bryson said.

"I love you too brother," he said to Bryson. He walked over to Brielle and hugged her kissing her cheek. "Love you sis."

"Thank you Bradon, that was beautiful."

He headed back to his seat as Chantae stood to her feet. "Well that is a hard speech to follow so beautifully spoken and so true. True love. I grew up with Brielle and we have shared so many hopes and dreams for our life. Her love that she gives to people is so genuinely pure. We grew so close, more like sisters than friends and I have been blessed to have her in my life. God takes us all on journey's in life and we never know where we will end up. We just hope for our happy ever after. Today and all the day's that lead up to today, I have witnessed my friend living in her happy ever after. True love is such an amazing gift given by God and anyone that has the pleasure of experiencing true love is blessed. It's something that should always be cherished and protected. That is something no one has to worry about when it comes to these two. From the moment Brielle met Bryson her eyes were lit up bright and you knew instantly she was experiencing true love. Brielle, I love you sister. I am so happy for you. Bryson thank you for putting that smile on my best friend's face, that beat in her heart and that happy ever after in her life. I love you both and congratulations to you both! To the Bride and Groom!"

Once again everyone lifted their glasses and toasted. Chantae hugged and kissed Brielle and Bryson embracing Brielle a little bit longer. "Congratulations my friend! I love you!" Chantae said to Brielle.

It was now time for the announcement of the baby. As Bryson and Brielle stood to their feet they announced to all their friends that they were having twins. Everyone was shocked, but everyone was excited and congratulating them.

Ameila and Kenneth were no longer hiding their relationship and were at the wedding as a couple. It was shocking seeing Kenneth out in public with a woman but it was good seeing him and Ameila happy. Love was definitely in the air. Isaiah was bringing a date but his new girlfriend backed out at the last minute. He saw Brielle's friend Vanessa Carols and ended up spending the evening talking with her.

It was time for their first dance of the night and as Bryson and Brielle headed to the dance floor, Bradon went over to sit closer to Chantae. He held her tight in his arms. "Your speech was beautiful baby." They watched as Bryson and Brielle danced then other couples started to join them. "You want to dance sweetheart?" He asked Chantae.

"Sure, let's dance. But I don't want to stay too much longer I'm tired. You know yesterday was very eventful and we stayed up all night long." She paused smiling, remembering the night before. "Seeing as how we had to be up early this morning, I am now exhausted. So not too much longer ok."

Bradon was smiling remember the night before. "Yeah you were a very bad girl last night. One dance and then we can go when you are ready." He grabbed her hand and they headed to the dance floor. After about thirty minutes Chantae told Bradon she was ready to leave.

"We won't be far behind, it has been a long day. Thank you both for everything! We will catch up after the honeymoon okay," Brielle said to Chantae hugging her good bye.

"Yes we will. You have fun on your honeymoon girl and congratulations again my friend."

They said their goodbyes and headed out the door. The party went on for a few more hours before the last person left leaving Bryson, Brielle, their parents and kids all sitting around talking. The kids were making plans for their grandparents to do while their parents were away on their honeymoon.

Once Bradon and Chantae were in the car she started crying tears of joy and of pain. She was happy for her friend but her heart was overwhelmed and hurting at the same time.

"What's wrong sweetheart?"

"I don't know. I guess I'm happy and sad at the same time. I mean, it was a beautiful wedding. Everything was so perfect for Brielle and Bryson. I have you and I love you. You make me happy. It's been a lot going on with the wedding and then I have the stress of preparing for my clothing line launch. It's just a lot going on lately." She paused for a moment. She figured she would tell him what was really bothering her. "I overheard that girl in the club mention to you about a girl who was pregnant by you or had a baby that was possibly yours. Then I saw the papers in your pants pocket when I was washing clothes about the DNA test you took. I assumed it was for the same girl from the club and I was talking to Brielle last night about it because I didn't want to bring it up to you if it was nothing. I figured it was your past and if you needed to tell me about a baby being yours you would. As I was talking to her about the baby and DNA test she assumed I was talking about Jewel." She looked up at Bradon for a response hoping he would say something to ease her mind.

"Baby I am so sorry I should have told you about everything from the beginning instead of trying to hide it. I thought I was protecting you." The driver of the limo closed the window in between them as he pulled off into traffic giving them privacy.

"I want to be the only woman having your babies. Having children were not a part of my immediate plans but seeing how happy and complete Brielle and Bryson are, I knew it was something I wanted to give you, to give us. And now." She started crying uncontrollably.

Bradon had never seen Chantae show these emotions before. He knew he loved her and he knew he couldn't fix what was done. He only hoped that both babies were not his. "I wish I could tell you that both babies were not mine but I won't know about Jewel until after she has the baby and I don't even know who this other girl is. I received a text from an anonymous number but I am clueless and don't think that girl is pregnant by me. But I promise I will handle the situations and find out for sure. Nothing will interfere with our relationship, our happiness. I promise you that. I'm sorry Chantae. My past is catching up to me and I don't want to lose you. You are my right now, you are my future."

Bradon comforted Chantae the best he could, holding her close to him. As the driver pulled up in front of their home he kissed her forehead then her lips. When he felt her response to his touch embracing his love he motioned for them to get out. "I need to make love to you. Come on baby." He held on to her hand never letting go. He thanked the driver tipping him and headed for the front door. "I love you Chantae," he said kissing her lips passionately the moment they were inside.

Chantae held on to Bradon as he picked her up in his arms. He started kissing her neck aggressively as he carried her to their bedroom. He held her tight to his body. He loved Chantae and did not want to lose her because of mistakes in his past. He undressed her body kissing her every moment he could. He buried his head in between her thighs kissing her, licking her and pleasing her like he wanted to be sure she knew he loved her.

Her moans made him please her more "Oh Bradon that feels good. I am about to cum baby." He kept on pleasing her with his mouth until he felt her honey flowing for him to taste.

He made love to her body facing her all night, looking into her eyes wanting to see her face and for her to see his. He wanted her to feel his love every moment as he looked at her and with his every touch.

Chantae felt better knowing that she told Bradon what she knew and his reassurance that nothing would mess with their happiness, that he would be sure to be a part of her happy ever after regardless of what life throws his way. The fact that everyone knew except for her weighed heavy on her heart and now she could be at ease knowing that she knew and that Bradon knew he could talk to her about any and everything, no matter how bad the situation may seem.

Chapter 17
Honeymoon
September 21

Monday morning Bryson and Brielle were packed and ready for their honeymoon. Both their parents were at their home to see them off. Their parents were taking advantage of the vacation away from home to take care of the kids and have people waiting on them hand and feet in the process. They were among good company and great kids. They had a fun week planned while the honeymooners enjoyed their vacation.

"Off you two go. We have everything covered here with the kids," Bryson's mom said.

"Yes go on now and enjoy your vacation," Mrs. Summers said.

They hugged the kids once more before heading out the door to their awaiting limo. "I think our parents enjoy hanging out together," Bryson said.

"Yes I believe they do. At least we know the kids are in good hands and our parents will have just as much fun as the kids," she said as they entered the limo.

"I am looking forward to this honeymoon. I will have you all to myself to love on every moment for a week. We never have to come out of the room if we don't want to."

"We can stay in bed making love nonstop if you want to but you must feed me, shower with me and sleep with me. Oh, and I want to go on the beach at least once," Brielle said.

Bryson laughed. "You are too easy to please you know. Although all that sounds like a great plan, we would probably only spend half our time inside. I have a full agenda of events planned for us to enjoy and it definitely includes feeding you," he said holding her close to him.

She laid her head on his chest. "I am looking forward to the rest of our lives together."

"Me too sweetheart," he said rubbing his hands through her hair.

They arrived in the beautiful St Lucia. The land was exotic at every turn. The water was crystal blue and the air was crisp and fresh from the beautiful exotic trees everywhere. The drive to where they would be staying was a tourist view full of excitement at every turn. Brielle was in awe of the romantic city and couldn't be happier to be experiencing all that St Lucia had to offer for the first time ever with Bryson.

They would be staying on a private beach in the Galaxy Sanctuary fit for a King and Queen. There were only three walls to the romantic getaway where they would be sleeping, eating and making love. They had complete privacy in this romantic place and an amazing view of the crystal clear blue water in front of them.

Once they were alone Bryson made sure Brielle had a tray full of fruits and vegetables to eat as she needed so she wouldn't become sick. He ordered dinner for them to eat in their room so they could spend the evening in resting from their travel. After dinner, he ran her a warm bubble bath in the enormous floor tub inside the bathroom. The tub was full of bubbles and red, pink and white rose petals. He undressed her and helped her inside the tub. He undressed and got in behind her. He had a plate of chocolate covered strawberries and chocolate covered pineapples sitting to the side for them to feast on as they enjoyed their bath.

"Babe this is so lovely, so romantic. You couldn't have picked a more beautiful place for us to enjoy our honeymoon."

"I'm so glad you are enjoying everything so far."

"Yes, I am and this room is amazing. We really could spend our entire vacation without ever leaving. The view of the water is perfect. So peaceful. We could take vacations here every year." Brielle was extremely happy and Bryson was happy because of that.

"If that's what you want to do it is a done deal sweetheart," he said kissing her forehead. He was sitting behind her with his legs straddled around her body caressing her shoulders.

"You are so amazing. Thank you Bryson."

"You don't have to thank me. Making you happy will be a pleasure for me and I will work hard to make sure I always make you happy."

"Bryson, can you make any changes to the movie?" She thought it would be the perfect time to ask.

"Within reason I can request changes. What do you want me to change?" he asked. Brielle didn't ask much of him and when she did he wanted to make it happen.

"The part you said they had of the wedding you know with Jewel. The humiliating part. Do they have to show that? Is there any way they can alter that part to not hurt her any more than it has and to protect Bradon and Chantae?"

"That's funny you say that. When we were married and everything was real to me regarding you and me, I thought about everything within the movie. I was so close to withdrawing the entire story but when you agreed to the movie I decided to change the terms and I focused on the part about Jewel. Not for her sake but because I had my blessing and I didn't want to hurt anyone else. So they have used pieces of that footage and blurred out her face and took out the humiliating pieces but the way they edited that part makes it look like a nightmare that I was awakened from. Its tasteful and I think you will be pleased."

"You are truly an amazing man of God. I love you so much." She turned her body to face him and straddled her body around his.

"I love you my Queen," he said kissing her. He picked up a strawberry and fed it to her. They ate several pieces of fruit before indulging in their kisses again. Bryson covered one of Brielle's breast with his mouth sucking on her nipple. He pulled her closer to his body holding on to her butt squeezing tight.

She could feel his penis rising hard as a rock and she started to move her hips back and forth. Unable to resist making love to her body, Bryson lifted them both up out of the tub sitting on the spacious ledge. With his feet still in the water, Brielle had her legs wrapped around his waist and he slid his penis inside her. The gentleness but aggressiveness of his thrusting inside of her honey pot hitting her overly sensitive erogenous g-spot made her moan out in pleasure. Her hormones were raging and she couldn't get enough of her husband making love to every inch of her body. Her breast were full and larger due to the pregnancy and her nipples were extremely sensitive screaming to be sucked and teased. Bryson gave her what she wanted, giving her satisfying orgasms one after another.

Her body was experiencing pure gratifying explosive orgasmic pleasure. "Baby you are making me feel so magnificently sexy and satisfyingly amazing." She was panting and expressing her pleasure grabbing at Bryson's back, shoulders and holding on to the back of his head.

Bryson picked her up with her legs wrapped around his waist and took her to the king size bed in the middle of the room. He laid her down flipping her over on her stomach and kissed the back of her neck. He ran his hand through the back of her hair as he gently bit her neck working his way down her back. He kissed her back making a trail of wetness to her butt, kissing and gently biting her there too before reaching her thighs. Brielle was reacting so sensually. "You like that baby?"

"Yes, every bit of it," she said with eyes closed clinching at the bed sheets.

"You ready to feel me inside you?" he said still seductively nibbling at the back of her thighs.

"Yes, yes baby. I am ready."

Bryson ran his hands up her back grabbing at the back of her neck massaging her head underneath her flowing hair. He mounted her from the back as she lay on her stomach. He grabbed her butt squeezing her cheeks before putting his hand inside her wetness. He then pushed his hard penis deep inside feeling the wet warmness, feeling the pulsation of her immediate orgasm. "Is that your spot baby?" he asked her as she moaned out in pleasure.

"Oh yes, yes don't stop. Keep going, faster, faster please don't stop." She moaned at every thrust inside her.

Bryson was loving every moment spent pleasing his wife. After another hour of pleasure, he couldn't hold his orgasm any longer. Afterwards they both collapsed from exhaustion. They repositioned their bodies with Bryson holding Brielle in his arms as they looked out into the amazing view of the water and the mountains behind. For the moment, it was as if no one else existed but the two of them embraced together as one.

The entire honeymoon was spent without technology or communication with anyone about anything. It was all about the two of them and their forever love.

Chapter 18
3 months of friendships and love
September 25 – December 24

Bryson and Brielle were glowing when they returned from their trip. The two love birds enjoyed their honeymoon spending quality time with just the two of them. They made a promise to one another to get away, just the two of them, at least one week out of every year. It was good for their marriage and building a stronger bond. The kids were excited to see them. They thought they looked different and that Brielle's belly had gotten bigger.

The next three months was wonderful in Bryson's home. He was happy with his wife and their children. He loved his new family and the happiness that he felt in his heart. His home was now truly a place he could call home. He was full of excitement anticipating the birth of their new babies. Bryson went back to work but instead of late hours he left work early and was always home to enjoy dinner with Brielle and the kids.

Brielle enjoyed being a stay at home mom. Their home was like a vacation before going on a vacation and she enjoyed every part of their home. Her and the girls were able to play dress up all the time, be movie stars in their own home. She would take the kids to school, go to the library, stay at home and read a book in a hot bubble bath if she wanted to. She would even visit Bryson at work for lunch. She would eat with him in his office and enjoyed many visits where she ate lunch with Bryson and she was his dessert laid across his office desk, his table or in the window seal overlooking the city. She was Bryson's dream and he was everything she imagined and more. Their life was perfect in every area. They didn't worry about anything, not even the DNA results of Jewel's baby.

Brielle didn't see much of Chantae since she returned from her honeymoon. They both were occupied with their men and new lives. Brielle called a few times but the conversations were always brief. Where she had time to do whatever she wanted to do,

Chantae was working hard to launch her clothing line off the ground.

Chantae was consumed in her clothing line. She had offers coming in from major distributors and spent all her time meeting with potential business associates, making deals and meeting deadlines. Her dream to own a major clothing line was coming true. What little time she did have to spare was being spent with Bradon. They didn't talk anymore about the women who could possibly be carrying Bradon's baby. There life was happy without mentioning a word about it. She figured if he didn't mention it there was nothing to mention. Chantae buried herself in her work so she didn't have to think about the situation.

Bradon was also busy with his new business venture and was taking over the industry with his exotic unique designs. He learned his work ethic from watching his brother all the years as he built his business and was now living the busy business life he watched his brother live. He enjoyed being the boss and being in high demand. It made him feel like he was the man. The same feeling he got when he was the man with all those women around him he was not feeling owning a successful business having only one woman. His time was consumed just as much as Chantae's. They both agreed to work on their business and if either felt neglected to let the other know. But they never missed a step in the love making department.

Chantae and Bradon were happy together. She was excited with the life they were living. She didn't have to work a nine to five job and could make her own hours for her business. She was living the dream even if she didn't have all the extravagant lavish material things that she thought she would have in the beginning of their relationship. She had genuine love with Bradon and working hard to build an empire with her man.

Isaiah was enjoying having a girlfriend. He thought they were building something towards a lasting relationship but he soon realized that she was no good for him. He found out after dating her for a couple months that she had a child she never told him about. He was willing to still date her and attempted to initiate a real relationship with her. She was flattered to have met a real man that genuinely cared about her, something that she was not use to.

But the moment she found out that Isaiah was only hanging around rich men, Bryson and Bradon, by association of his sister and never had their type of money she was quickly fading away from their relationship. She wanted to undo the love affair she had started with Isaiah but he was not ready to let her go. He was clueless to what was happening to him, he was losing his girl.

She first started avoiding his phone calls and cancelling dates. The day he decided to go by her house to check on her another man was coming out of her front door kissing her as she stood wrapped in a bath towel. She looked up at Isaiah smiled and went back inside of the house. When the man that was leaving passed him saying, "You next man? Home girl is freaky nasty and has some good ass pussy," Isaiah knew then the relationship was over. His heart was broken but he knew he was better off and saving his self a lot of trouble and heart ache in the long run.

Isaiah was a good man and a great catch for any woman who was lucky enough to have him. He was genuinely kind and gentle to women and wanted nothing more than to love a deserving woman. He would always think about how his mom and sister should be loved and never wanted to be any less of a man than his father was to his mother. He wasn't broke as she thought he was either. He was a man who saved his money and didn't need the finer things in life to flash and define who he was as a man. He put God first and worked hard enjoying the simple things in life. Isaiah took the break up as a lesson learned to pay attention to the signs in the beginning. After all, she did show him that she had hoe tendencies in the beginning of their relationship he just put his blinders on hoping to change what obviously was not changeable.

Kenneth and Ameila were enjoying and building their new love together. They did a lot of things in the beginning with just the two of them and eventually requested that they do things as a family. When Bryson came back to work, Kenneth took a couple days off to have an extended weekend and took them all to Disney land. Ameila and the kids had never been on any family trips and this was the first of many Kenneth planned for them to take. He was in love with Ameila and couldn't imagine how any man would treat her and the kids as horrible as her ex-husband did. He vowed to make her his wife and treat her like the Queen she deserved to be treated as.

They were cute working together in the office and before too long, everyone they worked with knew they were together because the chemistry between them was too electrifying. Anyone around them longer than two minutes could definitely feel the love they shared. Kenneth knew he would eventually make her his wife. He just needed to give her time to ensure she was over her ex. Ameila had not mentioned anything about him since their divorce. He also knew that it was a matter of time until her ex found out about her success and come crawling begging for his family back. Until then he would love her whole heartedly mending all the broken pieces her ex left behind. His love for her was genuinely true and Ameila could feel every ounce of it.

Brielle and Bryson's parents spent a lot of time together. They were bonding through their new-found friendship based on their children, church and similar principles and beliefs. When Brielle would call her parents to come hang out with the kids while she was away, Mr. and Mrs. Mathews would come along to hang out with them as well. And the same thing would happen when Bryson would call his parents, Mr. and Mrs. Summers would come along. The kids loved having two sets of grandparents around. They were free to be kids while the adults enjoyed adult company. It was fun for everyone.

The men would separate from the women when they were together and the women would do the same. It was their alone time to have guy talk and girl talk and still be together when they wanted to smoother the other with their love. They were happy that Brielle and Bryson found each other. They not only found love but gave their parents a genuine loving friendship. Everything was good. Whatever life threw their way they were sure they could handle.

Carter was celebrating his tenth birthday. He had everything he could ever imagined and the only thing he thought to ask for was to have his father's last name. He approached Brielle and Bryson a few days before his birthday to tell them of his wishes. "Mom I know what I want for my birthday. It's not much at least I don't think so but I wrote you a letter explaining why I am asking. I know you will make the final decision if I get what I am requesting or not. I love you with my whole heart either way."

"Okay son. I see you put a lot of thought into your gift to write a letter," she said to Carter looking up at Bryson before taking the letter from Carter.

"Yes, I have. You both can read it together. I have been convinced to attend Jayla's tea party. If you need me I will be in her room having tea," he said with his pinky out pretending to drink tea.

They all giggled. Brielle hugged her son before he walked away. "I love you son."

"Love you too mom." He held her tight. Then he went to Bryson and hugged him as well. "Love you too, dad." Then he quickly left the room heading up the stairs to Jayla's room.

"That's the first time he has called me dad. Wow that felt great," Bryson said happy but amazed that Carter called him dad. The girls had been calling him dad for a few months now but Carter had yet to call him dad. This was a big step for everyone.

"I am just as amazed as you are. I am so proud of him. You don't think he is trying to butter you up asking for something outrageous, do you?" She giggled.

"I'm sure it is reasonable. He is a good kid and hey he buttered me up really good just then," Bryson said smiling hugging Brielle's shoulders as she proceeded to open the letter. He decided to let her read the letter first letting her give him the ok to read it as well.

"Yes, he did," she said taking the letter out of the envelope.

Carter's birthday wish!

Mother dear first let me say that you are an amazing and beautiful woman. You have always put your children before anything and anyone else in this world. You are our angel and we thank God for such a wonderful mother. We all know what we went through with the man who helped you create us all and give us life. But just because a man helps create a life doesn't give him the right to call his self a father or a dad. Blood does not bond family. Our grandparents have always been wonderful to us. Grand daddy, grand momma, Isaiah, Chantae, you and us, that has been our family always and now we have more grandparents that love us, more uncles with Bradon and Kenneth and we now have a dad, a real dad, a real father in Bryson. He has been more of a father to us than we have ever experienced in life. He loves you and he loves us. He has given us more than we would have ever asked for. We love him for being that father we never had and for doing so because he wanted to, because his love for our mom is so genuine that he loves every part of you and we will always be a part of you momma. In my heart, I feel like he will always be a part of us all as well. So, since we have everything already including love, there is only one thing I am asking for and my sisters want the same thing. So, since it's my birthday I am happily willing to share my gift with them if you say it's ok. For my birthday, I want my father's last name. We want him to be our father on paper. Since you also have his last name we would like to have the same last name as you do. I have been practicing saying it and Carter Mathews sounds good to me. If it's ok with you momma that's all I want for my birthday. I know it may take some time to do if you decide it can be done. But besides cake this is all I need. I have everything else, and Christmas is right around the corner. Thank you momma, and thank you Bryson, for everything you do to take care of us and make us happy.

Your son, Carter

Brielle was in tears and she handed the letter to Bryson. "This letter was beautifully written by my son. He is so bright, I know but he always seems to amaze me."

Bryson was reading the letter and even when he was done he was choked up from Carter's words. He had a tear in his eye that he quickly wiped away as he held Brielle close in his arms. "You okay?" He knew she was feeling emotional realizing her past and Carter's truth.

"Yes, I am wonderful. I am so blessed Bryson. I am thankful for you and those amazing kids. I don't know how to address my son with this letter. I mean this is too much to ask of you to adopt the kids, give them your last name." She looked him in his eyes.

"If you are okay with me adopting them and giving them my last name you tell him yes. I would be honored Brielle."

"Bryson," she said his name as if she was asking him a question of confirmation to what he just said.

Bryson held her tighter looking down into her tear glazed eyes. "Let's do it. Let's officially make them mine and yours. We could have this done before his birthday. Give him his gift and his cake."

"Let's do it!" she said smiling tiptoeing up to kiss Bryson so passionately and thankful.

They were able to change the children's last name and give a copy to the kids on Carter's birthday. They were all happy with the change and it was an instant feeling of a stronger bond than ever before. A few weeks later a letter was sent to their biological father in jail letting him know that he was no longer listed as the father. He had already giving up his rights as a parent after the abuse on Brielle and Carter and now they were no longer legally tied to him.

The night of the Premier, Bryson was beaming with happiness. The news cameras were there interviewing and snapping pictures of him and Brielle and showing off her pregnant belly through her beautiful blue evening gown. She was gorgeous and glowing. The camera crews loved the happy couple. They were featured on several news channels. They made all of those around them happy just being in their presence.

Isaiah was there alone and seeing Dr. Carols there alone as well he grabbed her up happily. "You are too beautiful to be here solo."

"I could say the same about you sir. You are wearing that suit."

"As of this moment forward you are no longer solo. If you would join me as my pretend date, or for real date you can choose." He held his arm out for her to take.

"Well I am flattered. And I accept." She grabbed his arm and they both proceeded as if they were a happy couple that came to the premier together. The cameras took their pictures on the red carpet. They knew they were VIP's but were clueless as to who this beautiful mysterious couple was, only that they were Bryson and Kenneth's VIP guest.

Bradon and Chantae were beautifully dressed in Chantae's clothing designs and when the cameras were on them and the spokesperson asked what designer they were wearing, they both proudly smiled and revealed for the first time ever to the public the name for her new clothing line, "Tae Marie". She gave her speech to the media about her clothing line and the high fashion stores that will carry her line. It was a proud moment for them both.

Kenneth allowed Ameila to have her moment in the spotlight as the writer of the book and the face of the promotion. This was also her moment to shine and tell a little bit about her new foundation she was starting for battered and homeless women to get their life back on track. Kenneth admired her confidence and knew he would love her forever.

Everyone came out to support the Premier of the movie. It was a packed sold out theatre full of Bryson and Brielle's family, friends and tons of celebrities. Brielle's pastor who married them was also there. He invited everyone to church that Sunday to give thanks for all that was good with them. Everything was a success, even the after party. Brielle was pleased how well the movie turned out, even the part they edited about Jewel to not reveal who she was and the humiliating things she did.

Accepting the Pastors invite, Brielle and Bryson's friends all joined them for church that Sunday. Pastor Malone was excited to see everyone at church. The presence of God's true love brought joy and that was alright with him.

"Today's sermon I think we should talk about love. Protecting God's blessings of love. Amen."

"Amen." The congregation said in unison.

"Today I want to talk about three things. God's love is pure and genuine. Growing and strengthening God's blessing of love. And last but definitely not least, Protecting God's love. If you could turn in your bibles with me…"

Pastor Malone gave a powerful sermon on Love and had all the lovers in the building holding on to their true loves. He was sending out confirmations of God's true love all around him. True love was infectious. It made those that didn't have it want it more and those that did work harder to maintain their blessing.

Christmas Day Bryson had a huge party for everyone to come and enjoy Christmas at his home. Ameila and the kids came with Kenneth. Chantae and Bradon were there. Dr. Carols even made an appearance even though she didn't stay long. Isaiah and their mother and father stayed the night so they could all wake up and experience Christmas Day with Brielle and the kids. This would have been the Summer's first Christmas waking up without the kids so Bryson welcomed anyone wanting to stay. The kids opened lots of great gifts and everyone enjoyed Christmas dinner sitting around the beautifully decorated dining room table. Christmas joy consumed their hearts. As Bryson stood back looking over his family he was proud and extremely happy.

The past three months were wonderful for everyone. Love, success and happiness was all around with the Mathews and Summer's and their circle of family and friends. They were prepared and ready for whatever the future held for them, at least that is the way it appeared. Building a bond based on love strengthens a family and prepares them for whatever life could throw their way. Love is the secret ingredient in dealing with life and all of its joys and even its storms.

Chapter 19
Greg in prison
December 26

Day after Christmas was a busy day in the prison were Greg was being held. Inmates were still receiving Christmas packages, cards and letters from their family and friends. Even though they were locked up, this was a good time for some receiving gifts that were only allowed once a year. They anticipated these gifts even special cards and letters. Greg was sitting around with other men watching television when he saw a recap on the news of Bryson's movie premier. He could care less about what they were talking about until he saw a picture of Brielle and Bryson together.

"Hold the fuck up. I know that ain't my bitch with that nigga," he said to one of his boys locked up with him.

"Which one nigga? Your ass had a lot of girls, shit you still got a bunch of bitches coming up here for visits and shit."

"That is my baby mamma right there with that nigga," he said now standing up looking at the TV pissed off. His jaws were clenched and fist balled.

"Damn in the blue dress?" his boy asked.

"That's you man? Who the fuck is that nigga she standing next to?" another inmate asked hearing his conversation.

"Right, don't look like his girl. Look like that nigga on TV girl." another man said and they broke out in laughter.

Greg was looking at the TV watching the two of them standing, posing for the cameras, looking happy. Then he saw her belly and realized she was pregnant.

"Damn is that your baby she carrying? I know another dude ain't got what you say is your girl pregnant?" The men sitting around were all engaging in the conversation with Greg even if he was not talking directly to them. This was exciting entertainment for them. They made jokes and kept on talking about it.

"This motherfucker done got my girl pregnant. She gon always be my bitch. When I get out of here that nigga is good as fucked up. Believe that partner." Greg's jaws were clenched together in anger watching how happy she was with Bryson. He tuned everyone else around him out including the guard handing out mail calling his name.

"Greg, they are calling your name for mail man," his home boy said tapping him on the arm.

Greg retrieved his mail from the guard curious what was in the brown envelope. He knew it had nothing to do with Christmas. He was waiting to receive something regarding his parole hearing. Opening the letter and reading the content, his anger intensified.

We are writing to inform you of the recent change in government documents removing your name as father from the birth certificate of the named children below. Due to your release of rights from past convicted crimes involving the named minors below, the adoption and removal of name has been finalized. This is the only notification you will receive concerning this mater. If you have any questions please contact our office.

Previous father named has been removed from birth certificate and any other legal document concerning Carter Summers, Jayla Summers and Olivia Summers.

Greg read the letter out loud to his home boy standing near him. "I'm a kill that mother fucker," Greg screamed out in anger.

"Damn that's fucked up man. Can they do that without your consent?"

Greg ignored him pacing back and forth. "I swear I'm gonna kill that mother fucker."

"Inmate watch it you are verbally stating a threat," the guard said to Greg.

"Fuck you pig. Shut the hell up talking to me." Greg was in rage.

"We have a situation in unit Three-C," the officer spoke into his walkie talkie.

"Calm down man you ass is going straight to the hole you know they don't take threats lightly," his home boy said.

"Fuck them mother fuckers."

"Get down on the floor now, put your hands behind your head," the officer yelled at Greg.

"Make me motherfucker."

The officer had his stick out waiting on other officers to get there. "I said down on the floor inmate. Now." His tone was loud and demanding.

"Your punk ass called for backup. Y'all weak ass bitches wouldn't last on the streets. Fuck all y'all," he said right before screaming out in pain from the hit to his legs from the officer behind him. Greg swung at the officer closest to him and kept swinging causing the officers to hit him multiple times with their sticks until they had him pinned to the floor restrained.

"Your punk ass not so tough now are you?" the officer said handcuffing him while the other officers held him down with their knees in his back, neck and twisting his legs and arms.

"Fuck y'all motherfuckers," he yelled. Greg was enraged over the news of Brielle and his children. Even though he abused them while he was out, seeing her happy with another man and knowing he has lost all legal access to his children stung his heart.

"You are the one that's fucked. You just added assault on an officer on multiple accounts to your list of crimes. You can kiss your Parole good bye when you go in front of that board."

Greg was placed in maximum security holding. After being there a couple weeks he received his Parole letter in the mail. He knew any chance he had of having his release granted was now blown after his enraged assault on the officers. All he could think about was hurting Bryson and Brielle anyway he could and that was the only thing that consumed his mind. He didn't care about being in the hole, or any other charges they added. He was still pissed at the world and enraged at the fact that he completely lost his family.

Chapter 20
Interview gone wrong
January 12

Tuesday morning the Recruiting Manager came to see Kenneth as soon as he arrived. She walked up to him in the hallway as he was about to enter his office. "Mr. Cartwright if I could have a quick moment of your time. I have something you may want to know."

"Sure, come on in," he said opening his office door allowing her to walk in before him. "What can I help you with?" he asked.

"As you know we are hiring a new led writer for the Publishing team and I thought you should know that one of the candidates who actually meets majority of the qualifications we are looking for has an interview this morning." She went on to say.

Kenneth interrupted her, "I don't deal with candidates for any of those positions. The hiring managers always handle interviews for their departments."

"Yes, that is the process we follow sir but this man listed Ameila as a reference and I believe this may be her ex-husband. I don't want to over step my boundary here but I just wanted to make sure you were aware since I know she works under you," she said in a professional manner. Everyone was aware that Ameila and Kenneth had something going on between them that was more than a work relationship but it was not her place to say anything about it to Kenneth or anyone else.

"Oh, I see. What is his name?"

"Yes sir, it is Charles Churchwell Sr," she said opening the folder in front of her then handing it over to him.

"What time is the interview?" he asked.

"It is at nine this morning in the Boardroom."

"Thanks for letting me know. I really appreciate that. Go on with the interview as planned but I will be sitting in to observe and I may ask a few questions myself," he said looking down at Charles resume.

"Yes sir, I will let the hiring manager know." She stood and walked towards the door.

"Thanks again for letting me know. Good observation." And without any more being said she knew what he meant. Kenneth wasn't blind to the fact that people knew about him and Ameila being in love. He also knew everyone was aware of her story concerning her husband putting her and their children out of their home. This was his chance to meet the man that hurt Ameila and abandoned his family. It would also give Ameila a chance to see him since her divorce if she chose. He would be sure to be there to protect her no matter what. He closed the folder and picked up the phone. "Hey Jeff," he called the head of security by name. "Nothing is wrong but I need two of your best officers about eight forty-five to hang out up here by the boardroom. I have an interview at nine and because of who it is I want to be sure if a situation occurs they are close by."

"Yes sir. I'm all over it."

"Thanks my man," Bryson said before hanging up.

He didn't tell Ameila ahead of time. He wanted to be sure he had a chance to meet with Charles first. He went into Ameila's office before the interview and talked business and some lovers talk as well. He loved seeing her smile knowing she was happy. He wanted to be sure Charles and Ameila's path did not cross when he arrived. His phone buzzed letting him know Charles had arrived. He left Ameila with some work he needed to keep her occupied for the moment and headed to the interview.

When he arrived, Charles was seated across the table from the hiring manager. They both stood as he introduced him to Charles. "Mr. Churchwell, this is Kenneth Cartwright one of the Owners of the company and he will be sitting in on the interview this morning."

They shook hands with Kenneth looking down at Charles shaking his hand firmly. "Nice to meet you sir," Charles said.

"Likewise," Kenneth said before taking a seat.

"Alright let's get started. You have a very impressive resume. I want to start with your Magazine Company. Is this still an active company you are running?" the hiring manager asked

"Well I started the company a few years ago and it was a very successful Company but I had a few family issues that came up that prevented me from giving the dedication that was needed so I decided to close the company."

"Okay I see. That was one of my concerns with your resume. I know running a Magazine is very demanding and this position we are hiring for will be very demanding of your time."

Kenneth jumped in asking a question without looking up from his paper. "Mr. Churchwell, did you start and run the company on your own?" He knew the answer, that Ameila was the backbone of his company being started and successful. He also knew that when she left, his company started to fail without her. He just wanted to hear what he had to say.

"Yes sir I did start and run the company on my own for the most part. My wife would help out here and there when I needed her. The plan was to hire a team after revenue was established to grow the company. Although the company was very successful, with me having to close the company I never made it that far." Charles sounded nervous talking to Kenneth. He wanted to sound like he was a successful businessman.

The hiring Manager asked a few more questions before Kenneth jumped in and asked another question. "You have listed Ameila Churchwell as a reference on your resume. I assume you know she is an employee here with our company. An excellent and valuable employee. You once shared the same last name but how do you know Ameila?" he asked looking him straight in his eyes.

Charles felt like Kenneth's question about Ameila was personal but he was not backing down. "Ameila is my wife."

The hiring manager could sense that there was something else going on that he was not previous aware of but he quickly figured it out. He looked towards Kenneth and he knew that Charles would not be hired. "Excuse me for a moment I have a few documents I left on the printer that will need your signature." He stood to exit the room as the two men were still starring at one another.

"I assume you mean ex-husband?" he said leaning back in his seat. "We have a very strict policy here and we don't want any conflict of interest that would interfere with…"

Charles interrupted his sentence. "Me and Ameila getting a divorce was a mistake. I love my wife and I plan to make things right between us. We will be back together soon and no, there will not be any conflicts. My personal matters with my wife will not interfere with my work sir," he said with confidence.

Kenneth picked up the phone and all he said was, "Can you come into the Boardroom please. I have a gentleman here interviewing and I need you just for a moment." He placed the receiver back in place. "Your resume looks impressive. Since you listed Ameila as a reference she will need to verify the information listed."

Ameila walked in seeing Kenneth and Charles sitting on opposite sides of the table. "Charles?" she said looking at him then Kenneth and back at Charles.

Charles stood to his feet. "Hello Ameila. You look beautiful as always."

"What are you doing here?" She was not impressed with his compliment. She walked over to the side of the table where Kenneth sat standing beside him. "Kenneth what's going on?" she said in a softer tone to him.

"Mr. Charles Churchwell here is applying for a job with us and he stated you as a reference. Someone who could verify he started and ran his Magazine Company on his own and closed it due to family issues. He also stated that there would not be any conflict of interest working here with you who he referred to you as his wife. When questioned if he meant ex-husband he stated he loved his wife and divorcing her, well you were a mistake and he planned on fixing his marriage." Kenneth looked up at Ameila. "His resume is impressive and the hiring manager picked him because he thought he would be a great fit for the company. Since you know him and his work history I thought you should be involved in deciding and make the decision rather to hire him or not." Kenneth closed the folder and handed it to Ameila watching her expressions.

"How are the kids Ameila?" Charles asked her in a caring voice.

"Kids are great, no thanks to you," she said as she took a seat across from Charles.

"Ameila. I am sorry for everything, really I am. I miss you. I'm ready for you all to come home sweetheart." Charles looked over at Kenneth who was starring him in the face. "Can you give us a moment please?"

"Not a chance." Kenneth was not leaving Ameila in the same room with Charles.

"Charles you are nowhere near qualified to work as a writer for any company, not even your own. You are the reason your company failed and you are the reason our marriage failed. If you think you can apply for a job where I work in hopes of what? Getting your family back? You lost that opportunity the day you threw us out of our home with nothing more than the clothes on our back. And if you thought you had even a slight chance to get a job here, you must have been dreaming. You see, I'm the boss and I also know your resume is filled with lies. The next time you decide to use me as a reference be sure you want me to tell the truth about who you really are."

"Ameila wait. Let's go somewhere and talk please." Charles stood trying to sweet talk Ameila.

"We were done talking the day in court when you gave up all your rights to your children. We were done talking after all the days you laughed and belittled me when you had all your hoes answering our phone and the door to what was supposed to be my home when I tried to get in the house to get our children's clothes. We were done talking the day you put your hands on me. I suggest you leave willingly before I have your ass thrown out."

"Ameila, wait please don't do this. I need you baby girl please just come by the house so we can talk."

He started to walk towards Ameila and Kenneth stood up and moved in front of her. "This interview is over. I am going to have to ask you to leave." Kenneth said blocking his path to Ameila.

Security had come to the door just as Charles attempted to get around Kenneth. "I need to talk to my wife can you just give us a few moments."

"I need you to leave now." Kenneth said not moving. Security walked over to Charles.

"Your application for employment will be rejected. Charles please leave now. This conversation is over," Ameila said.

"Get off me." Charles said jerking away from the security grabbing his arm. "I'm leaving." He started to walk towards the door. "Ameila, I need you to come home please just think about it. Bring the kids with you. I would love to see them." When he didn't receive an immediate response, he started to plead his case more.

"I am about to lose our home. I need you Ameila. Tell me you will at least think about giving us a second chance." He stood in the doorway looking back at Ameila with security on his heels.

"You have been given more chances than you deserve. I have nothing to think about. I am so happy now and will never give up my happiness for an undeserving man. Goodbye Charles."

He looked as if he was choked up with emotions realizing she had moved on with her life. He knew he gave up the best thing that ever happened to him and he was never getting his family back. He took God's gift for granted and that reality hit him like a ton of bricks. He now realized all the girls he cheated with and his fun moments were not worth his family. But he realized too late. Ameila was gone and her heart now belonged to another man. Security escorted Charles completely out of the building.

"Are you okay?" Kenneth asked Ameila.

"Yes I am great." She thought for a moment then looked up at Kenneth. "You knew he was coming in for an interview when you were in my office didn't you?"

"I did. Sorry I didn't tell you then. I didn't know how that was going to play out, what his motive were for coming. Now I see he wanted you back." Kenneth kept his eyes on her.

"That would never happen in a million years." She looked up at Kenneth's smiling face. "Thanks for giving me the satisfaction of firing him before he was even hired." She smiled.

"I thought you would like that. Once I realized he was seriously applying I wanted to laugh in his face but thought you turning him down would be better." He walked over to kiss her lips. "I can't wait to make love to you tonight. Your authority and the way you handled him turned me on."

"Is that right? I am going to handle you tonight alright. You still could have given me a heads up before walking in like that," she said reaching for his awaiting lips. They kissed passionately embraced in each other's arms until they were interrupted by the head of security clearing his throat.

Kenneth still holding her looked up towards the door. "Sorry," he said turning back to Ameila. "We were discussing business plans for later tonight."

"Continue please. I just wanted to let you know the gentleman was escorted out of the building and everything is good." He had one foot out the door as he ended his statement. "Just come by my office to sign off on the incident when you have a moment."

"Thank you Jeff. I can sign now we are done here." Kenneth released his embrace from Ameila.

"I will see you tonight," she said as she headed for the door smiling. "Hey Jeff." Ameila left the room feeling empowered and in love with her man.

That moment with her ex, seeing him needing her help gave her strength she didn't even know she needed. She took back a piece of herself he took from her and knew she would completely heal and be able to move forward with her life.

Kenneth received his confirmation he needed seeing Ameila and her ex-husband together. Ameila never talked about him after the divorce was final and didn't say much about him before after the day Bryson and Kenneth rescued her and her children from the streets. He was now one hundred percent sure he would make Ameila his wife. He could see that her heart only had room for him and her ex-husband doesn't have a second chance to win her back.

Chapter 21
Love No More
January 13

Isaiah was laying across his bed thinking about his life, the mistakes he made with dating women who were not right for him. He also thought about his standards he stood by when it came to how he was raised to treat women. He said a quick prayer asking God to guide him on his love journey so that he would know who his forever girl would be. He thought about Melissa for a moment. He was really feeling her and thought despite her past they may have a future together. As he thought about Melissa knowing that she was now in his past, his phone buzzed and her name flashed across his screen. He debated if he should answer and on the fourth ring decided to see what she had to say. "Hello."

"Hey handsome, it's been a while, how are you?" she said in a sexy soft tone.

"Hey Melissa, what's up?" he said as dry and uninterested as he could. He was shocked she was calling him but interested in what she could possibly have to say after not speaking to him for over a month.

"I was sitting here thinking about you realizing I miss our conversations we use to have."

"Oh yeah."

"Yeah. I miss those calls. I miss you Isaiah." Silence was there when she hoped she would hear him tell her he missed her as well but she received nothing more than silence. "How have you been?" she asked instead.

"I'm great. No complaints here," he said forcing her to say what she wanted. He didn't care how she was doing or at least he didn't want her to know he cared.

"You don't sound so happy to hear my voice. Did I catch you at a bad time?" she asked trying to check his current status.

"I'm getting ready to go hang out what's up? I'm surprise you are even calling me." He was done with her but still needed to hear why she decided to call. It was like hearing her voice was giving him the closure he needed to move on.

"It has been a minute. Sorry about that. I have had a lot going on in my life," she said playing the sympathy card.

"I'm sure you do," he stated sounding as if he didn't care.

"So, are you hanging out like going on a date?" And there it was she was inquiring if he had moved on from her.

"Well I don't think you have any right to ask me about dating seeing as how you moved on a long time ago. According to the man leaving your house that day sexually satisfied by you. I think that would have been confirmation for us both that we were no longer together. At least it was for me which is why I am confused by your call," he said. What she was pretending never happened he made sure she remembered.

"It wasn't what you thought. I was confused about what I wanted then. My child's father came over and I thought I would give us a second chance at being a family but that was a mistake. I didn't sleep with him either, I was only in a towel because he popped up when I was getting out of the shower." Silence was heard and she wanted a response from him. "Are you there?"

"I'm here."

"I miss you Isaiah. Let's give us another chance. I need you. Come see me and let me show you how much I am sorry. How much I miss you," she said trying to sound as sexy as she could in hopes he would be turned on enough to give in and forgive her.

Isaiah was not feeling it. He was reading in between the lines and had the closure he needed. He knew she was lying and he know what he saw that day was more than a pop up visit. He didn't see the signs then but they all were crystal clear once he removed his blinders. "I don't think that would be a good idea. Maybe you and your kids father should try harder to work it out. Good luck to you and you can just lose my number." He wanted to hang up after his last words but being a gentleman decided to wait.

"Humph, you know what. I really was trying to get to Bradon anyways. Once I found out you two knew each other I knew it wasn't going to work out between us no how because he is my child's real father. He is the one with the money not your broke sorry ass. Fuck you nigga, your ass probably gay anyhow. What nigga turns down some bomb ass pussy because he trying to be a gentleman. Either you gay or your dick small." She was pissed that he turned her down. And she let the cat out of the bag about her motives and who she really was.

She revealed that she was the girl claiming to have a baby by Bradon. He remembered from the conversation he overheard Bradon and the guys talking about at the Bachelor party. A girl name Mel. He knew Bradon didn't know who the girl was but he planned to fill him in on the details. "A real nigga who respects women which you obviously know nothing about since you lay on your back for any and every man you meet. Bitch get some respect for yourself, for your kids' sake," he said and proceeded to hang up.

"Who you calling a..."

Isaiah hung up the phone while she was in mid-sentence. He was glad she called but even more so that he received the closure he needed. He received his confirmation that she was absolutely not the girl for him. He was ready to move on to never mention her again. Except of course to let Bradon know who his mysterious Mel was.

He called Bradon as soon as he ended his call and blocked Melissa's number. "Yo Bradon, you are not going to believe what I just found out."

He filled Bradon in on the story of who the girl was and the 'lonely missing your girl' feeling ended and his life was back to normal. He was a single and available man that would make some woman very happy. He had faith in God and knew he would find his Queen when it was time. Until then he would keep his standards being the respectful gentleman he was.

Chapter 22
Baby coming
January 14

Sunday evening Jewel was in her therapy session when she started feeling contractions. "Oh, these Braxton Hicks are painful at times," she said loud enough for her therapist to hear. She didn't know what to expect when she went into labor. She just knew it would be extremely painful, at least that's what she was told all her life. "When you go into labor it's the worse pain you could ever imagine," her sisters would say to her.

"Miss Taylor, are you okay?"

"Yes, they told me I would get these Braxton Hicks toward the end of my pregnancy but I am good now. It stopped," Jewel said. "We can continue."

"Okay then. Speaking of your pregnancy, what do you plan to do as a mother once you are released?"

"Well I can't raise a baby while I am in jail. Never thought about being a mother really. My mom as you know was not the best mother a girl could have so a part of me is afraid I would be a bad mother. I am hoping that Bryson is the father and he will take the baby. That's what my Dr. said she thinks he plans to do."

"You are not your mother Miss Taylor. The cycle can be broken. Just because your mom was not what you say a good parent should be that doesn't mean you have to follow in her footsteps. You can be a great mom if that's what you want to do. If Bryson is not the father, do you have plans for another relative to take the baby?"

"Well I have my dad but they did tell me I had the option to put the baby up for adoption you know let someone better take care of the baby. Give the baby a better life." Jewel had her head down rubbing her pregnant belly. "Ohh, these things are a little painful. I hate to feel what full labor feels like," she said making a face that said she was experiencing pain.

"Are you sure you are okay? That is the second contraction you have experienced pain with and it's only been six minutes."

"Are you timing them? Really I am ok." She leaned back in her seat and moaned a little from the pain of two contractions coming back to back. She was quiet and breathing her way through the contractions.

"Miss Taylor maybe we should take you to get checked out just in case," the therapist said becoming more concerned that Jewel was in labor.

"Really I am fine. Oh shit. Am I peeing on myself?"

"No sweetheart, your water just broke. We need to get you to a doctor you are definitely in labor." The therapist walked behind her desk to call for help.

"Can you call Bryson tell him we are about to have our baby. Ouch, ohh this shit hurts."

"We need an ambulance now. I have a patient who is in labor and her water just broke." The therapist spoke with a sense of urgency. "Help is on the way Miss Taylor, hang on," she said walking towards Jewel trying to comfort her.

"I hope they hurry I don't want to have a baby here."

"Everything is going to be just fine, hang in there."

Jewel was about to have a baby and soon she would know who here baby father is.

Bryson and Brielle had just walked through the door from church when his phone rang. It was Jewel's nurse calling to tell him she was in labor. She listed him as the father of the baby.

"Mr. Mathews, I am the nurse of the mother of your child. She has asked me to call you to inform you she is in labor. Everything is fine she is doing well, I just wanted to give you the room number and any other information you may need." The nurse was clueless to the situation but was lead blindly by Jewel's information telling her she was having Bryson's baby.

"Ok wait. First, thank you for calling me. We don't know for sure if I am." He paused looking up at Brielle and the kids. Brielle immediately knew what the call was regarding and she took the kids to get ready to eat dinner. "Sorry, thank you for calling me but I am not sure who the father is. We are waiting to have DNA testing done after the baby is born."

"Oh no problem. I understand completely. Simply going by the information that Miss. Taylor gave me."

"Thank you. I can write down the information if you give me a second to get a pen. Can you also call me once the baby is born so I will know?"

"Yes sir. Not a problem since she has listed you all over her paperwork."

Bryson wrote down the information the lady gave him and ended the call. He joined his family making sure everyone was ok, most importantly that his pregnant wife was emotionally fine. He knew she was understanding about the situation but he still treated her feelings delicately. "You okay sweetheart?" he said walking up to her embracing her in his arms.

"Of course babe. You want to talk about the call? We can go in our bedroom." Brielle knew Jewel had to be in labor. Bryson discussed everything with her openly and freely and she wanted to know details about the phone call.

"I was just about to suggest that. Maria, watch the kids please. We will be right back for dinner." Bryson took Brielle by the hand and they headed to their bedroom.

Sitting on the bed as Bryson closed the door, Brielle was looking him in the eyes. "Let me guess. Jewel is in labor," she stated.

"Yes, she is. That was her nurse. And typical Jewel listed me as the baby's father and asked them to call and inform me she was in labor."

"Do you want to go up there with her?" Brielle asked hoping his answer would be no but understanding if he did since the baby could possibly be his.

"Sweetheart I have no desire to ever be with that woman in anyway ever again, not even by her side to have a baby that could possibly be mine. I know that may sound harsh, but it's the truth."

"No, it's understandable and I'm relieved that you are not running to be with her."

"Hell no. Excuse my language," he said pulling Brielle closer to hold her in his arms. "We discussed this already I know. If the baby is mine, we will deal with it and if the baby is Bradon's we will raise him or her as our own. Until we find out the results there is no reason for me to deal with Jewel. Besides you will be with me when I go to find out the DNA results, even then there won't be a need to see Jewel."

"I love you sweetheart. You are such a wonderful man."

"You are the wonderful one. To raise a child that is not yours is a selfless and unselfish thing for anyone to do. The fact that we are having twins takes a lot of kindness and love for someone to take on another child. I thank you for your loving heart. Even if we find out the baby is not either of ours you are still amazing for even considering."

"That's the power of God's love," she said to him turning to kiss his lips.

After a few more moments they decided to join the kids for dinner. Bryson called Bradon to inform him about Jewel. He told him he would take care of the DNA results and let him know the outcome. Bradon insisted on being there when he went in for the results. He wanted to know as soon as his brother knew.

January 15

"Miss Taylor, it's time to deliver a baby. I can see a head full of hair," the nurse said to Jewel.

"Ok so what you need me to do?" Jewel asked.

"Don't push just yet. I'm paging the doctor so he can come and deliver this baby."

"Will it hurt?"

"Well you have an epidural so you shouldn't feel too much pain but you will feel a lot of pressure in your bottom."

"Will my vagina go back to normal afterwards? How long does that take?" Jewel asked with all seriousness.

The nurse laughed. "Honey that is the last thing to worry about right now but eventually you will go back to normal. But don't expect it to happen overnight you are about to push out a baby," the nurse said as she headed for the door. "I will be right back don't push."

There were people in her room setting up birthing tables and moving stuff around. "Can someone call Bryson, my baby's father?" she said to one of the ladies in the room.

"Oh yes of course. Let me go out and inform your nurse."

"Thank you."

When the nurse came back in the room Bryson was the first of her concerns. "Did you call Bryson?"

"We did and he asked for us to call him after the baby is born."

"He is not coming to be with me?" Jewel had tears in her eyes realizing she was alone.

"Well you have us and we will take good care of you. And your father is in the hallway."

"My dad is here?" she said with excitement.

"Yes, your therapist I believe called him. We told him you were about to push and he said he will wait in the hallway. He didn't want to see his daughter with her legs up in the air pushing."

"Ok. I'm glad he is here." Jewel laid her head back. She had tears in her eyes.

"You okay Miss Taylor?" the nurse asked seeing her tears. She knew Jewel wanted Bryson with her she asked about him all throughout the night, but she was also informed that there was a DNA test pending. She felt sorry for Jewel and made sure she felt cared for.

"I'm scared. Never had a baby before. I didn't want to be alone, I am glad my dad came."

"I will be here with you and hold your hand through it all. You are going to do great." The doctor arrived and they were about to deliver the baby.

"Push, push."

At two fourteen that morning, Jewel gave birth to a beautiful baby girl. After they stitched her up, put her legs down and covered her up, her father joined her and the baby. It took Jewel a minute to hold the baby and as soon as her father came into the room she gave the baby to him. She was so nervous and scared to fail as a mother. She hoped Bryson was the father so their baby could have a good life. She was still hopeful of a future with Bryson but knew in her heart that would never happen. That didn't stop her from wanting more for her baby, even if she wasn't ready to be a mother.

At two forty-five in the morning Bryson received a call from the nurse. "Mr. Mathews, Miss Taylor has had the baby a beautiful baby girl. We are taking the samples momentarily and will send them to the lab asap. Since I believe they already have your samples you should have results within twenty-four hours but you may want to call the lab and verify."

Bryson wrote down all the information. Brielle was awake sitting right by his side. He ended the call turning to Brielle. "She had a girl. The lady said baby's samples will be sent this morning and we should have results back tomorrow morning at latest."

"A girl, wow!" Brielle said thinking about Jewel's lifestyle and trying to imagine the life of her daughter if she had to witness her mother's past behavior with men. "How do you think Bradon will react if the baby is his?" she asked.

"With him excelling in his business I don't think he will take it too well and I don't want him to feel discouraged now that everything is going well. I think I am going to the lab tomorrow to make sure they give him negative results regardless. We will just make sure he is not affected."

"You don't think he can handle the truth and let us raise the baby? What did he say when you discussed it with him?" Brielle looked Bryson in his eyes. "You didn't tell him we would raise the baby as ours if it was his did you?" She searched Bryson's eyes knowing the answer before he gave it to her.

"I didn't. Only you, my mom and Kenneth know. I was going to deliver the news to him once I received the results but he wants to be there to find out his results at the same time I find out. So my only other option is to convince or payoff the lab to switch the results if his is positive."

"I stand behind you and whatever you decide. I do think he should know the truth but it's your decision and I support you either way." She kissed her husband's lips. "I'm assuming we will be going to find out the results tomorrow morning and not this morning so I'm going back to sleep."

"Yes, tomorrow morning. Let's go back to sleep. I have a few more hours before I need to be up for work. Love you sweetheart." Bryson laid behind Brielle holding her rubbing her belly. "Brielle." He called her name before she drifted off.

"Yes. I'm still awake babe."

"You and our kids are my priority. I know you know already but I would never do anything to hurt your heart. I want to make sure you know your opinion and your happiness matters to me. If you are not ok with anything that is happening around this baby situation you tell me and I will make it right."

"You are the best thing that has ever happened to me and those kids. You are our happiness. I feel your love and your protection every moment. Believe me when I say I am fine." She turned her head slightly so he could kiss her.

"Just want to be sure. I love you."

"I love you too babe." Brielle closed her eyes smiling feeling like the luckiest woman in the world.

The next morning Bryson's first stop before work was at the lab to bribe the doctor to alter the results if needed.

Bradon was up early and at Bryson's house waiting to go receive the DNA results. "I couldn't sleep man. I'm so nervous about this damn test."

"You look tired and nervous, calm down Bradon I am sure everything will be fine. I am nervous too but you look like you about to have a breakdown."

"You right. I'm trying." Brielle joined them and they all got inside the awaiting limo heading to the lab. "Andre is meeting us there too, just in case I need to go get drunk after the results."

"Get drunk? It's early in the morning?" Bryson asked looking at his brother concerned. He looked at Brielle confirming their discussion the night before.

"If the test comes back I am the father hell yeah I'm getting drunk. Chantae is going to be pissed, hurt, hell all that. I just hope she don't leave me. When Isaiah told me about that Mel chic or Melissa whatever her damn name is I had to convince her to let me take a DNA test as well. I'm hoping they have those results as well. If I'm the father of two kids, by two women I never intended to be with, let alone even remembered or well." He looked at Bryson. He never admitted remembering every pleasurable moment of Jewels seduction but he couldn't say that to his brother. "You know what I mean. My life is stressful right now."

"We will find out soon enough. Kenneth is meeting us at the hospital. I have some work to discuss while we wait."

"Cool, cool. Moral support we need our boys. No offense Brielle. You are surely one in a million."

"None taken Bradon. Everything will be fine."

They pulled up in front of the lab. Kenneth and Andre were there waiting and they all waited inside to meet the doctor for the results.

"Mr. Mathews." The nurse called. Bryson was concerned it wasn't the doctor he paid for and was hoping what he paid him for was taken care of.

"Yes." Bryson and Bradon both answered at the same time. Bradon jumped to his feet.

"Damn Bradon, we will need a drink either way I see just to calm your nerves," Andre said standing with Bradon.

"If you both can follow me." She noticed everyone walking with them. "If I can only have the two men please. Its policy."

"Kenneth, keep Andre away from Brielle." Bryson joked. He kissed her on the forehead. "I will be right back sweetheart."

"I will be fine. Hurry back."

"You know we got her. I don't bite, at least not family anyway." Andre said knowing Bryson was only joking trying to uplift everyone's mood.

"Good luck guys," Kenneth said as they headed to the back.

The men were separated into two rooms even after they protested they were brothers. The doctor was out and the nurse had to follow policy. "Only the doctor can break the rules not me," she said.

Bryson could hear Bradon screaming, "Yes I am not that baby daddy. Thank you Jesus!" He now hoped he was not the father. Knowing Michael Anderson couldn't have any kids and assuming they were the only three men Jewel slept with he knew in his gut that one of them was the father.

The nurse came in to his room. "Here are your results as well Mr. Bryson Mathews. I am sure everyone could hear your brother screaming."

"Yes, I could hear him. Did the doctor leave any instructions about the test?" Bryson asked wanting to know if the test were switched.

"No instructions. He had an emergency this morning and had to leave. He normally gives out the results of this kind of test," she said. "Looks like your test is negative. There is a note that says inclusive results, you may want to follow up with the doctor. But it does say you are not the baby father. But according to the test I'm looking at, the baby is related to you, just not your baby. You and your brother... Wow, the baby is definitely related, maybe another brother or a fath…" she paused hesitating to continue. "I would tell you to follow up with the doctor to see why he added these notes. I am sure it's what I said, the baby is not yours but related."

"Okay thank you. I think I know what that mean." Bryson had his confirmation that the doctor switched the test and Bradon was the father. He hoped the test came back that the baby was not either of theirs but would be sure to protect Bradon. He would stick to saying the baby was his.

He walked out into the waiting area walking right into Kenneth and Brielle waiting on him. Kenneth knew Bryson paid the doctor to switch the test he was just hoping Bryson wasn't the father as well. Bradon had already come out letting them know his negative results. "Where is Bradon?"

"He in the bathroom. Said his nerves were so bad he had to release his pent-up bowls now that he knew he wasn't the father." Kenneth said looking in Bryson's eyes for confirmation.

"What's the news babe?" Brielle said holding Bryson's hand.

"The doctor switched Bradon's test with mine. My test was negative so I'm not the father. But the baby is my family. We tell Bradon I am the father and protect him. No one says a word to him about none of this."

Brielle exhaled relieved that Bryson is not the biological father. "As always, I stand behind you and support your decision," she said squeezing his hand.

Andre was standing close enough to hear and understand what they said but walked further away not to let them know he knew. He was Bradon's closest friend but respected Bryson enough to not say a word. He walked over to the water dispenser and waited on Bradon to come out the bathroom.

"Man I feel great," Bradon said to Andre who was half-smiling looking and nodding towards Bryson. "Oh shit. He definitely doesn't look like he got good news." He walked over to Bryson. "Bro, what's the verdict?" He asked Bryson with a straight face.

"Not good news for me. But we will get through this as we get through everything."

"Damn. I am sorry Brys, Brielle you ok?"

"You can conquer the world with love Bradon. The joy and blessing of a baby in the home will be a breeze. So yes, I am ok," she said with a slight smile assuring him she was fine.

Bradon was relieved. He received the results from Jewel and Melissa and was not the father of either. At least that's what his test he received told him.

Bradon left with Andre to go celebrate. He figured they would eat breakfast and have one drink before he headed back to work and back to his new life. He called Chantae and told her the great news. She too was relieved and excited that he did not have any kids by another woman.

Bryson talked with Brielle for a few moments longer before heading to work with Kenneth. They would be making plans to bring the baby home with them after Jewel was taken back to serve the remainder of her sentence.

Chapter 23
Greg?
January 22

Monday morning, Greg was being transported to a maximum-security prison. He was on a secure van with several other inmates. What he did not know was that several inmates were planning an escape. The van started swerving and inmates were falling over onto one another trying to brace themselves from falling with hand cuffs on their hands and feet. "What the fuck is going on? Don't y'all mother fuckers know how to drive?" Greg lashed out.

Another inmate started laughing. He knew exactly what was happening. He knew Greg all too well for bucking up to the guards and not afraid to talk shit. "It's called an ambush nigga, so hold on tight and get ready to break out of this bitch." He started laughing louder hearing the guards in trouble. The van crashed and the officers were being taken over by several men in mask with big guns. The officers were shot and the doors to the van were opened.

"You a free man now. I suggest you stay out of sight. Lay low." The inmate said to Greg as the chains were being cut from their arms and legs. Greg was shocked but not surprised at what just happened.

"Thanks man!" Greg said as the men were heading to the awaiting car. He started running into the nearby woods. He knew he had to stay out of sight but he knew he had some business he needed to take care of first by any means necessary. Greg spent his free time in jail lifting weights and was an intimidating man to look at. He always had an angry look on face and when he walked up on a man at a nearby house getting groceries out of the car, the man was frightened and handed him his keys willingly. Now that he had a ride, he headed straight to find Brielle.

First placed he looked for her and his children was at the condo where they use to live. He didn't know she moved to a different floor and apartment while living there. And now she had completely moved. But that was the last place he remembered. He walked straight through the front door seeing a familiar face.

"What are you doing here." Mr. Floyd asked Greg. "Call the cops now," he said to the lady behind the desk.

"You know why I'm here old man. Let me up the elevator now before I break both your hips," Greg said standing so close to Mr. Floyd he could smell his breath. His fist balled up and his jaws were clinched tight, he was trying to intimidate Mr. Floyd scaring him into letting him pass.

"Can't do that son. You need to leave now the cops will be here soon," Floyd said without budging.

Greg had a half smile across his face. "Now I know you are not going to stop a man who is fresh out of prison from getting to his sweet pussy. You don't want me fucking my wife? You been fucking my wife Floyd?"

"You need to leave now," Floyd said sternly.

Greg grabbed Mr. Floyd and attempted to push him out of the way. Mr. Floyd grabbed his arms tight barely moving an inch. Greg pulled his arms away from him and swung his fist hitting Mr. Floyd. He then moved a step backwards swinging back at Greg missing. "It's called working out you should try it old man," he said laughing at him but a second later he felt Mr. Floyd's punch land on his face and he stumbled backwards at the powerful punch.

"That's called old school power mother fucker." Greg ran full force knocking Mr. Floyd backwards and they were in a full fledge fight. Greg was over powering Mr. Floyd but he was hanging with him and landing some powerful blows.

The lady behind the desk was terrified. "She doesn't live here anymore." She blurted out. Greg looked at her and then heard police sirens. "I will find her old man."

Greg left out the side door in a hurry running to get out of sight from the police. He left the stolen car where it was and knew he needed cash fast.

Mr. Floyd composed himself standing to his feet. He pulled out his cell phone and immediately called Bryson. "Hey Bryson, this is Mr. Floyd. How are you sir. I hate to call you with this news but you need to make sure Brielle is somewhere safe. Her ex just left my building looking for her. We had a fight but of course I didn't tell him where she was. I think he may have escaped from prison the way he was dressed. We called the police and as soon as he heard sirens he ran. I am about to give my statement now." Mr. Floyd could tell that Bryson was upset and in protective mode. He knew Brielle was in good hands and would be safe from Greg. Now that Bryson knew he would be sure that she was safe.

Greg went to a convenient store where it was only two employees working, went behind the counter and proceeded to rob the store without a weapon. He punched the man in the face knocking him to the ground and pushed the woman towards the cash register demanding she open both registers and the safe where they drop money. He walked away with a little over two thousand dollars, some jogging pants, hoodie, and a hat and gloves from the shelves in the store. He wanted to blend in with the crowd leaving the inmate clothing behind. He was now wanted for being an escape felon, trespassing, car theft, assault and robbery.

"Now where could that bitch be?" he said to himself inhaling the winter air standing on the corner looking around. He decided to hop on a bus and head towards his old stomping grounds in the hood where he would be off the radar to make plans to get to Brielle and Bryson, the man who too his children from him.

Chapter 24
The Summers are steaming
January 22

Isaiah was over his parent's house visiting Friday when they all received the news about Greg being out of jail. He was enjoying a meal that his mother had prepared for him and his father was watching television when Bryson called. "Hello." Mr. Summers said answering the phone. "Hey Bryson, what's going on son? Surprised to hear from you mid-day on a Friday."

Mr. Summers was quiet listening to Bryson tell him about Greg's escape and his encounter with Mr. Floyd. He stood to his feet. His wife and son came to join him sensing that something was wrong. "This all happened today?" Mr. Summers said to Bryson. He turned the television to the news and the escape was all over the local channels. News reporters and the police were at Brielle's old condos and the store Greg robbed. "It's all over the news we are watching it now."

"Are they saying Greg escaped from prison?" Mrs. Summers said panicking sitting on the sofa.

"What the hell. Excuse my language," he said to his parents. "How was he able to escape? Where is Brielle? If he went to where she used to live that means he is definitely looking for her."

"Honey what is Bryson saying?" Mrs. Summers asked.

"Ok, thank you so much son. Keep my baby girl and my grandchildren safe. We will be there shortly." Mr. Summers ended the call with Bryson. "Yes, he escaped from prison this morning and headed straight to find our Brielle. Mr. Floyd had a physical run in with him but he is okay and he obviously robbed a store. The other men that escaped are apparently off the radar but not Greg, he won't stop until he finds Brielle."

"Where is she? Is Bryson with her?" Mrs. Summers asked terrified.

Mr. Summers went to hold her in his arms attempting to calm her down. "He is increasing security and headed home to be with

Brielle now. They are making sure the kids get home safely as well. He will make sure they are safe." He reassured his wife. "I told him we will lock up and come to the house as well. He knows where we live and I don't want him coming here."

"I wish that son of a ... He just won't stop will he? What's up with this guy? Why can't he just leave her alone?" Isaiah was furious.

"Son we are all upset by this but I don't need you going off doing anything crazy and you end up in jail at the expense of someone who is not worth it. Protect yourself and your family yes but don't go looking for trouble." Isaiah was quiet thinking. "Son promise me," his dad said.

"I won't dad." He looked out the window seeing police officers pull up in front. He knew his parents would be safe and could only think about getting to his sister to make sure she was ok. "I'm about to head over to Brielle's now. Lock the doors when they leave and head out through the garage once you are locked in your car." Isaiah said as if he was the parent.

"You don't worry about us. I will shoot that bastard he come to this house." Isaiah kissed his parents before greeting the officers at the door and leaving.

"Mr. and Mrs. Summers, I am sure you heard about Greg by now. Is that your son leaving? Is he ok?" the officer asked standing in the doorway.

"Everyone is upset at the news. He will be ok. He is going to be with his sister. Once he can see that she is ok he will calm down. We are all a bit upset. How was he able to escape?" Mrs. Summers said.

"Please come in out of the cold." Mr. Summers said. They talked to the officer for a few moments as he reassured they had a full manhunting team all over the city for his capture. He advised that finding somewhere else to stay for a while was probably best. He stayed as they packed their bags, loaded the car and followed them out of the driveway. He made sure they were safe at the instructions of Bryson and doing his job. Everyone in their town remembered the incident with Brielle. Ensuring her and her family safety was more than a favor to Bryson but a priority for them as well.

Chapter 25
Special Delivery
January 22

Right before Bryson left work he received a letter in the mail from an unknown person. Thinking it was something business related in a brown envelope he opened it. As he was opening the envelope he noticed a stamp stating the package was from an inmate in a correctional facility. When he opened the envelope, he was not expecting what he saw. The picture that was inside was very disturbing. He immediately knew Greg had sent the letter before he escaped from prison.

"This man is crazy," Bryson said aloud looking at the picture. He found a picture of Bryson and Brielle with the kids from a magazine promoting his movie. The picture was cut separating Bryson from Brielle and the children. Bryson had his head cut from his body and the rest of his limbs were cut as well. He added a note to the picture.

I will kill you before I let you take my family from me. You think you are gonna adopt my kids, take them from me and take my woman? Partner your ass is a dead man. I'm coming for you and that cheatin ass bitch! I know you fucking her. You got my bitch pregnant? When I get to her I will fuck the memory of you away and make her pay for even thinking about another man. I would say watch your back but it doesn't even matter if you see me coming your ass is mine partner. Your bitch ass will regret trying to take my family from me. You dead motherfucker and my word is bond.

Signed this nigga coming for your head. You know who I am at least you will real soon.

Bryson would be sure to submit the letter into evidence as another weapon to use against Greg to ensure he never gets out of jail once they find him. He increased his security and was not worried about him getting to Brielle or the kids. Bryson would love to get his hands on Greg in a fist fight. Any man that can put his hands on a woman and child was not a real man nor worthy to be called a man. He wanted Greg to pay. First thing on his priority list was making sure his family was safe and then Bryson would make sure he felt the power he had to put him under the jail.

Bryson put the letter and picture back in the envelope and in his bag. He called the police chief so he could have someone meet him at his home to get a statement and collect the evidence. Bryson now had a case against Greg that he would be pursuing with no mercy. He knew his lawyers would bring every charge possible to put him away longer than he originally was in for.

Bryson left his office to pick up the kids and head home to Brielle. They were his main concern and became his top priority. He never would have thought this situation would be happening. Until Greg was caught and sent back to prison he would alert and aware of everything around him, even if he did have security. He couldn't imagine what Greg would do to his wife if he found them slipping. Bryson had to be smart in how he dealt with the situation. Any man protecting his family would kill someone before allowing harm to come. Bryson was no different. He made sure extra security would be in every place him and his family would be. Greg didn't realize the power he was up against but he would soon find out if he crossed that line.

Chapter 26
What is going On
January 22

"Hey Girl how are you feeling? How's the babies?" Chantae asked Brielle. They hadn't talked much since Brielle's bridal party. The news of Bradon possibly having 2 babies bothered her more than she let on that it did.

"Hey girl. Me and the babies are doing well. Tired a lot and feet swelling a bit. Other than that, babies are healthy, the kids are good and everyone is doing great. How are you girl?" Brielle replied to Chantae. She was happy to hear from her friend.

"Everything is good girl. My clothing line is launching as I planned. Bradon has helped me gain major distribution."

"That's great girl, I knew you would be successful at your clothing line. I am so proud of you going after your dreams."

"Thank you Brie. I appreciate that. Hey, I'm sorry I was distant from you. I was bothered when I found out about that Jewel girl possibly being pregnant by Bradon. I know you didn't know I was talking about another girl that night and not Jewel."

"Wait, another girl? I didn't know about another girl."

"Yes, but Bradon found out that both babies were not his and I am so happy about that. I mean I feel bad for you and all you know. You are having twins and then to raise a child that is not even yours. Life is not perfect, it never is huh."

"It's okay girl, we have to deal with the cards that life deals us and we are doing well. Bryson's mom has been a big help staying here, you would think she was the baby's mother getting up and tending to the baby. We enjoy having new life in the house. It's preparing me for our buddle of joy's."

"That is great girl. You have so much love in your heart and I admire that."

Brielle walked over to the window hearing the gates opening and hearing a car speed into the driveway. "Ahh thanks girl. I try.

We need to get together soon. Come see my big belly," she said laughing.

"I was just thinking the same girl. I will plan to come by this weekend to see you and the kids I miss my babies. I miss you too Brie.

"We miss you too girl. What is going on?" Brielle said looking out the window noticing something wrong with Isaiah.

"Huh, what's wrong girl?" Chantae asked.

"Isaiah is here. Let me call you later girl. See what's wrong with him," she said walking towards the door.

"No problem girl. We will talk later. Love you."

"Love you too, talk to you later." Brielle ended the call opening the door for Isaiah. "What is wrong with you Isaiah?" she asked seeing that he was upset with a frightful look on his face.

"Sis stay calm, you are pregnant and I don't need you going into labor." Isaiah said walking through the door. "I think I was followed."

"Isaiah, spit it out. What's going on? You are scaring me is Bryson ok? Mom, dad?"

"Yeah, everyone is ok. Greg broke out of prison. It's all over the news. And…"

"Wait, what? He broke out of prison?"

"Yes Bryson knows he has increased security everywhere."

"The kids. Oh my God, my kids. I got to go get the kids." Brielle was panicking.

"Bryson has the kids. He already went to get the kids and had security there before he even got there to ensure everything was ok. Brie, everything is and will be okay."

"Bryson, he got the kids?"

Isaiah had his arms on Brielle's shoulders. "Yes, calm down. This is why we didn't tell you before someone was here with you."

"Ok, Bryson has the kids. How did he break out of prison? Don't they have security and all that stuff to make sure they can't get out?"

"I don't know sis. But he went to your old place at the condo and got physical with Mr. Floyd."

"Oh no. Is Mr. Floyd ok?"

"Yeah he's ok. He may be old but apparently he can hold his own and throw a mean punch."

"So is Greg looking for me? Is that why he was there? Of course that's why he was there."

"Yeah, he is looking for you. They think after he broke free that was the first place he went." He looked at Brielle knowing the news would bring fear. "You know you are safe right? Bryson will never allow anything to happen to you. He can't get to you Brielle." Isaiah reassured her. At that point he thought he would only tell Bryson and the police details about the car following him. He had security take a picture of the car before coming in the house and get the license plate number.

"I know, I know. I feel safe here. I will feel even better once the kids are here too. I just know what he is capable of and he will hurt anyone who gets in his way. Momma and dad. He might try to go there," she said in a panic.

"Bryson handled it. Mom and dad are on their way here to stay for a while until they catch him and they will catch him Brie." He pulled Brielle closer to him holding her in his arms.

Bryson walked through the door with the kids and a couple of undercover police officers. "Hey babies," Brielle said as they ran to hug her. "Mommy is so happy to see you! How was school?"

"It was cool," Carter said trying to sound cool in front of the men in the room.

"I had fun at recess today momma, we played hopscotch and double dutch," Olivia said.

"It was good momma but I missed you and the baby," Jayla said.

"Oh yeah." Brielle was so happy to see her husband and children walk through the door.

"There go my little darlings." Mrs. Mathews said coming into the living room where they were.

"Hey granny is the baby sleeping again?" Jayla asked.

"Yes she is. Y'all come on here let grown folks talk." Mrs. Mathews was already informed by Bryson about what was happening and to occupy the kids when they were home.

Bryson held Brielle in his arms knowing that Isaiah had already told her the news. When the kids were out of ear reach he started talking. "You know you and the kids are safe and you don't have to worry about anything ok. I don't want you to be worried or stressed."

"Ok, I know we are safe Bryson. I hate that he is out though that man is crazy. There are no limits to what he is capable of doing."

"He won't be out for long they will find him. These two detectives want to ask a few questions. Are you okay with that?" Bryson had given his statement over the phone before he picked up the kids. He didn't want Brielle knowing about the letter he received from Greg and did not want her seeing the pictures. He gave the detectives the envelop as they walked toward the house.

"Yes, of course," she said turning towards the detectives.

"Sorry we have to bring bad news to you Mrs. Mathews. We don't want to take up any more time than we have to. Do you know where this man may be hiding out? We assume he connected with someone from his past. Any help with any addresses, familiar areas or names would be great."

Brielle could only think of one place where he would hang out and a club he used to frequent a lot. She answered the detective's questions best she could before they left. Her parents joined them at their home and everyone that was close to Brielle was now safe. She called Chantae back to inform her of the news knowing that she was safe with Bradon. Greg would have to get through layers of security and iron gates to get to any of them. Brielle would sleep safe knowing that Bryson was lying beside her holding her tight in his arms. She joined everyone in the dining room preparing to eat dinner that Maria had prepared. Bryson and Isaiah stayed behind.

"I think I was followed here Bryson. Your security guys took pictures of the car and has the license plate information. Greg could have followed me from our parent's house. I didn't see anyone following me and didn't notice the car until I was pulling up at the gate." Isaiah said in a quiet tone.

"I will get my guy to run the plates. He wouldn't make it through the gate alive even if he tried."

"I wish I could have one moment with him to fuck that nigga up so bad his momma wouldn't be able to recognize him." Isaiah said shocking Bryson. He never talks like that, at least Bryson has never heard him talk that way before.

Bryson turned and looked at him making sure he was standing next to Isaiah. All he could do was agree. "Yeah, I feel you man." And the men headed to the dining area to join the others for dinner.

Chapter 27
Eliminating the Competition
January 30

Greg met up with some men he met in prison. He wanted to go where he knew no one would suspect him. In the heart of the projects where the toughest thugs and drug dealers were. Everyone was sitting around drinking and smoking weed. Greg had made a little more money in the few days he was there dealing with drugs. He had women all over him since he had money and his physique was built. He was the new guy in the area and the men welcomed him into their circle. Greg had two half naked women sitting on his lap getting high with him. "I'm fucking the shit out of both you bitch's tonight sitting up here smoking my weed. You got to earn this shit."

All the men and women in the room laughed. "Ay nigga, what happened with that bitch you were talking about in the joint. You go see here yet?" The man he was locked up with asked. He was snorting cocaine with another girl and was high as a kite.

"She moved on me. I don't know where she at nigga but I am going to find her. I heard that nigga who got my girl pregnant owns that club downtown on West End. Some fancy shit," he said in between puffs.

"Oh word, I heard of that place. That's where all them stuck up bitches and niggas in suits be going. I think it's called Club Luxurious or some shit like that. We should roll up and see if that nigga there tonight. Teach him a lesson yo," the man said in between snorting cocaine.

"I was thinking the same thing. I ain't wearing no suit though. I will wear my nice shit but not no damn suit." They laughed.

"I need to be strapped though nigga. You can't get no gun up in there. They have that high-tech security shit. You can't even stash it on your girl. They don't play that shit there. Me and my guys tried and them niggas had a swat team swarm our asses, sent us on our way so quick. Some of them places you can pay the door and they let you walk right on in. Not that place. They have like an exclusive club where they try to protect high profile people and shit. I bet judges and shit be up in there," he said laughing.

"It's cool. We can leave our guns in the car just in case. I ain't gone need nothing but my hands when I see that nigga no how. I didn't tell you he adopted my kids from me. I didn't even get a say so in the matter, just a letter in the mail after the shit was done," Greg said. He had both girls dancing for him and he sat there rubbing on his manhood watching them, smacking them on their butt.

"But didn't you like beat up your son or some shit? Did you even want the kids?" the man asked. He was stoned, laid back on the sofa barely keeping his eyes open. The girl who was snorting cocaine with him was passed out laying her head on his shoulders.

Greg laughed. "Yeah I did. He attacked me like he was a grown ass man. I had to show him who his daddy was. Put him in a child's place," Greg said thinking about what he did. He laughed about it but he knew he was on drugs back then and not in his right man. He knew he took it too far when he was beating up his son when he was protecting his mother.

"Nigga that was child abuse. That wasn't teaching him no lesson. That boy couldn't have hurt you," the man said his eyes rolling to the back of his head.

"Yeah I know. Still, I bet his little ass wont step to a grown ass man like that again."

"You a fucking woman and child beater nigga," the man said right before passing out.

Greg stood to his feet moving the girls out of the way. "What the fuck you call me nigga?" he said standing over the man.

His homeboy who was only twenty sitting in the room playing a game on play station with another friend turned and said, "Chill man, you know he fucked up. He didn't mean no harm. Chill man." He could see the prison mentality to defend himself all over his face. "We people's man, chill out."

"Yeah whatever man, don't nobody talk crazy to me," he said walking away towards the back room."

"He higher than a motherfucker man. I done told him stop smoking that shit. Nigga ain't gone ever make no money smoking his own product."

"Y'all nigga's rolling with us to the club tonight?" Greg asked.

"I'm down," the other guy playing the game said without even looking up from the screen."

"I can't man, somebody got to stay and get this paper," the twenty-year-old man said.

"Aight then, y'all bitches get in here and get naked," Greg said to the two girls with him. "Nigga got a lot of fucking to make up for." Him and the other two men playing the game laughed. His plans for that night was to catch Bryson slipping at his club. He hoped to see Bryson and Brielle. One way or another he wanted to get to them both anyway he could. Greg thought the club was a good starting point.

Chapter 28
Headaches are Back
January 30

Brielle tried not to stress over the issue regarding Greg not being captured. She decided to stay home, not going anywhere until he was. Bryson made sure the kids were escorted to school safely and back home, making sure security stayed at the school the entire time. He did not want to chance Greg getting to any of the kids.

Saturday morning Brielle's head was hurting to the point she didn't want to get out of bed. Bryson thought she was just tired until he came back to check on her seeing her toss and turn with tears in her eyes. "Sweetheart, what's wrong?" he asked not sure if she was in labor or just sick.

"My head is hurting babe. I took some Tylenol but it is still hurting and I know I can't take the medicine I normally take for migraines."

"Do you need me to do anything? You want me to call Dr. Zackary?" Bryson was nervous. He had never seen Brielle in pain before. Since the beginning of them meeting at the park, he has seen her nothing but happy and full of life. He knew the fact that Greg was out added stress and could be causing her to have headaches.

"Yes call Dr. Zachary, he may know of something I can do safely. And can you call my friend Dr. Carols as well."

"Ok, I'm going to get you a cold wash cloth for your head and call the doctors for you. I will be right back sweetheart."

"Momma are you going to be okay?" Jayla asked sticking her head into their bedroom.

"Yes baby. Come lay up here with me." Brielle pulled Jayla into bed with her hoping having her close to her will help relieve some of her stress.

Bryson walked into the bathroom to call Dr. Zackary. "Hi, Dr. Zackary this is Bryson Mathews. I am so sorry to call you on a

Saturday, Brielle is having headaches again. She's been in the bed all day and I have never seen her like this. What do I do?" he said sounding nervous an out of breath.

Dr. Zachary was talking to him and for a moment and Bryson was standing still listening to his instructions. He was talking in doctor terms about her headaches and what could be causing them and the fact that she was pregnant. When he hung up he called his friend Rodger Maxx. "Hey Rodger, did you find out anything on the car?"

"Yes, sorry I didn't get back with you sooner. I did find out who the owner of the car was and it was Michael Anderson. I spoke with him and he rode by the house looking for Jewel. He said he rides by often because he has not talked to her. He thought you two were back together. I told him she was in jail and if he came by your home again he would be prosecuted for stalking. It was not Greg."

"Michael? Really?" Bryson said laughing. "Thanks man. I appreciate you. I owe you once again."

"This one is on the house. It was too easy."

"Thanks Rodger."

Bryson went back to Brielle with the wash cloth. Her mom, his mom and the kids were all in the room with her. He put the cold cloth on her forehead hoping it would relieve some of the pain.

"She needs complete relaxation, some good pampering. Take her mind off everything. I have Maria making her my special remedy tea. And a little laughter will heal her just fine." Mrs. Mathews said.

"Thanks momma. Dr. Zackary wants to see you in his office on Monday if the headaches don't stop. He suggested a few other things as well but let's see how this tea remedy and laughter works."

"What? Did he suggest some S E X?" Mrs. Summers spelled out sex due to the kids being in the room.

"Momma, the kids." Brielle nudged her.

"What? They don't know what I am saying." She saw the girls giggling. "Okay sorry, we are talking about your kids. They were always bright kids." She looked at them smiling.

"Dr. Carols is coming over. She said she wanted to check on you in person," Bryson mentioned to Brielle.

"Oh that is awesome. There is nothing like having friends that care about you when they are a doctor." Mrs. Mathews said.

"That Vanessa is a sweet girl and has always been a good friend to you. I hate she moved away when you girls were younger."

"I know momma," Brielle said.

"Here is your tea," Maria said walking into the room.

"Thank you Maria so much. It smells good, I hope it taste just as good."

"It tastes great child. We just want you to feel better," Mrs. Mathews said.

"I will leave you ladies be for a moment," Bryson said excusing his self from the room full of females.

"I'm coming with you," Carter said eyes wide. "I'm not staying in here with all these girls by myself."

The ladies laughed. They were all in the room trying to get Brielle to laugh and feel better.

The door bell rung and Isaiah answered knowing that Vanessa was coming by. "Hey there beautiful come on in," Isaiah said greeting her at the door with a hug.

"Hey you. I didn't know you would be here," she said kissing him on the cheek as she hugged him.

They both paused looking stunned that she kissed him. "So how is everything with you and with work?" Isaiah asked nervously.

"Everything is going well. My practice is thriving and I am doing great. How have you been? You're looking good."

"Well thank you. I'm doing well. We been here with Brielle since you know, Greg broke out of prison."

"I heard about that. How is she handling it?"

"She been good up until today when her migraines came back."

"Right. Bryson told me when he called. Can you take me to her?"

"Oh yeah sure. I'm sorry holding you up. I knew you were here to see her." Isaiah started walking towards the bedroom.

"But it's always a pleasure to see you Isaiah," she said with a smile a few steps before they reached Brielle's room.

Isaiah stopped in the hallway turning around to look her in her eyes. She paused still smiling standing directly in front of him. Her eyes were fixed on his lips and he said, "Woman, you are making it hard for me to resist kissing you. That childhood crush never left." He gazed into her eyes as she licked her lips anticipating his kiss.

"I wouldn't stop you," she said softly. Isaiah came closer to her and right before he reached her lips he heard Jayla's voice.

"You must be the doctor. My momma said you were coming." She looked at Isaiah and back at the doctor. They were acting strange to Jayla and she didn't understand what she just interrupted.

"Yes I am the doctor and you are a pretty little girl." Vanessa knelt to be eye to eye with Jayla.

Isaiah moved a couple steps backwards from Vanessa. "I thought you were in the room with the girls Jayla," he said to her.

"I was but I have to go get momma something from my room."

"Ok well carry on," Isaiah said before guiding the doctor in to see Brielle. Jayla was watching him close.

"Thanks Isaiah," she said walking into the room.

"We will talk before you leave," he said in a whisper.

Isaiah had a crush on his sister's friend when they were growing up but it was put on hold when she moved away. When he realized she was back, those old feelings resurfaced. Now that he could feel that she too was interested in him, he wanted to pursue more than just his crush. He sat with her during the wedding but didn't have a chance to really talk to her with everything going on. Then again at the movie premiere but he was nervous to approach her in any type of way other than friends because he was still involved with Melissa. Now that he was a free man and over his ex-girlfriend, Vanessa had his nose wide open. Isaiah didn't want to rush back into another relationship so soon, but Vanessa wasn't just another girl. She was his childhood fantasy that he now had a chance to possibly have a relationship with.

Brielle was starting to feel better after all the love and attention she was receiving. Dr. Vanessa also had a few tricks up her sleeve that she used as well, some of what she learned from Dr. Zackary. Before she left, Brielle confided in Vanessa about the eerie feelings she was having. "I have a bad feeling about Greg being out Vanessa. I keep feeling like something bad is about to happen."

"You know Greg is a bad person and after what he did to you and those kids it's understandable for you to feel that way. Try not to think about him and the past and trust that Bryson has you and the kids protected. He won't allow anything to happen to you and I do believe you know that."

"Yes, I do know that. Thanks for coming my friend." Brielle was on her way back to normal. Good friends, a little extra care and genuine love always seem to help make anyone feel better.

"You are welcome. Hey, your brother still seeing that girl?"

"No. She broke his heart. She was sleeping around with other men and was using him to get to Bradon I think. Just a mess. But I am glad he is over that girl. Why you ask?" Brielle looked at her and smiled. She knew Isaiah always crushed on her but now she was thinking Vanessa was crushing on her brother as well.

"Just wondering girl. You know your brother is sweet on me. I probably should have been your sister in law and your bestie."

They both laughed and let that comment be what it was, Vanessa letting Brielle know it was a possibility for Isaiah and her to talk and Brielle being ok with the possibility.

Chapter 29
Let's get out
January 30

Bradon was hanging out with his friend Andre Saturday morning playing basketball. Kenneth was occupied with Ameila and Bryson was keeping his family close to him dealing with the Greg situation. Their normal routine playing basketball was temporarily interrupted with all the men be there to play. But Bradon and Andre didn't let that stop them. It gave them some catch up time.

"How is your brother handling that ex-boyfriend situation man?" Andre asked Bradon.

"Ah man that's crazy but he is handling his business. I know they still haven't caught the guy."

"Yeah, but is that causing any issues in paradise by it being her ex causing this chaos?"

"Naw, I don't think it's causing any issues like that. He loves Brielle and he loves those kids like they were his own, so he is looking at it as just another nigga who threatened what's his. You know Bryson has so much power and influence to make anything happen so he is handling his business."

"That I do know, he definitely handles his business at any cost." Andre said loud enough for Bradon to hear but letting him know he knew of some things he has handled.

"Besides, he had his own issues with Jewel and Brielle was right beside him every step of the way."

"She is definitely a good woman. Especially dealing with a baby that's not his. I mean hers," Andre said trying to fix what he said. He was thinking one thing and said the opposite of what he meant, hoping Bradon didn't pick up on his slip up. He wanted Bradon to know but he didn't want to be the one to tell him.

"I really believed that baby was mine too and I was actually looking forward to being a good father. I know Chantae is not ready for any kids. I enjoy being around Brielle's kids though and when I do have kids I will be ready." Bradon was deep in thought for a moment. "I know Bryson was going to raise the kid as his if the baby was mine but honestly, I don't think I would have let him do that. Even if it did mean adjustments for me and Chantae. A child needs his father."

"How you know he didn't lie to you and have the doctors switch the test?"

"What do you mean? The doctors can't do that. Isn't that like a breach of oath or something that doctors have to sign?" Bradon thought about what Andre had just said to him. If anyone could pull something like that off it would be Bryson.

"Yeah, I'm sure they do. But we are talking about your brother here. You know the one that has the power and influence to make anything happen." Andre was telling Bradon without telling him. He wanted his best friend to know the truth, so he could then handle it the way he wanted to, but he didn't want to betray Bryson either. He knew once Bradon thought about everything he would figure it out on his own and do what he needed to do to find out the truth. After all he was Bryson's little brother and just as smart.

"Yeah we are talking about Bryson, if anyone could pull some shit off like that it would definitely be him." Bradon was now wondering if Bryson would have paid for them to switch the test. "The doctor said the baby was definitely related, that our genes were powerful enough to tell that one of the brothers were the baby's father. She even joked and said or our father." He laughed at the thought of his dad being the father of Jewels baby.

"Oh hell naw. Don't give me that visual. Your dad and Jewel. Now that would be a stretch for Jewel to be that low down. But hey she did fuck your ass. Or did you fuck her? Which one was it?" He joked and laughed.

"Ha ha mother fucker. I do all the fucking for sho." He laughed with Andre. "Hey, I don't like to visualize my pops either but according to him he used to be the man back in the day. Of course before he met my momma."

"Whatever he old now. I'm sure his shit shriveled up." Andre laughed.

"Let's talk about something else man." Bradon was still thinking about Bryson possibly switching the test. "You want to hang out tonight? Go down to the club?"

"I can't tonight man. My girl found some shit in my phone so I am kissing her ass tonight taking her out."

"I knew your dirt was going to catch up with you sooner or later." The guys laughed leaving the basketball court getting ready to head home.

Bradon was sitting in his car thinking of how he could find out for sure if the baby was his. He looked it up on line and saw that there was a paternity kit you could purchase and do the test yourself. He went to a pharmacy and purchased a kit. After reading the instructions he decided to stop by Bryson's house to swab the baby's mouth and mail the test off that day to find out for sure if he was or was not the baby's father.

He thought this news was behind him but after Andre reminded him of what his brother was capable of doing, he decided to find out the truth once and for all for his self and without anyone else knowing. He decided to call Kenneth and convince him to hang out with him that night. It didn't take long for Kenneth to agree sensing something was wrong. He knew Bryson was busy and after Bradon said Andre had other plans he agreed to hang out and have a few drinks.

Seven thirty that evening the guys met at Club Luxe headed straight for VIP. Bradon was hoping to get Kenneth drunk and get any information out of him he may know. The suspense of not truly knowing was weighing on him.

"Man tell the truth. Did you think I was going to end up being the father of Jewel's baby?" Bradon was trying to listen for signs of Kenneth lying catching him off guard with his comments.

"Naw, I had a feeling it was going to be Bryson's baby. After all, the way those two went at it, surely it would have been. I mean I know it only takes one slip up and you could have easily been the father but you weren't, so celebrate that brother." Kenneth was not trying to let the cat out of the bag. He knew Bradon was fishing but wasn't sure where it was coming from.

Bradon changed the subject trying not to think about it until he received the results from his test he took. It was close to eleven when Bradon saw a man approaching trying to get pass security. He nudged Kenneth and they both were standing to their feet just in case anything popped off.

"Ain't you Bryson Mathews?" Greg was mean mugging Bradon like he had beef with him thinking he was his brother.

"Who the fuck are you?" Kenneth shot back.

"I need you to leave now sir," Security said to Greg. Seeing he had several men with him he called for backup. "We have a situation in Mr. Mathews VIP," he said into his ear piece. Security was running to the VIP area knocking down whoever was in their way.

"I need to holler at you for a minute partner."

"Naw, you have nothing to say to me. Get his ass out of here," Bradon said to security.

Greg's friends were closer and got in front of the security guard so Greg could get around him. Once he did, one of his boys he was locked up with was right there with him. Greg looked at Bradon and said, "So you the motherfucker who fucking my girl and adopted my kids?" Greg walked straight towards Bradon.

Greg swung and Kenneth blocked his punch. Before anyone could stop the fight Bradon was punching Greg in a boxing match Greg was sure to lose. Kenneth even landed a few more punches to Greg and to his friend with him. Just as quickly as it started it was over. In a blink of an eye security had swarmed the VIP area restraining Greg and his friends throwing them out of the clubs back door.

"What the fuck was that?" Bradon said. He had several drinks but not too many to where he couldn't protect himself.

"I think we just met Greg and he thought you were Bryson. So now we know he is also looking for your brother."

"Damn we should have told them to hold him for the cops."

"Yeah, we should have. It all happened so fast and I just figured it out. I'm going to call my guy at the station and let him know. Once the situation is under control outside we can get the hell out of here before they come back if you know what I mean."

Bradon was drunk but the altercation sobered his mind up really quick. He followed Kenneth's every word. "Yeah, we don't need to give them fools no time to go get guns."

Kenneth made the call he needed to make and checked with security that the situation outside was resolved. After confirmation, Kenneth and Bradon decided it was time to leave. "Let's get out of here man."

"Yeah I need to get home to Chantae. She already texted me asking when I was headed home."

They headed for the front door after a final confirmation from his security team that all was clear. Kenneth made sure Bradon's driver was in front of the club and his truck was right behind him. They both walked to their cars to leave. Kenneth sat in his car waiting for Bradon and his driver to pull off when he saw the same guy from the club run up to his car.

"What you got to say now motherfucker." Greg opened the door where Bradon had just got inside. He had a gun aimed at Bradon's chest.

Kenneth reached in his glove compartment for his gun. Security ran towards Bradon's car. Girls standing in line to get in the club started screaming and running, "He's got a gun." Two shots were heard back to back. Then a third and a fourth and a fifth.

"Somebody call an ambulance now." One of the security guys screamed standing in the car door looking at Bradon laying on the back of the seat shot twice in the chest.

Kenneth ran to Bradon, "Fuck," he said in anger. "Hang on Bradon don't you die on me." He put his gun on the floor of the limo and grabbed Bradon to feel his pulse confirming he was still alive. He took off his dress shirt and then his t-shirt attempting to stop Bradon from bleeding so much until help arrived.

Bradon barely opened his eyes looking at Kenneth mumbling, "He shot me. Don't let me die. Call Brys. Call my brother." And Bradon closed his eyes with his head leaning back on the seat.

"Bradon wake up! Damit, don't you die on me! Open your eyes Bradon. Somebody help. Call an ambulance! God no!" Kenneth screamed out for help with tears rolling down his face.

Greg laid in the street shot three times gasping for air pleading for help.

Chapter 30
He shot your brother
January 30

Bryson was asleep holding Brielle in his arms when his cell phone rung. It was close to midnight and the ringing phone startled him. When he moved to answer the phone, Brielle sat up in the bed with him. "Hey Kenny man what's up? What time is it?"

"Brys, it's Bradon. That guy Greg came to the club looking for you and he thought Bradon was you, he shot him man. His in the ambulance now, they are on their way to Vanderbilt." Kenneth was so upset and an emotional wreck. He was standing in the street covered in blood with his shirt half button with his jacket open. He watched as they loaded Bradon in the back of the ambulance working trying to save his life. Greg had paramedics working on him but Kenneth was only focused on Bradon. As they started to pull off he got back in his truck to follow them.

"Kenny man, is he ok?" Bryson was sitting straight up in the bed, his heart beating fast, shocked at what he was hearing.

"He wasn't conscious man, I don't know. He was shot in the chest. Get to the hospital now man. I'm headed there. I'm right behind the ambulance." Kenneth was in his truck driving keeping up with the ambulance

"Kenneth." Bryson screamed not knowing what to say as tears flooded his eyes. He was choked up over his words and couldn't get it out. "I'm on my way man. Stay with my brother please." He stood headed to his closet to dress. Brielle was right on his heels.

"I'm not leaving him, see you when you get there. Bryson be careful driving man."

Bryson ended the call turned to Brielle putting on his pants. "Greg shot my brother."

"Greg? Why, how? Oh God, is he alive?" Brielle started crying.

"Come here." Bryson stopped for a moment and held Brielle close to him to calm her down. "I need you to try to stay calm for me and for our babies. I would tell you to stay here but I know that's not going to happen."

"No, I'm going with you. I need to make sure Bradon is alright. I need to call Chantae. Bryson I am so sorry." She couldn't stop crying.

Bryson held her tight in his arms. He had tears in his eyes as well. He didn't want his wife stressing and something happening to her or the babies. He knew Greg was no longer an issue since he too had been shot. Although he didn't know to what extent his injuries were or if he was even alive, he knew Brielle would be safe going with him. He needed her to be calm so he just prayed. "Father God, we need you right now. Father touch my wife and give her calmness in the middle of this storm. Father, I know you are with my brother and the doctors caring for him and Your Will is Your Will. God please lay your loving healing hands on my brother and give him favor right now Lord. It's not his time God. Heal him and allow him to be blessed with continued life. In Jesus name, I ask and claim these things already done." He released Brielle looking down at her calmer than before.

"Thank you babe. He is going to be just fine." Brielle went to get dressed leaving Bryson to finish dressing.

Bryson had a good cry when she left thinking about Kenneth's words. *"He was unconscious man I don't know he was shot in the chest"* Bryson quickly dressed meeting Brielle in their bedroom.

"I need to tell momma we are leaving so she knows to keep her eye on the kids," Brielle said.

"I need to tell my mom what's happening so her and dad can meet us there. Meet me at the front door." They both headed to the rooms where their parents were sleeping.

Moments later Brielle's mom was at the front door wrapped in her housecoat seeing them out the door. "We will be praying for Bradon and the both of you. He is going to be alright. Call me and let me know what's going on daughter." Mrs. Summers said standing next to her husband.

"We will momma." Brielle and Bradon headed out the front door to the hospital.

Mr. and Mrs. Mathews were right behind them. Mrs. Summers had the new baby and her other grand children to look after praying that everything would be just fine.

When Brielle was in the car she picked up her cell phone to call Chantae telling her the bad news. "Chantae, you need to get to the hospital now. Bradon has been shot."

Chapter 31
I am always the last to Know
January 30

Chantae arrived at the hospital in a nervous panicking state. Kenneth was the first familiar face to greet her. "Kenneth where is Bradon? Is he alright?" she asked hysterically crying and loud.

"He's in surgery. They haven't said much but no news doesn't mean bad news." He was talking to her in a low somber tone.

"Why was I the last to know? I am always the last to know everything concerning him." She cried out to Kenneth searching his face for answers.

"It all happened so fast and after I called Bryson I figured Brielle would call you."

"What happened? The news is saying Greg shot some body at a club, did he shoot Bradon?"

"Yes, he shot Bradon." Kenneth walked towards Chantae to hold her seeing her fall towards the ground weak, losing her balance.

"But why? Why did he shoot Bradon? Why?" Chantae was crying so hard falling into Kenneth's arms as he caught her keeping her from falling to the floor.

"He thought he was Bryson." Kenneth was trying to ease her pain knowing that would make matters worse but he didn't want to tell her a lie.

"Bryson? He was shot and now in surgery because Greg thought he was Bryson?" she said with frustration looking at Kenneth in his eyes for confirmation. She didn't understand why Bradon was shot. Her heart was hurting and she was in so much pain and did not want to hear this happened because of mistaken identity.

"Yes, we were at the club and when he asked him if he was Bryson he didn't say no and an altercation happened inside. After security diffused the situation, we confirmed that everything was good and they were gone before we left but he was waiting for us to come out. I'm sorry Chantae." He held her tight as she cried out in pain.

"Why is my life a shadow of hers? What did I do God?" Chantae sat down in the chair that was close to where they were standing. "I can't believe this is happening to me right now. I can't lose him I just can't. Not because of that damn man. I told her to leave when she first met him. She didn't listen to me and he almost killed her and her son and now my Bradon. Why me?" She cried out in pain. Built up pain from everything that has happened that she has been suppressing, starting with her father abandoning her. Not getting the house that she thought was Bradon's that is now Brielle's. The paternity test times two. And now this.

As she sat there, Brielle and Bryson walked up. "Hey Chantae, we are still waiting to hear something…" she started to say before Chantae loudly interrupted her.

"This is all your fault. If you would have left that damn man when I first told you to maybe we wouldn't be sitting here because he shot my man."

"Chantae calm down. It's nobody's fault but the person who did this to my brother," Bryson said.

"Oh yeah, but you are standing here in front of me, he wasn't looking for Bradon, he was looking for you." Chantae was upset and taking it out on people who cared about her.

"Chantae, I know you are upset sweetheart but we are all here for the same reason, we are all hurting over this," Brielle said softly trying to comfort her friend.

"Your man is standing here with you, alive and well while the man I love was shot by someone in your past. This was not supposed to happen to us," she said crying.

"I need for this conversation to be over right now." Mrs. Mathews came in the room hearing the yelling from Chantae. Her voice was stern and you could tell she meant what she said. "My son is in there fighting for his life. Now I don't wish this on anyone especially not either of my boys. Bryson is right, this is no one's fault but the man that shot my son. This is a time for prayer and all of us to come together as one. No more of this foolishness now you hear me!"

Bryson put his arm around his mother's neck seeing the tears and hearing the anger in her voice.

"I should have been notified first. I wanted to be there with him holding his hand before they took him to surgery, telling him to be strong. Telling him how much I love him, that I will be right here waiting on him. He needed me," she said as calm as she could, staring at the floor with tears in her eyes.

Kenneth never left her side. He knew she was upset. "He was in and out of conscious when he arrived and they took him straight to surgery. He is going to be just fine Chantae. He has the best doctors with him now. Bradon is a fighter." He wanted her to feel better considering the situation. He rubbed her back holding on to her for comfort.

"Thanks Kenneth."

"Chantae, can I sit with you?" Brielle walked closer to her hoping she was not mad at her for something out of her control.

Chantae turned to Kenneth ignoring Brielle and said, "I am going to go check and see if I can find out anything." She stood without looking at Brielle and walked away.

Bryson walked closer to Brielle rubbing her shoulders saying, "She is just upset right now sweetheart, give her a moment to calm down and think rational."

"No, she is right. It is my fault. He was looking for me and he is crazy enough to hurt anyone who gets in his way just to hurt me." She started crying and buried her head in Bryson's chest.

"Sweetheart, it is not your fault. You are not to blame for any of this. Chantae is hurting because Bradon is hurt. He will be ok. Everything is going to be ok." Bryson held Brielle tight in his arms, kissed her forehead closing his eyes and said a silent prayer.

Mrs. Mathews sat in a chair with her head down praying as well. Kenneth stood with Mr. Mathews giving him support as best a man could. Everyone was grieving and prayerful that Bradon would recover from being shot.

Moments later the doctor came out into the waiting area, "Is this the Mathews family?" Everyone stood to their feet to hear what the doctor had to say about Bradon. "Surgery went well, we removed the bullets that were lodged in his chest and abdomen. He suffered damage to his left lung and we were able to repair the damage in his abdomen. The bullets missed his heart, but he did lose large volumes of blood. Because of that he did need a blood transfusion. His body went into hypovolemic shock. He's in recovery now but he is not out of the woods yet. He is still in critical condition, we have him on a ventilator until he is awake and we can assess him further. We will monitor him around the clock. When he is stable and out of recovery the family will be able to visit. He will be allowed two visitors at a time."

"Is he going to be okay doctor?" Chantae asked softly. Her face was puffy and her eyes were red. She didn't understand everything the doctor was saying. She was pleading for answers hoping he was going to be ok.

"We are stabilizing him now, but we will not know anything more until he is awake. He could be in a coma for a day, a week or more. Until then, that is all I can tell you." The doctor knew she wanted to hear, "Yes he will be ok," but only time would tell.

"Thank you doctor," Bryson said.

Chantae was shaking and the tears were flooding her eyes again. Mrs. Mathews grabbed her hand squeezing tight praying out loud for everyone to hear. "My God, my God. I know you will not forsake me. God if it's your will, heal my son. God, we need you to show up and work your miracles Father God. Only you have the last say God, only you know and only you control the outcome. God please, my Bradon needs you. We need you!" Mrs. Mathews prayed and Chantae fell to her seat crying holding Mrs. Mathews hand. She felt her hands wrap around her and at that moment she felt Mrs. Mathews love for her. She never felt anything from Mrs. Mathews as a sign of acceptance until now. "I know you love my son. God has him and he will be just fine."

"Thank you. I really appreciate you." She enjoyed the embrace and stayed with her until the doctor came back and saying they could go back to see him. Chantae and Mrs. Mathews went back first and the site of Bradon unconscious with tubes in his mouth and arms was a frightening sight for both Chantae and his mother. All Chantae could do was lay her head next to Bradon wrapping her arms around him.

"Bradon is so lucky to have you Chantae. I used to worry about him and pray for him constantly. I could tell he met someone special. I could feel it in my heart. And at that moment I knew my Bradon would be alright. God told me then and God told me now that he would be alright."

"You really think Bradon is lucky to have me?"

"Chile yes. I could feel it. It was like a constant burden was lifted. I remember the day me asking him who you were. He acted like I was crazy but he had a smile on his face. I said who is the girl you met that has you acting like a new man? That's when he told me about you, how he felt about you and how you were the one. He said you were special and I told him yes, she is special to win the heart of my Bradon." Mrs. Mathews was smiling remembering the conversation.

"I didn't think you liked me too much. I mean you get along with Brielle so well and talk to her all the time. I just thought you favored her more than me."

"Oh chile no. I don't favor anyone more than another besides my boys. But any woman that truly loves my boys captures my heart. Brielle is special as well don't get me wrong. A woman who can love a man who is homeless and give of her heart completely is very special and a virtuous woman that anyone would instantly fall in love with. But you. You loved my Bradon even after him taking away everything you thought he had. Most women who thought they would be marrying the material things of a man, the things that actually belonged to Bryson, would have ran so fast. But you stayed. You still fell in love. You stayed with my Bradon and helped him to pull out the God given talents he has, to be the man God called him to be and that my dear darling is a blessing of true love!"

Chantae had tears of loving warmth in her eyes from the heartfelt words of Mrs. Mathews. She didn't care what made her tell her all those things at that moment, she was just glad she did. It gave her the strength she needed to get through this situation and the hope she needed that Bradon would be ok.

For now, Bradon's fate for his life was left in the hands of God, his fight for survival and his families constant prayer's.

Chapter 32
Bradon in Recovery
January 31

Early the next morning Momma Mathews and Chantae was still by Bradon's side. Everyone else had left for the night tired and emotionally exhausted. Bradon was in recovery but was still in a coma since surgery.

Bryson and Brielle had gone home the night before drained from the events that took place. Bradon fighting for his life from a bullet meant for Bryson was devastating for them both. Brielle felt like it was her fault that Greg came after Bradon thinking he was Bryson. She knew how crazy he was and what he was capable of doing. Bryson tried to comfort her assuring her she was safe and none of what happened was her fault. She told him she was ok but deep down she was hurting for Chantae, Bradon and his family.

Bryson and Brielle's parents were staying with them so they would have help with the baby. It was exhausting taking care of a new baby. But everyone knew the situation and agreed that babies were innocent and God didn't make any mistakes sending the baby to them. With Bradon in the hospital, Momma Summers, with the help of Maria, was on duty to take care of the baby. She knew everyone else was focusing on Bradon so she thought it best to take care of Brielle's kids and the baby. She knew that once the kids found out about what was going on with Bradon that they too would be asking questions and that morning Carter came in to help with the baby and to inquire about his uncle.

"Grandma, is Bradon going to be alright? I heard everyone last night talking about him being shot," he said with sadness in his voice. Even though Bradon was new in his life it felt to Carter that he had always been a part of their life. He was a true uncle to them and he looked up to Bradon.

"Baby yes he is going to be just fine. I am praying, your mom and Bryson are praying, everyone is praying for him and you should pray for him too," she said as she was burping the baby after her feeding.

"I prayed for him last night and this morning. Asked God not to take my uncle away from me."

"And you know and I know that God listens to young hearts. They are the purest and sincerest hearts and your prayers are answered. I know you love him, just keep praying and trusting God," she said trying to comfort Carter. She could see the pain of his heart in his eyes.

"I saw the news last night. I know it was Greg that shot him," he blurted out with tears in his eyes.

"Your father will pay…"

"He is not my father. I hate that man. He does nothing but hurt people." Carter started to cry a silent cry. He was releasing his hurt to his grandmother who he knew would listen. "He hurt people I love. He has always hurt people I love. I know you not supposed to hate people but I do, I hate him. I know it is not right but I prayed that God lets him die."

"Oh Carter come here." Mrs. Summers laid the baby in the bed and grabbed Carter in her arms. "I know you are hurting and I know Greg," she emphasized his name making sure not to call him his father, "Will pay for everything wrong he has ever done to your mother, to you, Bradon and everyone else. You don't need to fill your heart with hatred and anger allowing him to have a hold on you. Turn it all over to God. He will work it out son. It's ok to be upset. I know you are hurting so just cry and let it all out, I will sit right here and hold you." She held on to Carter tight as he released his anger through his tears. Women know that God gave them all tears to use as women please, especially in times of pain. Majority of the time we don't hold our tears back but often we must help men to know its ok to release theirs, even the young men.

The baby started crying and Carter felt selfish for crying in his grandmother's arms knowing that the baby needed her. "Granny the baby is crying," he said thinking she didn't hear.

"She is alright son. You need me more right now. The baby is ok," she kept her arms tight around Carter. She saw Brielle come around the corner seeing their embrace. She knew that what she saw was Carter releasing pain with his granny so she picked up the baby knowing her mom was working her magic.

Brielle knew Carter was smart enough to figure out what was going on. He took over being the man of the house after his biological father was gone. She never put pressure on him but knew her father taught Carter what it meant to be the man of the house and told him to take care of his mom and sisters.

Walking into her bedroom she walked right in to Bryson at the door, Brielle had a sad look on her face. "This whole situation with my ex is weighing down on everyone and Chantae is right, this is my fault."

"Sweetheart, don't say that. You didn't cause any of this. What that man did was all on him. I knew once the adoption was final that he would receive notification of his rights being ceased as a father."

"They told him? That's why he was after you?" Brielle was rocking the baby thinking about the adoption and how angry that must have made Greg.

"Yes, I should have told you that would happen but didn't want you to stress about anything nor change your mind out of fear of what he would attempt to do." Bryson stood behind Brielle knowing her mind was working overtime.

"That explains why after all these years he came back. He told me I would never be happy with anyone else and his kids will never have another father besides him. I can't believe all this has happened because he wants to control me, control my life." Brielle started to cry and the baby was crying.

"Brielle, look at me," Bryson said stopping her from pacing with his hands on her shoulders.

They both turned to the knock at the half opened door. "Sir, you want me to take the baby? I think it's her feeding time," Maria said through the door.

"Come in, yes Maria. Please take her. Thank you," Bryson said taking the baby from Brielle handing her to Maria.

Maria comforted the baby as she left the room closing the door behind her.

"Come sit with me," Bryson motioned for Brielle to join him on the bed. "I never want you and the children to worry about anything at all or fear someone hurting you. I pulled some strings to have Greg sent far away from here when I first met you. I didn't even want him in the same state as you and the children. They were in the process of moving him and several other inmates when someone intervened to break out another inmate. That's how and why he escaped not because he wanted to get to you or me. Yes, I am sure he was furious about his rights as a father being taken away but he didn't deserve the title father after what he did to you and his own children. Don't blame yourself or allow him to continue hurting you. He is a nobody and he will never get the chance to hurt you any longer. Bradon is a big boy. Going to a club, mine or any club, mixing alcohol with anyone hating or angry wanting to cause trouble, there is a chance for something bad to happen. That could have been anyone. Greg just saw an opportunity to harm someone and take out his anger. That has nothing to do with you.

"Thanks babe. It hurts knowing Bradon is fighting for his life and Chantae is upset with me. I am so happy and grateful me and the children have you." She laid her head on his chest allowing him to comfort her.

"You will always have me sweetheart. Chantae will come to her senses. If Greg survives he will be locked up so far away from us with more charges he will never see freedom again. I promise you that."

Bryson's cell phone started to buzz. "Hello."

"Hey son, I wanted you to know that I am leaving in a moment to come shower. I know you and Brielle didn't get to come in to see your brother so was hoping you were coming this morning. I sent Chantae home to get some rest as well."

"Ok yes ma'am, we are getting ready now to head that way. How is he? Any change?"

"No change. He is still in a coma. But you know your momma is a prayer warrior and my God has already informed me your brother will be just fine."

"Yes he will momma. We will see you in a moment momma."

"Alright baby."

"Chantae and my mom are leaving for a while we can take the morning shift if you are up to it." Bryson wrapped his arms around Brielle tight kissing her forehead.

"Yes, I would love that." They both hurried to get ready so they could head to the hospital.

Chantae was leaving the hospital when she ran into Andre. "Hey Andre, you headed up to see Bradon?" she asked with her eyes red and puffy from crying.

"Yeah, you headed out?"

"I am going to shower and rest for a minute then come back up here this afternoon. I been up all night hoping he would wake up. Momma Mathews is up there now."

"Oh ok, Bryson and Brielle been back yet?" He watched as she rolled her eyes. "What was that for?" he asked her with a frown on his face knowing it was directed at Brielle.

"Everyone always concerned about Brielle. It's her fault this happened." She waited for Andre to respond as he stood there looking at her. "What? Why you looking at me like that, it's the truth."

"Naw, shawty. That's not the truth. Truth is that's your girl. She loves you and you know that." He watched her roll her eyes and shake her head frowning. "As a matter of fact, she is the reason you been living your life so happy with Bradon after the baby drama. You better check yourself sweetheart. She doesn't deserve this treatment."

"What does that mean? That baby is not Bradon's."

Andre thought about what he was about to say out of anger realizing he already said too much. "Your girl, the one you mad at really has your back. You are mad at the wrong person Chantae, the wrong person. You have a good morning. I am going up to see my boy. Didn't mean to upset you," Andre said walking away from Chantae.

She stood there for a moment trying to figure out what he could have meant she was the reason she was living happy after the baby drama. She watched him walk away knowing that Andre was loyal to Bradon and wasn't too social with her beyond saying hello how you doing. She made a mental not to ask Bradon once and if he was better.

Andre headed to see Bradon greeting Mrs. Mathews standing beside Bradon's bed. "How you doing momma? How is Bradon?" he asked hugging her.

"Hey baby no change yet. He will wake up once he is done resting. He been up most his life you know thinking he gon miss something. God has him resting for the moment, he will be awake before we know it."

"You always do say the right words to encourage and uplift."

"That's what mommas are for," she said rubbing his back. She knows that he is Bradon's best friend and as tough as he looks he is hurting inside.

"I should have been there that night with him. I just feel like if I was then..." he stopped mid-sentence to take a breath to keep from crying.

"There is nothing that you could have done. So stop beating yourself up over it. You are here with him now so talk to him, I'm sure he can hear you. It will do him good to hear your voice. Bryson is on his way up here. Will you stay here at least until he gets here?"

"Yes ma'am I will." Andre stood looking at his friend laying in the bed with a tube in his mouth. A site that no one wanted to ever see someone they love be in.

"Alright, I will be back a little later. Call someone if anything changes with my Bradon." Mrs. Mathews grabbed her purse heading for the door.

"Yes ma'am I will be sure to call you if something changes." Andre stayed with Bradon telling him stories trying to hold back his tears as long as he could before he broke down crying releasing his pain. After a moment, he wiped his face and sat in a chair next to Bradon's bed until Bryson and Brielle arrived.

Everyone was hurting and in pain but prayerful for Bradon's recovery.

Chapter 33
News having a field day with the story
January 31

The news reports were having a field day with the story of Bradon being shot in the club. "Last night the club owners brother was shot while sitting in the back seat of his limo. Witnesses say he was leaving the club after an altercation happened inside Club Luxe between Mr. Mathews and the man that shot him known as Greg Philips just moments before the shooting happened outside the club. Mr. Philips escaped from prison during a routine transfer of prisoners a little over a week ago. He was also shot by the security team and he is now in critical condition. As soon as he is stable if he survives he will be arrested and taken back to prison where he will recover.

"Any reports on what caused the shooting or the altercation in the club Jennifer?" her coworker back at the station asked.

"Well we do know that Greg is the father of the victim's brother's wife's children if that makes sense and Bryson and Brielle were recently married. Witnesses say he asked his brother inside if he was Bryson and Bradon never identified who he was to Greg. That was right before the fight inside the club. Bryson and his wife may have been Mr. Philips motive in coming to the club and we believe the brother Bryson was the target and not Bradon. We are not sure but that could have something to do with the altercation and the shooting. Looking at a photo of the brothers they resemble one another to the point where Bradon Mathews the victim who was shot by Greg Philips could have been confused with being his brother. Some people that were interviewed think this was a case of mistaken identity but either way the two men are brothers and neither one of them deserved to be shot or fighting for their life."

"Any reports about how Mr. Mathews is recovering?" her coworker asked the reporter.

"We have not had any new updates at this time. The last update we received was that he was in surgery in critical condition and the details of if he will survive the shooting have been sketchy. Doctors are doing all that they can to save his life. His family is said to be at the hospital praying for his survival including his brother Bryson. Now although Bryson is said to be the intended target I witnesses are saying that Bradon Mathews did not deny being Bryson when asked by the shooter during the altercation inside. It is very possible that the shooter believed he was Bryson Mathews and the bullet was intended for him. We have new information here about the escaped inmate Greg Philips. The woman and child he was convicted for beating to near death is now the wife of Bryson Mathews and her son. Brielle Summers was involved with Mr. Philips and their relationship was very abusive so he was known to be a violent man. And the bullets that hit Bradon were very likely meant for Bryson because he is now married to Mr. Philips ex Brielle."

"Do we know the medical condition of the shooter?"

"Not at this time. The ambulance took him away and they had several EMT's working to stop the bleeding where he was shot by security trying to save Bradon's life. There is no word on his condition at this time."

"Jennifer how do you think Mr. Philips found out about Brielle's new relationship?"

"Well Bryson has a new movie he is promoting and it has been advertised on television and its possible that he saw them together at his Movie Premiere or read an article in a magazine. Bryson is a popular and powerful man and everyone has been talking about the most popular bachelor and the woman that stole his heart becoming his wife. I am sure he heard about it through some type of news outlet circulating at least it is a huge possibility that could be the case. I know his brother Bradon is the owner of an Architecture firm that has taken the industry by storm with his creative and unique designs. The demand for his work has increased more than any other company in the industry in his line of work because of his unique amazing gift. But his fans will have to wait and pray that he makes a full recovery from this tragic event taken place here tonight." The news showed pictures of Brielle and Bryson standing together with their children at the movie premiere as well as magazine articles form their wedding. They also showed some of Bradon's art work and the building he was designing and building. They spent the entire morning talking about the incident. It was the top news story at that moment.

"Jennifer thank you for the updates. This is a sad situation and we will keep that family in our prayers and keep you the viewers updated as new information is received."

Chapter 34
Wake up baby
February 3

After days of waiting for a change with Bradon's condition, everyone was concerned and worried if he would make a full recovery. Chantae barely left the hospital. She packed her a bag to shower and change at the hospital so she wouldn't have to leave. She loved Bradon and didn't want to lose him. She was taking it hard that he has yet to awaken.

The doctors and nurses were in and out changing his fluids, medicines and doing vitals. No one could give her an answer about his condition improving. He was in the same state as he was after surgery. The waiting game was hard for her not knowing what the outcome of Bradon's fate would be.

Everyone took shifts coming to see Bradon to give Chantae and Momma Mathews a break. Chantae did not want to leave his side. She would leave out to grab a bite to eat from the cafeteria or if Brielle came into the room she would step out. She was not speaking to Brielle, still blaming her for what happened.

That evening, Chantae was finally alone with Bradon lying beside him in the hospital bed listening to his beating heart. She couldn't take it anymore and she started crying. "Baby please wake up. I need you to be alright. I don't care about anything else but you waking up, coming back to me. Please Bradon I need you. Please wake up. I love you so much. I want to spend my forever with you. Only with you. I can't lose you. I just can't lose you Bradon. We are going to have babies and raise a family together. You have to wake up. You have to come back to me. Please don't you dare die on me. You can't die on my Bradon." She sat up in the bed, turned to kiss his face. She lightly smacked his face trying to wake him. "Baby wake up, please wake up. Her voice was a little louder.

She lowered her head to his bed crying. "There is so much I want to share with you, tell you. So much more of life for us to experience together. God, you can't take him away from me. God please. I deserve to be happy. Bradon deserves to be happy. Whatever we did before us I apologize, please forgive us! Just don't take my Bradon away from me God. I need him. I love him. Please wake up Bradon." She buried her face in her hands and cried.

After a moment longer she walked into the bathroom to wash her face. She didn't want anyone to walk in and see what a mess she had become. She lost her father at a young age and her mom never got over losing him. It not only affected her mom but Chantae felt like she lost her father and her mother. Her mom was physically there but mentally had checked out. She understood where her pain was coming from but didn't want to experience the unbearable pain of losing the one person she loved most in the world.

When she walked out of the bathroom she walked straight into Bryson and Brielle.

"Hey Chantae, how are you holding up?" Brielle asked.

Chantae looked her in the eyes without responding, turned to look at Bryson. "Since you are here, I am going to run home grab some more clean clothes and then I will be back. Give you time to spend with your brother," she said as she grabbed her purse and her overnight bag.

"Sure I will be here when you get back. We will call you if anything changes."

"You call me if anything changes. Just you," she said firmly letting him know she didn't want Brielle calling.

"Chantae, can we talk?" Brielle asked.

"No, we have nothing to talk about. I don't even know why you are here. Just stop."

"Chantae! Brielle is your friend, you need your friends and family right now. You know this is not her fault," Bryson said upset that she was hurting his wife trying to be sympathetic that she was hurting too.

"Maybe it's your fault then. After all the bullet was meant for you. Either way, Bradon doesn't deserve to be lying in that hospital bed and we don't know if he is going to live or die."

"Chantae. I never wanted this to happen and you know that. I know you are hurting I just…"

"You don't know how I feel. You are not standing over Bryson wondering if he is going to live or die. You don't know my pain and you don't get to tell me how I'm feeling." Chantae had tears streaming down her face again as she walked out the door. She was hurting and deep down she knew it was not Brielle's fault. She was the closest person to her and the only one she could blame and hurt because she was hurting. We always end up hurting the people we love when they are always never at fault of the source of our pain.

"Are you ok." Bryson knew Brielle was hurting. He knew Chantae didn't have anyone to comfort her pain either.

"Yes. I know she doesn't mean it. I need you to go check on her for me comfort her since she won't allow me to do it. Please. I am going to sit here with Bradon for a moment," Brielle said as calm as she could so Bryson would go after Chantae and not feel obligated to stay and comfort her. She knew she was his priority and if he saw pain he wouldn't go after Chantae.

"Are you sure you are ok?"

"Yes. Please go after her." She insisted.

"Ok I will be right back." He left out of the room and saw Chantae leaning up against the wall bent over crying.

"Come here I got you?" He wrapped his arms tight around her squeezing her tight allowing her to release her anger and pain.

She cried so hard in his arms releasing her lonely frustration. Sometimes a simple embrace from those who matter is enough to help a hurting soul through difficult times. "I can't lose him Bryson. I love him so much. He should be awake by now. I just need him to wake up." She held on to him squeezing her tight, expressing her pain and frustration.

"We all need him to wake up and be ok. My brother won the lottery when he met you. I was so glad to see him fall head over hills for someone and to know that you loved him like you do makes me feel good. That love is going to make him fight harder to come back to you. Keep on praying."

"Thank you Bryson. Can you loosen your grip I can't breathe."

"Oh sorry." He released his grip releasing her making sure she was ok. "Are you going to be alright alone?"

"Yes, I have been alone majority of my life, well until Brielle and…" she paused thinking about what she had just said. She knew Brielle was and has always been there for her. Her anger was not directed towards her because it was her fault. Chantae finally had someone to love her in a way she desired to be loved and cared for and losing Bradon scared her more than anything. "Hey thanks again for coming after me. I needed that hug even if I couldn't breathe." A half smile appeared on her face.

"Brielle insisted I did," he said wanting her to know her friend really does care about her.

"I will let you get back to your brother. I will be back in a few hours," she turned to walk away. Her pain she was feeling was directed at Brielle and she now felt bad. She knew she would have to apologize soon, she just hoped Brielle would forgive her.

Chapter 35
Visiting Bradon Alone
February 3

After Bryson left to go after Chantae, Brielle took that alone time to spend with Bradon and talk to him. She saw a man standing close to Bradon's room looking in and for a moment she thought it was Bradon standing there. When the man noticed her looking at him he immediately turned and walked away. *That was weird, he looks like he could be related to them. I wonder why he left so suddenly,* she thought to herself.

She walked closer to Bradon's bed knowing he was in a coma but knew it was a chance of him hearing her as well. She started her visit by praying over him. The moment she reached his bed she touched his face, his arms, his chest and back to the top of his head. She reached for his hand holding it tight and with the other hand on his head she closed her eyes to pray.

"Father God, I am coming to you right now with a bowed head, open heart asking for your blessings and miracles right now. Lord I need you to touch Bradon's body, his mind, his soul. Give him life, give him health. Lord please touch his body and perform your miracles giving him back to us all. Allow him to be in his right mind just as he was before this tragic but better in your image. Lord if it is a will and a way you are that will and you are that way. Lord heal broken hurting hearts, mend relationships, give us peace and happiness back. Give us Bradon back Lord. We need him, Chantae needs him, Bryson and his parents need him, my children need him, Lord I need him. I need him to be alright Lord. Please Lord. You have done so much for me already and I am so thankful and grateful but Lord I need this one last favor if you do nothing else for me in life I need you to heal and wake Bradon up in his right mind. Give Chantae her forever love back. Mend the brokenness right now Lord, in Jesus name perform your miracles. You are a miracle worker, a healer, a way maker and right now I need you to be here and make a way for Bradon to be better, to be healed. I thank you Lord, I thank you Heavenly Father for already granting my prayers. In Jesus name. Amen!'

She released her grip on Bradon's hand and removed her other hand from his head. "Bradon I am so sorry this happened to you. The kids send their love. Carter is taking it pretty hard so I need you to wake up assure him you are going to be ok. You are going to have to hurry up and get better for us all now. You are going to be the God father of our babies. They need you too. We all need you. Chantae needs you. She is taking this pretty hard. She blames me for what happened to you. I understand her pain and why she thinks that but I never wanted any of this to happen. I need you to be ok Bradon. Please, it's time to wake up now. You have been resting enough." Looking up to the ceiling she paused briefly before continuing. "I know it's not my fault what he did to you. I'm sure you were taking up for your brother but I still feel bad because he is someone from my past. What he did to me and the kids was horrible so I know what kind of monster he can be. I wish you never had to experience that. I know he was looking for Bryson and if he would have found him instead of you I might not have him right now. I know he wishes he could trade places with you and fight for your life just as hard as you fight for his. I love that about you two. You have to fight through this Bradon. You have to be ok. I need you to be ok Bradon."

Brielle stood there looking at Bradon rubbing the back of his hand in complete silence. She placed his hand in hers again still rubbing the back of his hand looking down towards the bed with tears in her eyes. At that moment she felt him squeeze her hand. She looked from his hand to his face and his eyes were open with a slight smile on his face. He held her hand tight letting her know he was going to be alright.

"Oh Father God thank you!" She leaned down and kissed his forehead. "Bradon you are a wake." She turned to Bryson walking through the door her eyes filled with tears.

"What's wrong Brielle," he said panicking unaware Bradon was awake.

"Bradon is awake. Call your mom. I will call Chantae."

"Hey bro, welcome back. You scared the hell out of us all," Bryson said standing over his brother. He reached down pressing the nurse button.

He dialed his mom number. She answered on the first ring. "Mom Bradon is awake."

"Praise God, I am on my way."

"Hey Chantae, Bradon is awake. Hurry back I am sure he wants to see you," Brielle said to her answering machine.

Bryson and Brielle was excited to see him open his eyes.

The nurse called into the room, "Can I help you?" yes, he is awake. My brother is awake," Bryson said with joy.

"I will tell the nurse and notify the doctor. That's great news," she said.

At that moment Brielle leaned over in pain. "Aarrghhhhh."

"What's wrong Brielle? Are you ok?" he ran over to her side. He noticed water on the floor.

"I think my water broke." She winced out in pain. "I was having some mild contractions but thought they were Braxton hicks nothing to worry about. Ooohhhhhhhh," she screamed out again in pain. "These are hurting Bryson."

"Hold on sweetheart. Bro welcome back. I love you. We have babies to deliver." He picked Brielle up in his arms as the doctors and nurses came into the room to assess Bradon. They noticed Brielle needed assistance as well. A couple of them guided Bryson to the labor and delivery floor. He refused a chair and insisted on carrying his wife where they needed to be asap.

They worked on Bradon making sure he could breathe on his own and was out of the woods. They checked vitals, ran test and more test. Chantae arrived moments later. She was in the parking lot when she checked Brielle's voice message. She wasn't ready to answer her call instead chose to listen to her voice message and was glad to hear Bradon was awake. She stood by Bradon's side as the doctors worked holding his hand.

Bryson stood by Brielle as they hooked her up to monitors and checked the babies heart rate and to see how far she was dilated. She was definitely in labor.

He let everyone know she was in labor and that Bradon was awake. He was happy with his wife waiting on his twins to be born and knowing his brother was going to be ok.

Everyone was back at the hospital playing the waiting game but this time for a joyous occasion. Brielle to have the babies and Bradon awake and well.

Chapter 36
Baby commotion
February 4

"Brielle I feel the head. When I tell you to push I need you to push and keep on pushing as we count to ten."

"Ok," she said breathing heavy.

"I'm right here sweetheart. Squeeze my hand as hard as you need to. You are doing great," Bryson said holding Brielle's hand and stroking her face and hair with his free hand.

Brielle's water broke and started her labor earlier the evening before and now here she was about ten hours later having her babies. It was a little after four in the morning and the anticipation for Bryson to see his first-born son was growing tremendously as he encouraged Brielle through the labor.

"Brielle here comes another contraction, when I say go I need you to start pushing. Get ready. Ok go, start pushing now." The nurse was doing most of the coaching as the doctor worked. Her take charge momentum and Bryson being by her side is what helped Brielle through the pain.

She screamed out as she pushed through the ten seconds until the nurse told her to relax.

Not even thirty seconds later the nurse had her to push again. "Brielle here comes another contraction. I need you to push and really push down one of these babies. Push Brielle, push." She held Brielle's other leg up helping her and coaching her to give a really good push. "Stop, relax for a moment." Moments later she shouted out, "We have a beautiful baby boy."

Bryson looked in amazement at his son. He kissed Brielle on her forehead. "He is beautiful sweetheart," he said smiling looking towards his son.

After the doctor clipped the umbilical cord, the nurse took the first baby and he was ready to deliver the next.

"Brielle, you did great on the first baby. The second baby should be easier let's get ready to push this baby out." She grabbed her leg and the other nurse grabbed the other. Bryson held her hand tight and everyone was ready to start the pushing all over again.

Baby number two was born and Brielle was exhausted. She was glad the labor and delivery part was over. Now they both anticipated holding their babies.

"Here you go momma baby number one." The nurse placed the first born on her chest wrapped in a blanket.

"He is so beautiful," Brielle said kissing his forehead.

"Just like his momma." He looked into Brielle's eyes when she looked up at him. His smile was heart-warming. They were at peace knowing that Bradon was recovering and their babies were born healthy.

"Here is baby number two daddy." The nurse handed Bryson his other son. He leaned in closer to Brielle and their other son laying in the bed. "If someone has a camera or a phone I can take a picture," the nurse said looking at their picture-perfect moment.

"Yes, that would be great," Bryson said handing her his phone after getting the camera ready. The nurse took several pictures of the four of them capturing their happy moment.

Moments later a knock at the door and momma Mathews entered. "I heard I have two healthy grandsons' in here."

"Hey momma. Yes your grandsons are here." He motioned for her to join him and Brielle and handed her the baby he was holding.

"Oh Father God they are absolutely gorgeous! Bryson they look just like you did as a baby. Head full of hair and just beautiful as they can be. Brielle sweetheart how are you doing?"

"I am just fine now that these two bundles of joy are here."

"They are a blessing from God I tell you. You two have done such a beautiful job making these two handsome boys."

"Thanks mom," Bryson said standing behind her looking over her shoulders at his sons.

"Have you two thought of a name yet?" Momma Mathews asked admiring the baby she was holding glancing over at the other.

"Well I thought Bryson should name his son's. I told him I would leave that part up to him." Brielle calmly stated smiling at Bryson.

"Well I thought since me and my brother had the same letter to start our name that our boys should as well. So since Carter starts with a C, what do you think about Caden and Carson?" he said looking at Brielle for confirmation.

She was surprised at the fact he included Carter in his decision and was elated. "I love that idea and love the names Caden and Carson."

"Caden and Carson. I love the names too Bryson. Caden and Carson." She repeated to herself. "Hey Caden. Your grandmother loves you so much."

"There you have it. And you my sweet baby will be called Carson," Brielle said to the baby she was holding.

"Let me get a picture of you all so I can send it to your father. Let me give you the baby Brielle and Bryson you stand there." Momma Mathews was excited about her new grandchildren. She took her pictures and stayed a moment longer before giving them private time together with their babies.

"You did good Brielle. I am such a proud husband and father," Bryson said staring at Brielle as she attempted to nurse the babies.

"We did good babe. Thank you for being with me every step of the way. I couldn't have done it without you."

"I wouldn't have had it any other way," Bryson said.

A couple hours later after Brielle completed recovery, they moved her and the babies to a new room. Their first visitor was Bradon being pushed into the room in a wheel chair.

"Knock Knock. Uncle Bradon is here." He was being pushed into the room by Andre.

"Oh Bradon I am so happy to see you," Brielle said smiling at Bradon.

"Hey Bryson, how are you Brielle?" Andre said speaking as he pushed Bradon closer to where the babies were in their crib.

"I'm good Dre. Thank you for bringing Bradon to see us."

"What's up Andre. Hey brother I see you're feeling better. Sitting up is good. Glad to see you awake and moving around. How are you feeling really?" Bryson asked his brother.

"I'm feeling ok. Of course they have me pumped with pain killers. Look at these two beautiful babies right here." He reached his hand into the cribs and grabbed their little hands.

"We are naming them Carson and Caden," Bryson said.

"Beautiful names for beautiful babies." After a moment of quiet in the room with everyone looking at the babies, Bradon broke the silence. He knew everyone was scared he wouldn't make it. "Your uncle got shot but there was no way I was going anywhere and miss the opportunity to see my god children and my nephews grow up." He wanted Brielle to know that her plead for him to be ok was heard. He turned and looked in her direction smiling.

"I knew you could hear me. Glad you are ok Bradon."

"Thank you Brielle, seriously. I heard every prayer and every word everyone spoke. I wasn't awake but I could hear everything. And when you were there visiting I could hear every word you said. Not to bring any sadness to this joyous occasion but I know that Chantae wasn't a pleasant person to be around, and for that I am sorry."

"No need to apologize for that." Brielle softly said.

"What happened to me had nothing to do with you or Bryson. I can be hot headed at times and I always take up for my family no matter what, that includes you too. This was one of those times. He just caught me slipping you know. It was never your fault, I don't think that and Chantae doesn't believe that either. I know she was just hurting. But Mixing alcohol with confrontation is not a good mix. But the important thing is, I am alive and we have two beautiful babies who will make us forget about all the pain and focus on happiness.

"Thank you Bradon!" Brielle said squeezing Bradon's hand with a tear running down her cheek.

"Yes we do. Glad you are ok brother. Where is Chantae now? She coming to see the babies?" Bryson asked. He walked over to Brielle wiped the tear from her face, kissing her forehead.

"I don't think she is ready. She experienced so much pain with all of this and I think she knows she directed her pain in ways she shouldn't have. Give her time she will come around. She went home to change clothes and grab me some decent clothes. She will be back soon." Bradon was enjoying the babies. "I am your God Father and Uncle Bradon is going to spoil you both rotten."

"So Brys man this makes five for you all now. Almost a basketball team," Andre said.

"I know man. I am going to cherish every moment."

"Congratulations to you both. Twins is a big task. Double duty. Literally," he said laughing.

"You don't have to tell me twice. But I am ready for the job." Bryson laughed with Andre.

Bradon and Brielle were adoring the babies. Bradon attempted to wake the babies. He wanted them to open their eyes to see their uncle for the first time.

Brielle couldn't be happier. Her older children were on their way to the hospital, Bradon was well and she had Bryson right by her side. She knew in time Chantae would come around, at least she hoped she would. Until then she had plenty to be thankful for and to keep her heart happy.

Chapter 37
Slip of the tongue Uh Oh
February 4

When Chantae returned to the hospital she helped Bradon get dressed. His mother and his best friend Andre were still at the hospital waiting on his discharge papers with him. Chantae helped Bradon get his clothes on over his wounds and bandages.

"Be careful with my arm baby, it is still painful," Bradon said helping the best way he could. He didn't like the fact he had to have someone help him dress but he knew Chantae loved him and would do anything for him.

"I got you baby. I'm trying to be as gentle as possible." Bradon could see down Chantae shirt while she was trying to get his shirt over his head. He leaned in to her chest and put his head in between her breast, biting at her right breast. "Ouch boy stop. I'm trying to help you and you want to be freaky." Her voice was low so his mom wouldn't hear what she said.

"I miss those all in my face," he said putting his free arm around her.

"I missed you too. All of you. I was so scared that…" She paused not finishing her sentence. "I am just so happy to have you back with me Bradon. Don't you ever leave me you hear me?" She looked into his eyes with tears in hers.

"I promise sweetheart. Thank you for being here every day around the clock. I really appreciate that. I love you so much and I don't want to see you hurt like this ever again." They kissed passionately for a moment for the first time since he had awakened from the coma. They were interrupted by a knock at the door. "Yes." They both said in unison.

"Son the doctor is here to discharge you." His mother spoke through the door.

"Coming mom. Almost have this shirt on." He smiled at Chantae. "Let's get home so we can be alone." He grabbed a hand full of her bottom.

"You so freaky nasty," she whispered.

"I need to ask the doctor about sex before we leave. But my mom… maybe he will tell me without me asking." Bradon was thinking. He didn't want to discuss having sex in front of his mother. He really hoped he would just say it as part of his discharge instructions.

Hearing the doctor discuss his discharge instructions he did indeed mention sex restrictions. "Try to restrain from having sex for a couple weeks. We want you to completely heal. You don't want any sutures to open and risk infection."

"Doctor we are talking about my son here, a grown man who I know is going to have sex. You see that beautiful lady next to him?"

"Mom, really." Bradon was shocked his mom asked the question he dared not ask in front of her.

"Son, we need to know these things before you go home. So doctor if he does have sex let's say slower than normal but his heart rate gets up, he starts to sweat."

"Mom." Bradon was feeling like a little kid in the doctor office with his mom asking all the questions needed to take care of him.

"Boy hush, as soon as you and Chantae get home you two are having sex. So, doctor what is the worst that can happen?"

Chantae's eyes got big from embarrassment but she didn't say a word. Bradon looked toward the doctor for an answer to the questions his mom asked on his behalf.

"Well I don't advise it for two weeks but," she said and paused. "if you do decide to go against doctor's orders and have sex before two weeks take it slow and how can I say this, try to simply enjoy without doing work. The worse that could happen is too much strain on your wounds, they open and start bleeding and you have to rush back to the hospital so we could stop the bleeding and your wounds be sewn back up. But I advise you to wait as long as you can."

"Got it. Thank you doctor. We will try our best to follow all the doctor orders. So, are we free to go now?" Bradon didn't want his mom asking anymore questions. He was ready to get home and simply enjoy Chantae without doing work as the doctor said.

"Yes. If someone will go get the car and meet us at patient pickup we will roll you down in a wheel chair." The doctor looked up at Chantae and Andre.

"Of course, I will go pull the truck around baby," Chantae said.

"I will stay here and walk out with you son." His mother insisted.

"I will walk with Chantae. I will follow you all to the house man if that's ok, keep you company make sure you don't need anything else," Andre said to Bradon.

"Yeah that would be great man thanks."

"We will get that wheel chair and all your things and meet you all there," the doctor said.

Andre walked out with Chantae. They chatted a bit and before they walked out into the parking lot Chantae made a comment that Andre didn't like. "I am so glad to be leaving now I don't have to run into that bitch Brielle everyday coming to see my man. You know he defended her."

"Are you hearing yourself right now?"

"What?"

"You are calling your best friend a bitch and acting like you hate her when she has done nothing wrong."

"I don't want to see her every day, and she doesn't need to be coming to see my man every day. He was alright without her coming up there every damn day."

"Your man is also her husband's brother. Her brother in law. You know what you sound real ignorant right now. I don't understand you."

"What is it to understand? It's her fault he was even in this situation. He almost died because of her."

"You need to check yourself. That girl loves you. It is not her fault."

"Fuck you Dre. You just like everybody else all up her ass. Her life is perfect, well almost perfect," she smirked. "Her man does have a baby by another woman." Chantae had a moment smiling thinking about what she said.

"No, your man has a baby by another woman. Bryson and Brielle agreed to take care of the baby if it was Bradon's and Bryson convince the doctor if the test revealed Bradon as the father to say it was Bryson's."

"What are you talking about?"

Andre realized he only spoke out of anger and he immediately regretted telling Chantae the way he did. He knew it wasn't his place. "It wasn't my place to say that to you but you need to lay off your girl. She has your back and you don't even realize it."

"That don't even make sense."

"Brielle nor Bryson wanted you to be hurt if Bradon was the father That's what family do. Stick together no matter what and take the bullet to save someone else. Bradon never denied he was Bryson that night. He would do the exact same thing over even if he knew what the outcome would be. So you need to ease up off your girl. The same girl who has your back and always will."

"Your lying," Chantae said with tears streaming down her face standing in the parking lot.

"Look, it wasn't my place to mention that to you and for that I am sorry. Hell, I am not even supposed to know. I just overheard Bryson and Kenneth talking about it." He watched Chantae's face change from sad to horrified. "Look, I didn't mean to hurt you or spill the news. I was just upset. Bradon doesn't know the truth. With everything that is going on I don't think this is the best time to have this conversation with him."

Chantae was quiet staring into space. "Yeah, you right. At least I am not the last to know this time. I won't mention anything until he is better."

"Thanks Chantae. I was going to tell him before all of this happened. But you really need to fix this mess with Brielle. That's your girl. Friends don't treat friends foul like that. You know damn well none of this is her fault."

"I know. I am sorry. I was so scared of losing him." Chantae started crying hysterically.

"Come here," Andre pulled her closer to him holding her. "Sorry Chantae. I shouldn't have lashed out at you." He rubbed her back and held her tight until she was calm.

"Not mad at you. I needed that tough love and glad you told me about the baby situation. A lot of things make sense now. But I don't care. I will help him raise the baby if that's what he wants to do. I am just thankful to still have him. I love him Andre."

"I know you do. We all know you do. Everything will be ok. Let's get this man home.

"Yes, I am glad to be going home. I forgot where I parked." Chantae started looking around for her car.

"Come on follow me. You are down here. I saw your car when I parked. Your Tae Marie Boutique sticker is big as day. No one can miss it."

"Well that's a good thing. Thanks Andre seriously!" she said grabbing his hand. "I really appreciate you not only for now but for being there for Bradon as well and respecting me and Bradon's relationship."

They left the parking lot after the intense then calm moment. Andre felt bad but relieved that his comment didn't run Chantae off and Chantae felt better knowing that Brielle was trying to protect her. She now understood why Brielle was not upset after hearing the news. It is easier to accept a child when it's not your man's but then again Brielle is just an accepting person. She didn't allow things that hurt her to show on the outside.

Chantae took Bradon home and Andre followed. They all interacted as if nothing was ever said. They focused on taking care of Bradon. Chantae knew they would eventually discus the baby situation but also knew Bradon didn't need any added stress until he was better. Her life had been altered but she had her man and knew that with Bradon she could accomplish and deal with any situation coming her way. Even a baby that wasn't biologically hers.

Chapter 38
Making Mends with my friend
February 5

Early Friday morning, Chantae woke up to get her day started so she could go visit with Brielle. Andre stayed the night so she knew Bradon would have someone looking after him while she was gone. She fixed breakfast for them both and made sure Bradon took his medication the doctor prescribed. She knew it was time to make amends with her best friend and put the foolishness behind her. "Baby are you comfortable? You need anything else?" Chantae asked Bradon before she showered getting ready to leave.

"No, I'm good sweetheart. Are you headed to visit with Brielle?"

"Yes. I'm going early before she has other visitors."

"Yeah that will be good so you two can talk. This is a pleasant visit, right? You are apologizing to her?" Bradon wanted to make sure she wasn't leaving him with ill intentions for Brielle. He loved Chantae but he also loved his brother and Brielle was a part of his brother. Hurting her was hurting his brother and he couldn't knowingly allow that to happen.

"I am going to apologize and hope she will talk to me again. I know I acted like an ass to her. I was hurting and I was scared I would lose you. I am not happy about how I treated her. I never wanted to be one of those people who hurt the ones you love when you are hurting. It happened and now I am going to apologize and make things right again." Chantae was being sincere. Knowing what she knew now from Andre she knew Brielle deserved more respect and kindness from her. Any woman that can raise another woman's child who tried to destroy her life was an amazing woman. For Brielle to make her own sacrifices just to protect her relationship with Bradon, she knew Brielle had always and will always have her best interest at heart, even when she didn't need her to.

"I am glad to hear you say that sweetheart. Thank you for doing this."

"I just hope she accepts my apology. Brielle is sweet but she has a little stubbornness in her as well. I grew up with her trust me I know." She laughed a little thinking back to when they were kids.

"She will welcome your apology I am sure. Come give your man some sugar."

"You know you have restrictions for two weeks. All you can have is some lip sugar for now."

"I will take whatever I can get. Come here woman."

Chantae walked over to Bradon sitting up in the chair. She straddled his lap kissing her man passionately. Bradon grabbed her butt pulling her closer to him with his lips locked with hers she could feel his erection. Chantae pulled back. "No sir, that's it. I feel you getting excited wanting more than lip action. No need to get yourself all worked up and I can't take care of you." She tried to get up but Bradon's grip was tight.

"Come on baby just sit on it." He was trying to convince her to have sex with him.

"Bradon I love you. I promise to always satisfy your every need sexually and non. I will always be your yes girl. Whatever daddy wants daddy gets."

"So we can…"

"Nope, let me stop you there. I already had a terrifying experience thinking I would lose you. Two weeks to completely heal is nothing compared to a life time. So, I don't want to chance anything bad happening to you."

"Woman when I am cleared by the doctor or you whichever comes first, I am going to wear that ass out," Bradon said smacking her on the butt as she started to walk away.

"Ouch. That hurt," she said giggling walking towards the bathroom. "You always wear this ass out."

"You just be ready."

"Always for you babe. I'm going to get ready. Go wake your friend up. I made breakfast for you both. It's on the stove."

"Umm. Thanks baby, I'm starving."

Chantae got herself ready and headed to the hospital. When she arrived, she sat in the parking lot for a few moments longer nervous about seeing Brielle. She got up the nerve to get out of the car and headed to see Brielle.

When she got to the room Bryson was walking out to go fill the water pitcher for Brielle. "Hey Chantae. Is Bradon ok?"

"Yes, he is at home, he is doing well. Andre is there with him. I wanted to visit with Brielle and see the beautiful babies," she said with a smile. She knew Bryson wanted to make sure she was not coming to upset Brielle.

"The babies are in the nursery they should be back soon. Brielle just got back in the bed. I'm sure she will be happy to see you."

"Good. I have some apologizing to do. I owe you an apology as well Bryson. I know I acted hateful when I was hurting. It's not an excuse and I shouldn't have…"

"Chantae, we family. No need to apologize to me. I'm sure your friend would love to see you. I will give the both of you some time and wait outside the room so you two can talk."

"Thanks Bryson."

"No problem, thanks for taking care of my brother. Go in, the babies will be back shortly." He opened the door for her to enter the room."

"Hello beautiful," Chantae said nervously hoping Brielle would accept her being there.

"Hey Chantae, I was wondering when you were going to make it up here to see me. How is Bradon, and how are you?"

He is doing good. He is at home now. Andre is there with him."

"Well that's good. So glad he is awake and getting back to normal. And you, how are you holding up?" Brielle sincerely wanted to make sure her friend was doing better.

"I am ok. Thanks for asking. Look Brielle, I owe you a huge apology. I am so sorry about how I acted towards you. You are my dearest friend and I love you girl. I know you love me and how I acted towards you was just unacceptable."

"Yeah you were something fierce girlfriend."

"I'm so sorry if I hurt you in any kind of way. I should have been comforting you, us comforting each other. And I missed the babies being born. I wanted to be here with you but that stubborn side made me miss an important and special moment with you my friend."

"Come here and give me some love. You know I forgive you and love you dearly." They embraced in a long tight hug that was well needed for them both. "I surely missed my friend."

"I missed you too. We have so much to catch up on." Chantae was happy knowing that Brielle forgave her. She knew she had a gem of a friend in Brielle and probably didn't deserve her forgiveness but was happy she was so forgiving.

"Yes we do. I can't wait for you to see our beautiful babies."

"Speaking of babies. I know that you and Bryson are taking care of the baby but I also know the baby is really Bradon's."

Brielle looked at her without saying a word for a moment. "I'm not sure I am following you."

"I know you all were trying to protect me. Bradon doesn't know and he doesn't know I know."

"Chantae…"

"No need to say anything. As soon as he is better we will discuss the matter and if he wants to raise his child I will help him raise the baby. I love him and everything that comes with him. Even if it's the child of that evil woman." She laughed a bit causing Brielle to laugh with her.

At that moment, Bryson walked in. "I hear laughter so I assume everything is good in here."

"Hey baby yes everything is good. Everything is just wonderful." Brielle was happy to have her friend back and that she knew about the baby. She felt bad keeping that secret from her friend but was happy she now knew and they were in a good place.

Chantae leaned over to hug her friend, "Can we please keep this between us."

"Of course. I missed my friend so much." She squeezed her tight before letting her go. They heard a knock at the door. "This may be our bundle of joys now." She released Chantae and looked towards the door.

The nurse brought the babies into the room. After washing her hands, Chantae picked up one baby and Bryson handed the other baby to Brielle. Moments later Brielle's mother, father and her other children walked into the room. Everyone was loving on

224 | Donna Christopher

the new babies and Bryson and Brielle couldn't be happier. Chantae looked over at Brielle winked her eye and smiled. Things were finally getting back to normal.

Chapter 39
Why did I give up my baby
February 9

Jewel was due to be released from jail soon and had a couple more therapy sessions to attend as part of her release. Therapy was helping her to uncover her past and the hurt she endured as a child that led her into the trouble she endured as an adult.

"Last time we met Jewel you were telling me about an uncle who left you when something bad happened to you. Can you elaborate more on what happened that day?" Her therapist had a calm soft tone. She really wanted to help Jewel uncover her pain and deal with her illness in a healthy way.

"I don't know why I even brought that up. That was so long ago and I have moved passed that."

"Jewel, you were very emotional last time we talked. You mention that day briefly but I can tell that what you have been experiencing in your adult life has something to do with your childhood. Often times people ignore what happens to them at a young age not realizing how it can hurt them as an adult."

"I don't see how that has anything to do with me being in jail and away from my daughter? I lost my man over this. I suppose to be living in that mansion with my man and our baby. I should be his wife now. But no, I ran a car through his building and ended up in jail instead of out fighting to get him back."

"Jewel, you are aware that Bryson has moved on. He has since married and having a baby with his wife."

"I know. She is having twins. It might not even be his babies. I could have had a fighting chance if I was out of this place. My life is so messed up. All because I couldn't keep my damn legs closed. If I would have kept my legs closed all those years ago maybe I would be a different person now."

"See how you always reflect back to your past? How old were you Jewel when you lost your virginity?"

"What does that matter? I don't want to think about that time of my life?"

"Why not? Is it a painful memory? Is it an exciting memory?

Jewel was quiet thinking about her past. She tried not to think about her childhood and when her innocence was taken from her. The chain of bad events that started to happen to her flooded her mind and tears flooded her eyes.

"Jewel, I know bringing up past memories can be an emotional experience but I do believe that your past has everything to do with your sexual addiction and the anger that you hold on to."

Jewel had her head down in the palm of her hands in between her legs crying uncontrollably. "My uncle, he hurt me as a child. He left me in a room where these men, they were supposed to be his friends and they raped me. They raped me and hurt me. They drugged me, made me have these uncontrollable orgasms and it felt good but it was wrong, all wrong. They hurt me. It felt good but it hurt all at the same time. That orgasm feeling grew into a constant craving. I crave that feeling at all times. That day, that feeling, something happened to me inside that wouldn't go away. They really hurt me. And I wanted to hurt them back. Hurt them and every other man for what they did to me that day. I lost my daddy, my innocence and my life wasn't the same after that day. I was only fourteen years old." She held her head down once again realizing that her past is the reason her adult life was filled with her sexual addiction and anger.

"How did you lose your father Jewel?"

"He tried to murder the man who was responsible for those men hurting me. He went to jail for attempted murder. But when he left he left me out there all alone and my uncle..."

"What happened with your uncle Jewel? Did he continue to hurt you?"

"I can't do this." Jewel started shaking her head. She didn't want to talk about her past anymore.

"We can change the subject for now. Talking about the source of your pain is therapy in its self. It is the starting point to healing. I am glad that you shared what you shared with me. I want to try some methods to help you cope with what happened to you and overcome the sexual addiction."

"Ever since I was raped in jail, the urges haven't been the same as they were. I still want to have sex because I like it but it feels different now. It's like the rape did something."

"Sometimes a traumatic event, the same traumatic event that caused your addiction, can cause the start of a reverse effect and start your healing. Now I am not saying it will heal you but it does have some effect. Let's end our session for today and pick back up when we meet again. At that time we can discuss a treatment plan for you."

"Thank you for trying to make me better. I do want to get better."

"Jewel when you want to be better the healing process becomes easier. Still hard work and it won't happen overnight but it's a step in the right direction.

Jewel was sincerely wanting to be a better person for herself and to hopefully one day be a good mother to her daughter. Becoming a mother unexpectedly and losing everything you had that was good in your life is a wakeup call. Jewel has a choice to move forward leaving her past behind her or drown in her own misery. Her heart was telling her to move forward.

Chapter 40
Raising our baby
February 9

Chantae was taking care of Bradon, she developed a routine since he been home from the hospital. Helping him shower, fixing him breakfast, giving him his medicine, checking and cleaning area around his wounds if needed and even trying to please him sexually without causing strain to any of his stitches. She loved her man even more now than ever. The thought of losing him hurt her to her core so much that she vowed to overlook the little things and enjoy every moment she has been given back with Bradon.

"Good morning baby. How are you feeling?" Chantae started rubbing Bradon's chest gently.

"I'm sore and I feel like I have been shot. I tried to not take the pain medicine last night and I am paying for it this morning."

"Babe why did you do that? The Doctor said not to miss a dose for at least the first week."

"I know. I don't want to become dependent on those pills. Hell, they make me feel like I can run a marathon. Can you get me one now please?"

"I will be right back." She left the room to get him some water and his pills. "Here take this. Here are your other pills."

"Thanks Chantae for everything. I am so use to mom doing everything for me when I'm sick you know. It feels good to have you here by my side. You have not complained once and I can feel your love."

"I do love you. I can never replace momma of course but I can take care of you too. In more ways than she can." Chantae smiled winking at Bradon.

He smiled looking at her walk towards the bathroom. "Yes you can," he said. When she walked into the bathroom he winced in pain not wanting her to know how much pain he was in. The quickie they had the night before may have hurt him more than the pleasure. He should have waited as directed by the doctor. The pain pills couldn't start working quick enough.

"Babe you are in a lot of pain. Let me check your bandages."

"I will be alright. This pain medicine will kick in soon."

"Your bandage feels wet. Maybe you need to go to the doctor just to check things out."

"No I don't feel that bad babe. This medicine will kick in soon and I will be just fine."

"Ok. But if you are feeling more pain and your bandage starts…"

"Baby I am fine. Trust me. I am ok." Bradon grabbed Chantae by the hand pulling her closer to him. He kissed her lips. "Calm down sweetheart. I am fine."

"And you are not getting any either, not until you are completely healed." She pushed off his chest on the opposite side of his wound and he winced from the pain. That's it babe I am calling your mom. If she says you need to go to the doctor then you will go."

"I'm fine babe I promise. I should have just taken the pain pill last not. It's not in my system yet so I'm feeling everything. I was shot baby. My body needs to heal and I need to keep the pain pills in my system until I do. But you can call my momma. Ask her to come visit. I know she been helping with the baby."

Chantae was on the phone calling his mom before he could finish talking. She knew that he would listen to whatever his mom told him to do. "Your mom is coming over. She is bringing the kids with her."

"Brielle's kids? It will be good to see them."

"And the baby." She looked at Bradon knowing she knew something she should share with him.

His facial expression changed. "Oh ok." He remembered the test he took and became nervous to discover the results.

"Baby you know I love you right?"

"Of course I do Chantae."

"I have to tell you something but I don't want you to get upset. I don't even know if I should be telling you right now."

"Just tell me. You can't say you have to tell me something and then don't tell me that's more stressful than telling me."

She took a deep breath. "Andre told me the baby might be yours that Bryson may have paid for the test to be switched. But I don't care. I still love you regardless and I still want us to be together and happy even if that means raising a baby. I love you and I love everything that comes with you. Even if it's a baby that I didn't give birth too. And if it is your baby, maybe we should raise your child together. I mean Brielle has twins now so I am sure we would be helping her out as well." Chantae was rambling nervously fast and nonstop.

"Andre told me he mentioned something like that to you. I was wondering how long it would take for you to mention something to me."

"I didn't want to stress you out or cause anything to happen to you that would make me lose you. You are my everything Bradon. I love you!"

"I love you too. I figured my brother would pull something like that and I already had a test done without anyone knowing. I bought one of the home test and swabbed the baby one day I was there and myself. The test takes about two weeks. So between me and you I should have the results in a few days. Sorry I didn't tell you I just needed to be sure for myself."

"Ok that's good. So, we will know in a few days and we can take it from there. And no matter what, I will be right here by your side." Chantae reassured him she was not going anywhere kissing him on his lips.

"Chantae I love you so much. Thank you!"

"Baby I am happy we are together. God blessed us with a second chance and whatever that brings we will deal with that together. I love you forever!"

"I love you forever Chantae."

Bradon's pain decreased after taking the pain medicine. His mother and the children came over. The pain pills kicked in and he felt much better to entertain his company. His mother checked his bandages, changed the one that was wet and decided he was okay for now. He was able to enjoy the children and even hold the baby. If the baby was his he needed to get to know her and she needed to know who he was. As soon as he found out the true results and was well enough he planned to ask Chantae to marry him and bring his child home to raise as his own.

Chapter 41
Valentine Love
February 11

Isaiah was walking from his car to meet Vanessa for their first official date. He saw Melissa walking with another man towards the same restaurant. She looked back at him smirking as she was all over her new man. Vanessa saw what was happening and put two and two together. She walked quickly over to Isaiah wrapping her arms around his neck saying, "Hey baby there you are. I have missed you so much. This morning was so amazing I couldn't wait to be back in your arms." She wrapped her arms around his neck tighter locking her lips with his.

He picked her up kissing her back. He didn't know what she was talking about but figured she was being the amazing woman she was and trying to make Melissa jealous. Whatever the reason, he was not about to ruin a perfect kiss with the girl of his dreams. Smiling, he placed her on her feet and said, "You are a great kisser."

"So are you darling. I saw your girl trying to make you jealous, thought I come save you."

"Save me huh."

"Although that guy has nothing on you babe. Her loss, my gain." She was smiling from ear to ear reaching for his arm to walk into the restaurant together. She looked over at Melissa and her date upset that she was paying attention to another man.

"Shall we?" Isaiah said escorting her into the restaurant. Their reservation allowed them to be seated immediately.

Vanessa sat across from Isaiah. She wanted to be able to look him in his eyes as they talked about where they wanted to go with their relationship. "Sorry I was so forward just then. I saw that girl smiling hanging on the arm of another man looking at you and I knew she was trying to make you jealous. So, I thought I would give her a taste of her own medicine."

"Alright Dr. But, did you mean that kiss like I took it?"

She smiled trying to hide the fact that he made her blush so easily. He wasn't her best friends little brother any more. Now he was a grown man, sexy and just her type. "Isaiah, the kiss was real. I would have kissed you when we were kids but you know back then I wasn't into boys. I was the shy girl you know."

"What about now? Are you still shy?"

"Not really."

"Do you have a special someone in your life? I mean, I might as well ask before we go any further, just to be sure."

"No, there is no one special. That's where the shyness comes in I guess. And the stubbornness. Now that I think about it, I never really allow men to get close enough."

Isaiah looked at her smiling, "Is that why you wouldn't let me pick you up? Insisting we meet here?"

"Well, if this didn't go well I figured it would be easier to leave separately and not together. You know, no pressure."

"I am a no pressure guy. But you also know I like you. More so love you and I have since the beginning. Even if we didn't end up together that wouldn't change."

"You are too sweet. I know how you feel and that makes it easier for me to be comfortable with you."

The waitress walked up to take their order. They ordered quickly reacting to one another as if they had been married and in love forever.

"Do I have a chance with the beautiful Vanessa Carols?"

"It depends on what your intentions are with me?"

"Girl if I could marry you today and spend forever with you I would but whatever you give me is what I will take until you give me more. You lead. If I move too fast you tell me."

"I can lead?"

"If you want? If I lead it will be like we have always been together. No holding back."

"I think your ex is heading this way."

"She has a date why is she coming over here?" He turned to look in her direction. "And he looks pissed."

Just then Vanessa got up to join Isaiah on his side of the table. "Baby you shouldn't have. Yes, yes, yes I love you too!"

"You are a great actress." Isaiah kissed her lips grabbing her up in his arms.

"I'm not acting Isaiah and yes, I want you to lead."

He kissed her passionately for what seemed like forever. He couldn't believe that he was kissing his childhood crush. He would make sure to treat her like the Queen she was. They could hear Melissa screaming, arguing with her date. They came up for air looking in her direction as she stormed off mad. Her date went in the other direction.

"We have pissed her off." Vanessa said.

He ran his hands across Vanessa face smiling down at her. "I can't believe my dreams are coming true with the one and only Vanessa Carols."

"You want me to pinch you? Wake you up?" She joked.

"Never wake me up. If this is a dream I want to stay asleep forever." He kissed her lips and pulled her close to him. "I wonder what Brielle is going to say when she finds out?"

"Well I kind of mentioned it already to her the day she was having headaches."

"Wait, you asked her permission?"

"Kind of, in so many words. You know she was my best friend as a child. Got me through a lot. After my dad found the picture of me and you and her with your hand on my hip he freaked out. He said it was too close of an encounter with a boy. He caught me looking at the picture smiling and he told me he knew I liked that boy. He thought I was using Brielle to be with you."

"That's why you had to leave so sudden?"

"Yep. He sent me away. He was for sure I was going to be a doctor. He didn't want anything distracting me, especially not a peanut head boy, his words." She smiled.

Isaiah laughed "Peanut head. Yes, your father was real protective over you and I don't blame him. I will be protective over my daughter too when I have one. But look at you, you turned out great don't you think?"

"Well I knew I wanted to be a doctor. Even if he wasn't as strict as he was. I love my dad dearly but wish he would have allowed me to live a little."

"Maybe that was all in God's plans for you, to get you to this point. I mean if we would have fooled around then who is to say we would be all cuddled up about to get married now."

Vanessa raised up looking him in his eyes. "Married? We just skipping the dating part and getting straight to the wedding?"

"I mean if you want too. It's cool with me." Isaiah was comfortable with Vanessa. He knew her well. He fell in love with her as a kid. When she moved away he would always ask his sister about her until he was able to follow her career. He knew that if she said yes, he would definitely marry her.

"How about we start with dating. I mean I got to make sure you not a peanut head little boy like my father said. He does have to approve of my man before I could even think about marrying him." She was blushing ear to ear.

"So, I'm your man? Your words." Isaiah smiled.

"Do you want to be my man?"

"Vanessa?"

"Yes Isaiah?"

"Will you be my girl?"

"If that means exclusively then yes I will be your girl."

"Exclusively! I'm not sharing you with anyone woman."

"Neither will I. Not sharing you with anyone!"

Isaiah wrapped his arms around her tightly squeezing, kissing her lips. She wrapped her arms around his neck as their tongues danced entangled together as they sealed the commitment of being in an exclusive relationship. They were completely engaged in one another until they were interrupted by their waitress.

"Excuse me," she said clearing her throat. "Your food is ready." The waitress herself was blushing watching the two lovebirds. "Didn't mean to interrupt you two. I love seeing true genuine black love."

"Thank you," Isaiah said. The waitress walked away and he turned to Vanessa grabbing her hands, shall we pray.

When they started eating, Vanessa continued their conversation asking, "So you said you would be protective over your daughter when you have one, how many kids do you plan to have?"

Isaiah stuffing his face turned to her and said, "When you become my wife, as many as you will give me."

Vanessa blushed and continued eating with her new man. Isaiah was now in a meaningful relationship with the love of his life. God's timing was perfect for them both.

Chapter 42
Charles Churchwell
February 12

"Amelia, please just hear me out." Charles was not giving up on his family but decided to try a different strategy. "I just want to see the kids. I miss them."

"Charles if you try anything funny I swear to you…"

"I'm not I promise. Can you just please meet me."

"We can meet at the park close to your house. I will be there with the kids at three."

"Ameila, the house is still your house too."

"Whatever Charles. You asked for the house in the divorce settlement and you got it. The house belongs to you.

"I'm sorry 'Meila. You can have the house if you want. I can leave and you and the kids can move in. Let me make it up to you. I'm really sorry for everything Ameila. I messed up bad. I ruined our family but if you move in and…"

"Charles what don't you understand? There is no us! That home stop being my home, our home when you brought all your whores into our bed. You think for a second I would entertain the thought of being back with a man who cheated on me and oh let's not forget the fact that you hit me, then threw me and our children out in the front yard. Such drastic measures just to be with your whores who don't even give a damn about you. Where are your whores now? Huh?" Ameila had frustration and hurt in her voice.

"I don't have anyone Ameila. Everyone left." The sadness in his voice was enough to bring tears. He was choked up on his words and could hear the sigh in Ameila's voice. "I will see you all this evening when you bring the kids. I promise to be on my best behavior."

"I will see you at three Charles." Ameila was over his begging to be back with her. She felt bad for him having no one but would only bend with the kids. She had no plans to go back to him.

"Thanks Ameila, see you then."

After ending the call Charles started thinking of a new plan to try and win his ex-wife back. He took off his shirt, looked in the mirror then dropped to the floor and started doing pushups. "Twenty-five... forty-seven... sixty-three... eighty-two... one hundred." He grunted out the numbers as he completed one hundred pushups. He headed to the shower to freshen up and get ready for his date with the kids, hoping Ameila would stay. He picked out some dark blue ripped jeans and a short sleeve shirt to show off his built arms. He knew Ameila liked muscular built arms. His plan was to smell good and look good in hopes of stirring up memories.

When Charles arrived at the park he watched as mothers played with their kids and fathers played football with their sons, some playing basketball. He used to be a great father and missed his kids. His life was turned upside down when the greed of money and the fast life took over. He wanted to make up for neglecting his family. He hoped to win his wife back, but even if he doesn't he planned to be a great father to his children again. He had a lot of making up to do.

He saw a black Escalade pull up and nervously started fidgeting. He knew it had to be Ameila and the kids. "She is living the good life now. Damn, I fucked up," he said out loud to himself. He watched as the driver got out of the car to open the door for Ameila and the kids. "I thought drivers had to wear suits. This nigga got on a t-shirt and some jeans. Damn, she is beautiful." He watched as Ameila stepped out of the car with the assistance of her driver's hand extended to her. Then his arm was around her back and she tiptoed up to his awaiting kiss. "What the fuck? That's the guy from the damn interview. Ah hell naw." Charles was mad and he knew once he saw Kenneth that Ameila was never coming back to him.

"Hi, you must be Charles." An older lady with a briefcase approached Charles distracting him temporary from Ameila.

"Yes, and who are you?" he questioned.

"I am Amanda, your children's caseworker appointed by the courts to supervise your first few visits with your children. Supervised visitation was court ordered in your divorce. Do you

238 | Donna Christopher

remember signing off on that? I have a copy for you here." She reached in her bag to pull out the paperwork for him.

"I actually forgot about that. So you will be here for the entire visit?" Charles asked stunned. His plans were ruined and the situation was not getting any better.

"Yes sir. First visit is an hour and it increases with each visit. After I review my reports with a judge he will then determine if the visits continue or stop."

Charles was looking at Ameila and his children. His perfect family was in the hands of another man. He now felt defeated. "Thanks," he said to the lady and started walking towards his children.

"Daddy, daddy..." his son yelled as he ran towards his father. He picked him up swinging him around.

"I have missed you so much."

"I miss you too daddy. You been gone too long. We live in a new house now daddy. When you coming to our new house?" His son was full of questions.

"We will see about that son. You and your sister have gotten so big." He placed his son down on the ground and took his daughter from Ameila's arms when she walked up to him. He took his daughter and looked up into her eyes. For a moment, he thought she still felt something for him. "You look beautiful."

"Same as I always have. I won't be too far. I'll be back in an hour to pick up the kids."

"I see you have a new boyfriend. What is he your boss?"

"That's none of your business. I will be back in an hour," she said in a sassy happy tone turning to walk back to Kenneth.

"Tell mommy bye-bye," he said to the kids. He watched as Ameila walked away from him looking up to see Kenneth looking back at him with a smirk on his face as he embraced Ameila. He felt a sharp pain in his chest, the feeling of heart break.

Charles focused on the children and enjoyed his supervised visit. He didn't want to jeopardize his visitation by getting a bad report so he fixed his face and forced a happy smile. He played with the kids and made them smile. Mending the pieces of his marriage may not happen as he planned but he would start with their children and hold on to hope.

Chapter 43
Jewel's baby
February 12

Jewel was released early Friday morning. Her father was there waiting to pick her up. "Hey daddy. Thank you for picking me up." She wrapped her arms tight around his neck holding on seconds longer.

"How you feeling baby girl? You don't even look like you had a baby a month ago."

"I feel good daddy. I started doing sit-ups a couple weeks ago. Even though I wasn't released by the doctor yet."

"Well you look good. Just make sure you are taking care of yourself."

"I am daddy."

Her father started the car and pulled off into the midnight quiet. There were no cars on the street in sight. "I know you want to see your baby…"

"Yes, I do. Where is she daddy?"

"Bryson still has her but his mom is taking her to a doctor appointment tomorrow and she invited me to come if you want to take my place."

"Of course yes. Do you mean tomorrow as in today? Like when normal people wake up?" Jewel was nervous about seeing her daughter and Bryson.

"Well yeah today. The appointment is at ten. We can get some rest before its time. Mrs. Mathews will meet us there."

"Wait Bryson won't be there? Someone else is caring for my baby besides him?" Jewel was upset that another woman was caring for her child. Her voice was high pitched and filled with anger.

"No, Bryson won't be there just his mom. She is helping Bryson and his wife care for the baby." Her father glanced over at Jewel. "Wait, you were upset because you thought I was referring to Bryson's wife?"

"I don't like the thought of another woman raising my baby. I want my baby back so I can raise her myself."

"Jewel, you know Bryson has full custody of the baby. And his wife is not going anywhere."

"I know daddy." Jewel's voice was low and sad.

"We will see the baby tomorrow and then you can focus on getting your life back on track. Once you do I will help you get custody back, or at least joint custody."

"I do want my daughter back daddy but I am so scared that I won't be a good mother."

"Nonsense child. It's something about a mother daughter bond that come naturally. Motherhood won't be that bad at all. What you don't know you will figure out and everything else love will take care of. Your mother didn't know how to take care of a baby and she did ok with you and your sisters."

"Yeah before you left daddy. After that well..." she paused for a moment. "You know what happened after that. All my problems started after you left us."

"I am sorry for that baby girl. I truly am."

"I am not trying to make you feel bad daddy. I am dealing with everything from my past and trying to become a better person. I do want us to sit down and talk about the past one day soon, the good, the bad and the ugly. Just not right now."

"When you are ready you let me know. I'm here for you Jewel, no matter what."

"I know that daddy. You have always been even when I tried to close you out."

"You are my precious Jewel and you always will be."

"Thanks daddy. That means a lot to hear you still say that."

"Let's get some rest so we can see that baby in the morning."

They pulled up in front of her father's home. Nothing big and fancy as Jewel was used to with Bryson but it was the home of her father. A safe place where she knew and felt love.

The next morning, they arrived at the doctor's office. Jewel looked up and immediately spotted Bradon. She thought he was Bryson at first until he turned to the side. Her facial expression turned from extremely happy to a subtle smile. She stared at Bradon thinking about Bryson.

Chantae looked at Jewel with her eyes fixed on Bradon. "Babe there is a gorgeous woman looking at you," she said through her teeth and a forced smile on her face.

"Hello Bradon."

Bradon turned to look at Jewel and was not expecting to see her. "What are you doing here?" he said with a confused look on his face.

"Hey son. I was expecting to meet your mother here for the baby doctor appointment." Her father interjected shaking Bradon's hand and stepping in between Jewel and Bradon.

Jewel saw the baby in the car seat sitting in the stroller and walked over to the baby. Chantae had her eyes glued on Jewel still trying to figure out who she was. Jewel reached down pulled the cover back on the baby. She squatted down next to the baby touching her face and holding on to her finger.

"I'm sorry, who are you?" Chantae blurted out.

"Jewel."

"Chantae this is Bryson's ex, Jewel. She is the mother of my niece. My mom wasn't feeling well so while I was there I told her I would bring the baby. She didn't tell you were coming."

"The test came back that Bryson is the father?" Jewel stated more so than asked a question. Knowing all the dirt she did to Bryson she was relieved that the test revealed Bryson as the father. She knew he would get tested. She knew he agreed to take the baby.

"Oh so this is the famous Jewel everyone has been talking about." Chantae stated.

Jewel smirked at Chantae's comment. "How is my darling baby?" She reached in to pick her up.

"Jewel the doctor is ready to see her, hand her to me please." Bradon didn't know what to do. He didn't want Jewel trying to take her.

"Bradon can I join you please? Just let me go back with you please. They took her out of my hands when she was born and I have been waiting to hold her close. Please Bradon."

Bradon looked up at Chantae nodding in agreeance to allow her to join him. "I can wait out here for you Bradon."

"Please Bradon. I can wait here with your lady friend." Jewel's father said.

"Sure. Let's go." He walked behind Jewel into the back room to see the doctor.

"The doctor will be right in," the nurse said.

"Thanks Bradon. How are you? I heard about what happened and glad you are okay."

"I am doing a lot better. You are not plotting to get Bryson back are you? He is happily married now."

"I know that and no. I am trying to change my life around so I can be a mother to my little girl. I know he is married and I am not up to anything."

"He is happily married so I hope not."

"I'm not Bradon. Look I am sorry for what I did to you, really I am. I had a lot of time to think while in jail. I am so sorry."

Bradon felt her sincerity in her voice. "It's cool. Well it wasn't cool what you did but I'm good. Glad you are getting help."

"Thanks Bradon."

Bradon knew if it was a chance the baby could be his instead of Bryson's that be needed to establish a relationship with Jewel.

The doctor walked in the room asking if they were the baby parents. Bradon said yes turned to Jewel and said, "Well I am the uncle and she is her mother."

Jewel smiled glad that he acknowledged her as the mother. She held the baby the entire checkup, bonding and rocking her. Bradon watched as she seemed so natural and hoped that what she said about changing to raise her daughter was true. After the doctor was done he walked over to help Jewel change the baby diaper. She turned with a tear in her eyes telling Bradon, "Thank you for letting me have this moment. In spite of everything I done to you…" Jewel was choked up on her words. "Thank you Bradon."

They finished dressing the baby and headed towards the door. Jewel was so happy. Chantae watched as she placed the baby back in the car seat. Jewel looked up at her and said, "Thank you pretty lady. You take care of that man of yours." Turning to the baby she kissed her forehead. "Momma will see you soon."

From that moment on Jewel vowed to get her self together so she could get custody of her daughter.

Chapter 44
Love Talk
February 14

Since Brielle was a new mommy, Bryson wanted to bring dinner and fun company to her on Valentine's day. He invited other couples to join them for a romantic dinner. The music was playing setting the ambiance of romance, as the cooking staff he hired prepared a feast of appetizers and dinner. Chantae and Bradon were the first to arrive. Bradon joined Bryson in the living room and Chantae joined Brielle in the nursery to tend to the twins before joining everyone for dinner. "Hey darling, you made it. Is Bradon down stairs?"

"Ye...Oh look at these two precious babies." Chantae headed straight to the babies enthralled in their cuteness. She heard Brielle but was side tracked when she saw the babies laying in their bed. "Brielle they have gotten so big since the last time I saw them. That breast feeding is plumping them right on up."

"They eat literally every two hours, keeping me busy." She stood next to Chantae admiring the babies.

"Oh girl yes, Bradon is downstairs. Seeing these two beautiful babies, my mind went blank."

"I heard you met Jewel yesterday," Brielle mentioned in a low voice.

"Girl yes! And she is absolutely beautiful and damn sure didn't look like she was fresh out of jail. She walked in that doctor office like she owned the damn place."

"Yes that's Jewel. I didn't have much of an encounter with her but I did see some sex videos of her and Bryson."

"Shut the front door. You did not," Chantae was shocked but wanted to know more details as Brielle nodded yes. "Were they good videos or boring?" she said joking laughing at her comment.

"They were actually very good videos. The girls sex drive is by far un heard of. She wanted more and more and more."

"Damn. I bet that was hard for you to see, you know, her and Bryson."

"Yeah it was. I was supposed to be looking at childhood videos and ran across the wrong set of videos."

"Oh wow. Were you by yourself?"

"Yes. This house is so big it is easy to find alone time."

"I guess Jewel is trying to be in the baby's life since she is out of jail. Bradon wasn't too happy to see her but he ended up in chill mode seeing her interact with the baby and really wanting to be a mommy."

"Girl, she can be a mommy but I have a feeling she is not done trying to come for my man."

"She did perk up when she first saw Bradon. She thought he was Bryson. But you already know Bryson ain't going nowhere. You the love of his life and that man is staying with you forever."

"I know girl. I still don't want her bringing that drama my way." Just then Brielle looked up to see Vanessa walking in the room. "Hey girl, what are you doing here?" she said hugging Vanessa.

"Well, I was invited. This is a couple's dinner so I came with my new boo." She walked over to the babies. "Oh look how big they are getting. They are too cute," she said touching their little hands.

"Wait who is your boo?" Chantae wanted to know.

"Yes, who is your boo? I think I already know but I want you to tell me." Brielle had a smirk on her face waiting to hear Vanessa's answer.

"His name is Isaiah," she said with a big smile on her face as if she was talking about someone other than Brielle's brother.

"Isaiah as in Brielle's brother Isaiah?" Chantae asked?

"Yeap that's exactly who she is talking about," Brielle said.

"Yes, that's my boo," Vanessa said standing over the babies in their bed.

"You ladies in here discussing me?" Isaiah said walking in the door. Everyone wanted to see the babies while they were there at the home visiting, and he too walked straight towards the babies. He stood behind Vanessa putting his hand around her waist.

Chantae watched the two of them before saying, "Vanessa and Isaiah. Okay I see you. You two look good together. I didn't see it coming but you look good."

"All this love in the air. I just love it!" Chantae said.

"Alright ladies and gentlemen, dinner is almost ready and your presence is needed down stairs. I will take great care of the babies now go on and enjoy yourself," Maria said. Bryson paid her a whole lot of money to stay and help with the kids.

"Okay, I just fed them both and changed their diapers."

"Don't worry. I got them. You all enjoy your dinner. Now go." Maria directed them towards the door.

"Ok, but if you need anything at all you come get me."

"Yes ma'am. Now go." Maria was like family and she loved Brielle and her children. She would do anything for them just as she would for Bryson.

They walked down the stairs towards the living room. Isaiah and Vanessa had their arms wrapped around one another walking and acting like two love birds. Chantae was watching them. She cleared her throat and asked, "Now how long have you two been dating?"

"Feels like forever but just a few days," Isaiah said. His eyes were still fixed on Vanessa. He leaned towards her kissing her lips.

"Yeah it does feel like forever," Vanessa said kissing him once more.

"Damn, you two are all over one another. You sure you staying for dinner?" she laughed.

"Girl they secretly liked each other growing up. This is nothing new for me. They are just acting on their feelings now," Brielle said.

"Wait. I never said anything or did anything when we were kids?" Vanessa replied.

"You didn't have to. You lit up every time he was around. You both did. I was just shocked you didn't start dating then." Brielle revealed to them that she knew then they liked one another. "I didn't want to say anything because you were my friend and he was my brother."

"Well I didn't try to hide it. I was in love the first time I met you. When you came to sleep over the first time I wanted to join the sleep over too just to be next to you. Even if I had to do girly stuff. You had me then and you have me now."

"Ah that is too sweet." Chantae said. "This is going to be a romantic Valentine dinner with all this love around."

They walked in on the guys talking about the upcoming movie premier. Kenneth and Ameila had arrived and the ladies joined her to say hello. As the ladies took their seat they noticed the men huddled up. The music changed and John Legends song 'Spend my life with you' blasted across the radio. The men formed a line and started to dance to the music. They were trying to do a rendition of the dance from the movie "Best Man."

As the song was playing their moves were not all-together. The ladies were laughing and enjoying their efforts. Then Bryson's father said, "Follow my lead," in a whisper to the men. He started two stepping and walked to his wife. "Baby the day I met you was the best day of my life. God showed up and showed out when he gave me you. Through all the good times and bad, I count my blessings and you my darling are my greatest blessing of all times. My true love that I will always cherish and adore."

He stepped back and Brielle's father walked towards his wife. "Girl you are the light in my world, the sun and the moon, the stars and sparkle in my eye. It's all because of you girl. There is no other that could compare or match the love we share, the love you give to me. You are my everything and so much more. I love you sweetheart."

The women were going crazy about the sweet words being said. They were cheering each man on, smiling and enjoying the show.

Kenneth went next speaking to Ameila. "Beauty is your name. Pure bliss is what you bring. From day one, God told me you were special but I didn't know how special until you touched my heart with your beautiful kindness and your love. My heart knew you were the one long before my mind threw in the white flag to surrender to love. A sweet love. Girl you are the one and only love, sent from the heavens above."

All the men were high fiving him on his words. They were now trying to outdo the next.

Isaiah walked up and took Vanessa's hand. "I don't have all that relationship swag talk like all the other cats but what I do have is a genuine love for you. Three days into a committed relationship and I can truly say I love you and mean it with all my heart. You see girl when I was a little boy with buck teeth and nappy hair not even knowing what it meant to be in love, I know I fell in love with you. Your smile, your looks, your feisty attitude and all. But I also fell in love with your heart girl. All those years went by and the love never faded and here we are today girl the two of us and forever is where we are headed together."

"Damn bro, I thought Kenneth was a hard act to follow. And I know Bryson will put us all to shame. Now I got to go after you," Bradon said, but before he could go next Bryson had already took Brielle's hand making Bradon go last.

"Brielle, my darling sweet love. You are a gift wrapped so beautifully and perfect for me. You are a breath of fresh air, my sun, my moon. You are the beating of my heart. I thank God every day for blessing me with what I know is his most valued and precious gift who he created just for me. Brielle Mathews, mother of my children and the apple of my eye, you are my everything and so much more and you are my forever. My heart beats for you, my smiles are because of you and you are loved whole heartedly forever."

Bradon looked at his brother with a look of disbelief. The guys were cheering him on telling him he would be fine. Chantae was looking at him with a smile anticipating what he too would say to her. As the song was ending the sounds of John Legend singing spend my life with you blared through the silence. Bradon looked Chantae in her eyes held on to both of her hands. As the music silenced so did everyone else.

"Chantae. Girl you know I I I I love you." Mimicking the Lenny Williams song 'Cause I love you'. "From that moment I saw your beautiful smiling face and my heart skipped a beat, I knew God sent you for me to find. There you were right in front of me and we instantly came together as one. God never makes a mistake. You changed my life. It's no secret I was wild and out of control but it all stopped instantly when you became a part of me. I didn't know God loved me so much to bless me with one of his angels who is equally yoked with me that I can share her heart, her love, her life, her everything with me. God loves me enough to allow me to love another, to love you whole heartedly to love you forever. I feel all the mushy stuff just like everyone else does here, you are my moon, my stars and my everything as well but what you are not…" he paused. He got down on one knee still holding on to Chantae's hand. Everyone was sighing at the anticipation of what was to come. "You are not my wife and I need that to change right now." He watched as Chantae started fanning herself and tears rolled down her face. He pulled a box out of his pocket opening it to expose a beautiful diamond engagement ring. "Chantae, will you do me the honor of allowing me to love you forever as your husband, will you spend your life with me, will you marry me?"

"Yes, yes, yes." Chantae screamed as he placed the ring on her finger. "I love you Bradon, so very much!" she got down on her knees to be face to face with him, wrapped her arms around his neck and kissed him like a woman in love. As their tongues entangled and danced, they savored the sweet taste and passion they shared. They kissed like they were the only ones in the room until the sounds of everyone around them cheering them on became louder and louder.

They ladies were happy and love was in the air. After the newly engaged couple was celebrated, dinner was served. They shared a perfect Valentine evening with family and friends that were like family surrounded by true genuine love.

Chapter 45
Fellas hanging out
February 20

Saturday morning all the guys gathered at the gym to play basketball and hang out. Their old habits died down a bit with everyone living their lives. After their Valentine night of passion, the guys vowed to hang out more often.

"Bradon man that proposal was nice. I'm sure when you got home your girl showed you a lot of love." Isaiah said.

"Man, nothing new. We always freaky as hell. Another incentive to marry her besides being in love."

"Right right. One day I hope to marry Vanessa."

"Yeah, you two happened real fast. She was your childhood sweetheart right?" Bradon asked.

"Yeah except I wasn't hers. Her father didn't allow her to have a boyfriend."

"For real?"

"Yeah, when he found out she even liked a boy he sent her away. That's why her and Brielle lost touch and so did we. But my love for her never left," Isiah said remembering.

"What y'all young cats talking about?" Kenneth said walking in to join the two in the gym.

"What's up Kenny. Bryson here yet?" Bradon asked.

"Right here brother. What y'all up too?"

"We are talking about Isaiah and Vanessa being so in love after only a few days," Bradon said giving his brother a hand shake.

"Ah yeah, Brielle filled me in on the child hood history of you two. That's some real love right there. I'm happy for you two. Bradon you already know I am proud of you stepping up making an honest woman out of Chantae."

"Thanks bro! Chantae is already planning the wedding," he said to Bryson. He looked up to see his boy walking in the door. "What up Andre. My man." He walked up to greet his friend.

"What up man I figured I better come hang out with my friend now before you tie the knot," Andre said shaking Bradon hand giving him love.

"Ah I'm still going to be the same man you know."

"What up Kenny." Andre spoke to him and to the other men. "Kenny, I hear you all in love too. Did she ever get a divorce?"

"Yes and yes. In love and she did get a divorce and now the man trying to get her back."

"Get the fuck out of here! That's how them no good nigga's do," Andre said. "But I'm happy for you!"

"Thanks man! I appreciate that."

All the men were now there playing ball. Bryson set the first game out since it was five men. As he sat on the floor watching a game a familiar face walked up to him.

"Bryson? Bryson Mathews?" the young lady asked.

"Yes that's me. You are the doctor who performed testing for me and my brother."

"Yes sir. I thought that was you. I went to my car to retrieve this paper work I have been holding on to trying to figure out the best way to get it to you."

Bryson stood to his feet and took the letter from the lady. "Oh yeah. Did I need to sign something? My accountant did say the check has not cleared, was something wrong."

"No, nothing was wrong. I was not there to talk with you when you returned for your results but..." She paused briefly. I cannot take your money even if I could help you I shouldn't have even considered taking your money. It goes against the oath I took as a doctor and my morals. This has bothered me since I last spoke with you and now that I see you face to face I need to make this right," the doctor said.

"What are you saying?" Bryson spoke in a quiet voice, "You cannot tell my brother he is the father." He glanced over at Bradon and the guys who were now concentrated on Bryson seeming upset.

"See that's the thing..." she started too say.

"Bryson man you ok?" Kenneth asked.

"What's up bro? What's going on?" Bradon asked.

"Sir, can we talk somewhere in private?" The doctor asked.

"No, Bryson is this about you paying to switch the test because I already know about that. Just tell me the truth. Am I the father of Jewels baby?" he attempted to say in a hushed tone to Bryson but everyone standing there could here.

Bryson looked him in his eyes and could feel his readiness for the truth. "Just speak freely in front of us all."

"Well are you sure?" she asked.

"Yes. I was trying to protect my brother but seeing as how he already knows, spill it. What's up? What are the true results?"

"Ok well. Neither one of you are the father. The test results are here in this envelope and your check. However, the baby is related to you. Another brother or perhaps a father."

"Daddy? Ah hell naw. I know Jewel didn't stoop that low. Ah naw not my daddy!" Bradon said walking away.

"At least you are not the father." Andre said.

Bradon walked away and retrieved his phone. He checked his email to reveal the exact results from the test he took, he was not the father of Jewels baby. Exciting news for him but devastating at the same time.

Bryson was still having a conversation with the doctor trying to understand her findings. "Are you sure about these test results?"

"Bryson! She is not lying. I took a home test myself and I am looking at the same results."

Everyone turned and looked at Bradon taking his phone to see the results in his email for themselves.

"So if we are not the father who the hell is the father that could be related to us?" Bryson looked Bradon in the eyes.

"Ah hell naw. This keeps getting worse" Kenneth said.

"It can't be daddy. Ah hell she got to daddy. Damn," Bradon said looking at Bryson.

"Don't worry I will discuss with dad and get to the bottom of this. Thank you for telling us," Bryson said to the doctor.

They all watched as she walked away. The men leaned against the wall, their basketball game now over at the hearing of this news. As everyone was deep in thought Bryson finally broke the silence and said, "How in the hell am I going to ask my father if he slept with my ex?"

"Good luck with that my friend!" Kenneth said.

Chapter 46
Release preparations
February 22

Monday morning bright and early Bryson, Kenneth and Ameila were at the office to meet about the upcoming Movie Premiere. Bryson was still bothered by the news he received from the doctor at the gym. Ameila could tell something was wrong but didn't know what. She didn't want to pry but considered him family and wanted to help if she could.

"Bryson, is everything ok?"

"Yes Ameila. I'm ok. Just have some things on my mind."

"Ok well if you need anything you know I am here for you even if you just want to talk," she said with a reassuring smile on her face.

"Thanks, I appreciate that but really I am fine."

"Okay if you say so." She dismissed the conversation and went back to discussing the movie premiere. "Well, I saw portions of the movie and I am so excited for everyone to see the premiere Thursday night. We have the guest list confirmed and it will be a full house."

"Did we get all the news stations on the list to show up?" Bryson asked.

"Yes, we confirmed and have everyone on the list showing up. Interviews will be conducted as people are entering the premiere to hear what they are expecting from the movie and when they are leaving to get their thoughts of the movie afterwards. This should boost the attendance for opening night."

"That's the plan we are hoping happens," Bryson said.

"Everything will be great. We have worked long hours and hard to make this movie just as good if not better than the first." Kenneth said.

"I must say they got some very good footage of everyone this time around. Mostly because they didn't have to hide the camera crew I'm guessing but this movie is full of the passion and love from everyone. It's going to be a hit."

"Good. That's what I want to hear. I can't wait to see it in its entirety Thursday. We have a lot of important people coming so make sure we have increased security…" Bryson started to say.

"Brys, I got this. Trust me. Everything has been taken care. We do need to confirm a few things for the after party at the club." Kenneth said.

"I'm going to step out for a second let you two talk about that. I will be right back."

The two men watched as Ameila left the office before either of them said a word.

"Brys man what's going on? Is it business or is what got you down about your father?" Kenneth asked. He couldn't ask in front of Ameila because he didn't want to discuss Bryson's business in front of anyone else.

"It's my father."

"Well, did you talk to him about it yet?"

"No not yet."

"Why not Brys? You must talk to him and you need to do it before Thursday. I need you to have your head right when we are talking to all those people and in front of the news cameras man."

"I know but I can't just walk up to my dad and say 'hey dad did you smash my ex? Turns out the paternity test was negative for me and Bradon but the baby is related so that leaves you.'"

"Well, okay no. Don't say it that way but you could have a conversation and explain to him what the doctor said and then maybe he will confess."

"Easier said than done. I wish I could ask my mom for advice."

"No, no, no. that could never happen in this situation." Kenneth said in a panic.

"I'm not doing that. I could never hurt my mom that way."

"You still need to talk to your dad man and do it soon."

"Yeah I will. I can't believe that shit man. How the hell could she stoop that low. How the hell can my pops keep that from me?"

"You don't even know if he slept with her. Damn, that sounds bad saying it."

"The lady said it was a brother or could be a father. If it's not me and Bradon it must be my dad. No one else has been around and besides there is no one else left for it to be."

"Well you got to talk to your dad."

"I will soon. That bitch has made me look like a fool."

"Good thing she is out of the picture."

"Exactly! Let's finish the movie preparations."

"Yeah let's do that. Get your mind off that situation."

The men worked in silence for a moment until Amelia returned to the conference room so they could finish up their meeting preparing for the movie premiere.

Chapter 47
Movie Premiere Night
February 25

Today was the greatly anticipated movie premiere day. Cameras and news stations were lined up everywhere waiting to take pictures and do interviews. Bryson, Brielle and their entire family and friends were arriving to have their pictures taken on the red carpet. He had celebrities arriving as his VIP guest and the media was going crazy taking pictures trying to get to them for exclusive interviews. Everyone was amazed but not surprised at all the support Bryson was receiving. This time the movie was not all about Bryson but included his family and friend's stories and how they were a big part of their circle of love.

"Wow babe. I knew there would be camera's here but this is more than I expected," Brielle said to Bryson as they pulled up in their limo.

"Are you up for this? I can have the driver take you home and come right after the movie is done."

"Baby no. I am with you all the way. I'm ready."

"Hold on to me the entire time. This crowd is thick."

Bryson and Brielle exited the limo and the cameras were flashing away. Brielle held on to Bryson tight. She had on a flowing red evening gown that sparkled as she moved. Her hair was flowing down her back. Her breasts were sitting high and full showing just enough cleavage. Her stomach was snatched in her girdle appearing flat in her dress as if she didn't just have a baby. She looked amazing. Bryson had on a black tuxedo with a red tie to match Brielle's dress. They were picture ready and beautiful for the cameras.

Kenneth and Ameila arrived moments later. Ameila had on a royal blue beautiful evening gown. Her hair was in a sexy updo exposing her neck that was decorated with a diamond necklace Kenneth bought for her. She was a star just as the rest of them. She was the author of both books to the first and second movie. Her very own story that was reflected when she was homeless and now living the lavish life from her blessing the day Bryson came into her life touched millions. Fans instantly fell in love with Ameila.

Bradon and Chantae arrived right after. Knowing that Bradon was shot and had to fight for his life was also another major storyline. Chantae had on a white dress that fit her curves and came up to her neckline. The long elegant beaded dress was her design. She was beautiful from her hair, makeup, down to her shoes. Bradon also had on a suit that she created as well. They were the best dress of the evening.

Everyone was there. After all meet and greets, pictures and interviews were done, Bryson and Kenneth said a few words before the movie started.

You could hear laughter during the movie. Some ahh moments and even some sniffles. All the emotions that were expected for people to have as they watched the movie happened at some point.

At the end of the movie everyone was screaming and shouting praise of greatness giving Bryson, Kenneth and the entire cast a standing ovation. Ameila had tears of appreciation rolling down her cheeks. Kenneth picked her up swinging her around and as he placed her to her feet he kissed her lips. He looked up and saw Charles standing in the back looking directly at them. Bryson held on to Brielle and Bradon held on to Chantae. Isaiah and Vanessa joined them as well as Andre and their parents. Everyone was happy and the love for them and one another was all around them.

As everyone was breaking away Bryson looked towards the back of the room when Brielle whispered in his ear, "That's the guy from the hospital that I saw outside Bradon's room that I was telling you about. Who is he? He looks just like you and Bradon." Bryson was clueless as to who he was but could see the strong resemblance. He caught the eye of the young man and watched as his father approached him furious at the sight of him.

"I am not sure but I am going to find out," he said to Brielle. People were all around them shaking their hands and talking to them. Bryson decided to excuse himself and head towards them. He saw his father walking away from the man after pointing towards the door for him to leave. The guy started walking through the crowd towards the door. Bryson stopped him before he reached the exit. Grabbing him by the arm to stop him Bryson was face to face with him looking in his eyes. "Who are you?" he asked him.

The young man looked back at Bryson's father. Bryson turned in the direction he was looking and saw his dad embracing his mother looking over at them with a disturbed look on his face. The man replied, "I better go."

"No. don't let my father intimidate you. Look at me." Bryson paused looking at the young man. The resemblance was so strong that Bryson knew he had to be related but didn't understand how. "Who are you?" he asked again.

"I came by your house. I'm sorry. Some lady answered the phone and told me it was okay for me to come by. So I did. She gave me the address and told me a time to come. You weren't there but she invited me in anyways. I shouldn't have come. I am so sorry. I didn't know she was your fiancée. I found your number in my father's things and wanted to meet you." He was rambling on as a nervous exposed man asking for forgiveness.

Bryson had a knot in his throat now assuming the worse. A dark secret that his father never intended to be exposed was now coming to light. "Who is your father?" he asked again.

The young man looked back at Bryson's dad again. "He is. We are brothers. You, me and Bradon. He is my father too. My name is Byron Mathews."

Bryson looked over at his dad. He was helping his mother with her shall as they prepared to leave. He knew he was trying to protect his mom from finding out this way. But Bryson would make sure he faced him and answered all the questions racing through his mind. "Well, brother. Here take my cell number and call me tomorrow. We can do lunch, sit down and talk, catch up on life."

"Thank you. I would like that," his newly found out about brother said looking down at the card.

Bryson's mind started racing and everything about his life started to make sense. His father's road trips when he didn't come home at night. His mom telling him stories about how things were not always good at home but her prayers were consistent and saved their family. And now a brother that could possibly be the father of his ex's baby. He looked at his brother's happy face and asked, "Hey when you came by my home the woman that answered the door…" He paused seeing his brother's face turn sad. "Never mind it doesn't matter. We will talk later. How old are you anyways?"

"I am nineteen first year in college."

"I see. Congrats on college that makes me proud."

"Thank you. That means a lot."

"Well I have a crowd to host so call me tomorrow and we can meet and talk ok."

"Yes sir." He looked at Bryson's smile. "I mean ok, talk to you tomorrow."

"That's better brother."

Byron took Bryson off guard and hugged him quickly letting go. "Talk to you tomorrow," he said as he walked away.

Just as he walked away Kenneth walked up to Bryson. "Who was that Brys?" he asked.

"That my friend is a dark secret of my father's that he has some explaining to do. That young man is my brother." He stood watching as his brother walked out the door of the movie theatre.

"Oh wow," he thought for a moment. "Wait a minute, could he be?"

"Yeap, he could be one of Jewel's victims and the father of her child."

"Damn. You okay?"

"Actually, I am ok. Have a strong feeling he is the father. I rather it be him than my father. I just went from having one image of my father to now another," he said watching his father walk out the door with his arm around his mom.

"That's a hard pill to swallow." Kenneth looked up to see what Bryson was looking at, his father leaving. Distracting him he said, "You coming to the after party?"

"I'm going to show my face but I have to talk to my father before he leaves to head home."

"Cool. You know I will hold it down for the both of us if you want to skip it all together."

Bryson watched as Brielle headed towards him. Her smile making him smile. "I want to show off the star of my life. She is stunning in that beautiful red gown and I want to make sure she feels every bit of special and seen tonight. Having twins is a hard job and she deserves to have her moment you know."

"You are a good man Brys. A great friend too but a damn good man."

"There you are handsome. I thought I was going to have to go party alone," she said leaning in for his kiss.

"Never that my darling. You ready to head to the after party?"

"Yes if you are."

"You ready Kenny?" Bryson asked.

"Yes. Let me grab Ameila and I will meet you at the limo."

"Sounds great. Grab Bradon and Isaiah if you see them as well."

"Aight see y'all in a moment." As Kenneth headed towards Ameila he walked right into Charles. "What the hell are you doing here?"

"Look I don't want any trouble. I just wanted to see the great job Ameila did. She has always been great at what she does with her writing. With everything actually."

"Okay well the movie is over. What, you waiting on an autograph or something?" Kenneth was not being nice and would rather have him thrown out. He would do it himself if he didn't have to maintain an image.

"Look. I'm leaving. I just wanted to apologize and tell you congratulations. I surrender. She is happy and she deserves happiness. You have a real true gem, a precious gift. Just make sure…" he paused seeing Kenneth's face turn to look at him with anger in his eyes. "I know she will be well taken care of. Congrats man." Charles turned to walk away. He left after saying his peace to Kenneth. He wanted him to know he wouldn't be bothering Ameila anymore trying to get his family back. He knew that they were now Kenneth's family.

Kenneth gathered the others and they joined Bryson and Brielle in the limo to head to the after party. They were celebrities and treated as such.

As they were partying and toasting to the beginning of their success Bryson saw his father standing in the crowd looking at him motioning for him to join him. He left his friends and followed his father into a back room. "Dad. Glad you came."

"Let me start. I know you spoke to the young man at the theatre…"

"You mean my brother?" Bryson said with anger in his voice.

"Yes, he is your brother but it's not what you think."

"What do I think dad? I was confused when I found out that Bradon and I both was not the father of Jewel's baby. But then the doctor tells me the baby is related to me and it could be a brother or my father's baby."

"What I have never slept with that woman."

"Which woman dad, Jewel or my new brother's mom?"

"I have never slept with Jewel. Your brother told me about Jewel coming on to him. He was a virgin before she…" he looked up to see Bryson's face sad and tears forming in his eyes. "Son. I'm sorry. I was drunk and at a party and this lady was there. She was beautiful I was so drunk that I didn't know if I was coming or going. I don't even remember sleeping with her but the DNA test confirmed he was mine."

"Does mom know?"

"No! She doesn't know. I thought I was protecting her and my sons by keeping him a secret. I would schedule pretend business trips so I could go spend time with him. He is a great kid just as you two were. I wanted to make sure he had a great life as well."

"I guess the saying is true. What's done in the dark always comes to light. You are going to have to tell mom. I plan on having my brother in my life." Bryson wiped his eyes stood straight looking his dad in the eyes. "I still love you dad. Disappointed you didn't make this right nineteen years ago. But make it right now."

"I will son. I promise."

"I have a wife to attend to dad. Oh and I will be the one to break the news to Bradon myself so you don't have to swallow all that pill. He will take it better coming from me."

"I will talk with Bradon about this son, you don't…"

"I'm having lunch with Byron soon and I won't keep this secret from him any longer. Nineteen years was long enough."

"Ok." Bryson started to walk away. "Son I love you and I am very proud of you and all your hard work."

Bryson looked back at his dad deep in thought and managed to say, "Thanks."

He went to his wife who comforted him in every way a man needed from his wife. He kissed her on her forehead.

"Babe are you ok?" Brielle asked her husband.

"Everything is good darling."

Bryson, his family and friends enjoyed the party celebrating the success of the movie. He received some much needed answers. He was happy to know his father never slept with his ex but was shocked at the news of a brother that could possibly be the father of his ex's baby. Jewel was another person outside of the woman he thought he knew. He was glad she was not in his life anymore and he was not the father of her child. Life as he knew it was great for him. Everyone has a past and where there is darkness light shall shine.

Chapter 48
Greg's Final Words

"Get up, you have a visitor," the officer said coming to buzz Greg out of his jail cell.

"A visitor? I haven't had a visitor since I been here. Who even knows where I am now?" Greg asked as he stood to be hand cuffed to go meet his visitor.

"I don't keep a log of who is here to see who. You have to go find out for yourself," she said with a no-nonsense attitude.

"I'm coming." He walked into the visitation room and couldn't believe his eyes. "Brielle?"

"You murderer. You murdered my husband. How could you! You ruined my life twice you evil bastard."

"Brielle, I'm sorry. I am so sorry. I love you. I am sorry for everything. I am sorry please forgive me. Please forgive me, please forgive me, please forgive me…"

I was having a nightmare that felt so real and deserving. I don't know what happened after that night. I haven't been able to see the news, read a paper, nothing. But what I do know is my life flashed before my eyes. Being shot multiple times, losing so much blood and laying in the middle of the street without one person who cared if I live or die was the worse feeling in my life. Those niggas I was with that night I thought had my back, but they didn't give a damn about me. They left me there to die. Strangers stood over my body laid out in the middle of the street. Have I been that cruel in life to die alone?

I had a good thing with Brielle. My kids. Damn I fucked that up. I had a great time in the clubs getting high, getting drunk. Those hoes were coming a dime a dozen giving up the pussy for free. What a life I had having my cake and eating it too. I was a greedy man and it cost me everything. I abused the woman I loved and what I did to my son was not human at all. I deserved to go to jail. That wasn't me. I was strung out on them drugs I didn't know if I was coming or going. I was a horrible man and a horrible father.

No wonder God saw fit to have me lying in the middle of the street alone to die. That's not how my life was supposed to be. Now here I am defeated in all areas of my life. I am recovering but I may not be able to walk again at least not the same. I don't know why God spared my life that day. I am not a praying man but I prayed to God that day to save my life. Told him I would change my ways if he spared me this one time even though I know I don't deserve to be saved. I beat the shit out of the only woman I ever loved. My momma abandoned me for a john and some drugs. Sold me off for a hit. If it wasn't for my uncle saving me I would have been dead a long time ago anyhow.

Fuck them hoes. That's all I use to think and say until I met Brielle. But I guess I am more like my mother than I thought, strung out on drugs. I took all my girl money. When that ran out I started selling any and everything we had just to go out, get high and get laid by the junkie getting high with me.

My life was fucked up from the beginning and Brielle was my angel. I didn't cherish what God gave me and he took her away. Hell, I wish she would have left after the first time I hit her. That may have been a wakeup call for me to get my life in check then. She was my everything. I hurt her, I hurt my son. I feel like scum left on the street for the rain to wash away. The scum that doesn't even deserve to be left on the bottom of a shoe. I was left all alone in that street to die. Fucking up your life and ruining the best thing that ever happened to you, ruining the one that saved you deserves to be left for dead alone. I remember being high feeling like the devil himself raping and hitting her repeatedly. I was so fucking mad at myself for fucking up my life that I took it out on her. Those drugs fucked with my mind something terrible. My momma abandoned me, the man that molested me, the streets that mistreated me after my mom sold me for drugs, it all haunted me and I thought I buried those memories.

Those drugs. Those fucking drugs had my mind. The devil had my mind. I fucked up. I hit a woman. A woman I loved. I hit a child. A child that is mine. How could I even fix my mouth to even ask God to save me? I want my life back before drugs. I want my woman back, my children back. I know now that God took her from me. Prepared her for another man.

I surrender God. I surrender all my sins to you. I surrender all my wrong doings to you. I surrender every breath I have left in my body. I surrender everything to you God. Fix me. Although I may never again see the light of day outside a prison wall I still surrender and ask you to fix me. Fix my mind, fix my heart, fix my ways, and just fix me Lord. I'm broken. Me, a man who claims to be hard. This ghetto gangsta. I am repenting my sins, laying here with nothing. I am asking you Lord to please forgive me. Make me anew. I accept losing everything I had but I thank you Lord for giving me a second chance at life.

Chapter 49
Mrs. Mathews

What a journey of love and pain this has been. My son Bradon gave us all a scare but my God is so awesome! He is doing well and now he is engaged to be married. Chantae really stayed true to loving him when he was on his death bed. She never gave up.

Bryson has two beautiful twin boys. He still has Jewel's baby in his home even though he knows that baby is not his. They think I am in the dark but momma is never in the dark. I know what I need to know, what's important for me to know. So I know the baby is not Bryson and I also know the baby is not Bradon's.

I saw the young man my husband was talking to at the movie premiere and my Bryson talked to him too. My husband thinks he has kept me in the dark all these years but he hasn't. Heartbreak comes in all forms. My heart was healed the moment I found out. I followed him one day and saw him with his son. Yes, I was upset and hurt but to see a man own up to what he has done and be a father and raise his son without sacrificing our home I forgave him instantly. I saw the picture he kept and I had to know for myself. He didn't deal with the woman, only the child and my heart was ok.

I never said anything to him about that day. I have always waited on him to reveal his dark secret. I just let him tell me about his fishing trips or out of town meetings and trusted he would always be faithful. I was happy he was being a man and taking care of the baby he had while married to me. I am a Christian woman but don't get it twisted, I wasn't having him sneaking around dealing with another woman he was or could have been sleeping with. I did all the things a woman who wanted to feel secure would do. A man will always be a man but I checked and I was content enough to be alright.

I love the men in my life and I hope the news that my Bryson bas received does not harden his heart against his father.

He is a good man but good men can be hurt too. I know that news hurt him. When my Bradon finds out I don't know how he will react but I am afraid that his hurt will be deep. He loves his father, they both do. Being the baby son is special to him. He will soon find out about his father's lie.

What's done in the dark will eventual come to light and in my husband's case the light is shining bright. I just hate it took all those years to be revealed. Now we all are wondering if this child is and could be the father of Jewel's baby. I wouldn't put anything past that girl. I just hope her having that baby has changed her ways.

I pray to God that all wounds are healed and our family will not be broken. May God bless the Mathews both new and old.

If you enjoyed Love Never fails and the sequel Naked Truth of Love, please show the author some love by sharing with your family, friends, book clubs and social media fans. Rate the book and share your comments on amazon.

About the Author

Naked Truth of Love is the sequel to book one, 'Love Never Fails'. Donna Christopher is working on a spin off series about Jewel Taylor, Chronicles of a Sex Addict. Be on the lookout for that series before the sequel to Naked Truth of Love will be released. She is also working on a book titled Beautiful Curse to be released before Christmas 2017.

You can follow the author on Facebook at Donna Christopher, on Instagram @donnachristopherauthor, on twitter @donnachristphr
And periscope donnachristopherauthor

If you would like to share comments or contact the author you can e-mail her at
donnachristopherauthor@gmail.com

Notes:

www.ingramcontent.com/pod-product-compliance
Lightning Source LLC
Chambersburg PA
CBHW050357260626
47156CB00003B/772